Praise for "Clockwork Boys"

"Hands down, probably the best piece of traditionally western epic fantasy I've read ever."
— Cassandra Khaw author of *Hammers on Bone*

"As stories give us maps to unknown possibility, Clockwork Boys shows us how to do that nearly-impossible thing—how to go on after we have screwed absolutely everything up. A must-read for anyone trying to be a decent human being and/or competent adult!"
— Sigrid Ellis

Praise for "Bryony & Roses"

"The writing. It is superb. Ursula Vernon/T. Kingfisher, where have you been all my life?"
—The Book Smugglers at Kirkus Reviews

Praise for "The Raven & The Reindeer"

"…an exquisitely written retelling of Hans Christian Andersen's The Snow Queen… I love this book with the blazing passion of a thousand suns. I'm sitting here almost crying at the thought that I had to wait until I was fifty-seven (almost fifty-eight!) years old before having a chance to read this book."
—Heather Rose Jones, Daughter of Mystery

Other Works

As T. Kingfisher

Jackalope Wives and Other Stories
Nine Goblins (Goblinhome Book 1)
Toad Words & Other Stories
The Seventh Bride
Bryony & Roses
Summer in Orcus

As Ursula Vernon

From Sofawolf Press:

Black Dogs Duology
House of Diamond
Mountain of Iron

Digger Series
Digger Omnibus Edition

It Made Sense At The Time

For kids:

Dragonbreath Series
Hamster Princess Series
Castle Hangnail
Nurk: The Strange Surprising Adventures of a Somewhat Brave Shrew

Anthologies:

Comics Squad: Recess!
Funny Girl
Best of Apex Magazine
The Long List
Peter S. Beagle's *The New Voices of Fantasy*

CLOCKWORK BOYS

Book One of THE CLOCKTAUR WAR

By T. Kingfisher

Argyll Productions
Dallas, Texas

Weasel Invicti!

CHAPTER 1

There are a number of smells one expects to encounter in a dungeon. Fresh rosemary generally isn't one of them.

Slate grimaced and blotted her nose on her sleeve. It wasn't that the herbal scent wasn't a vast improvement—the ancient stone keep had been meant to hold prisoners in, not let odors out. The entire lower level stank of centuries of unwashed bodies, tallow candles, and despair.

The problem was that there was no earthly reason for the rosemary to be there. She knew already that there were no guards with a fondness for scented aftershaves, no potted herbs on the warder's desk, and if she asked anyone else, they'd stare at her like she was crazy. The rosemary was all in her head.

Slate sighed.

It happened occasionally. Sometimes it meant "danger!" and sometimes it meant "here, look more closely, this is important!" As near as she could tell, the scent of rosemary flooded her nostrils when it was very important that she pay attention to... something.

Her grandmother had been a minor wonderworker. Slate figured the rosemary warning was probably inherited, and that she'd gotten the short end of the family stick.

Still, of all the magical odors one could be afflicted with, it could have been a lot worse. Goat. Skunk. Old cheese.

The rosemary hit her again, a direct blast, as if the crushed leaves were directly under her nostrils. Slate put a hand over her nose and wrinkled her eyes shut.

Fine, fine, you've got my attention...

"Sorry," said the warder, "smells pretty rank down here. You get used to it. I hardly smell it myself."

Slate nodded. It had been pretty thick before the rosemary choked her, although she'd smelled worse.

"Who's left?" she asked, dropping her hand.

"Six in for assault, three murderers."

"Lovely. All right, let's see the ones up for assault."

The warder opened a door and went inside. She heard shouting and muffled grumblings while he prodded the prisoners up to the bars. Slate tried to clear her head, got another whiff of rosemary, and pinched the bridge of her nose to steady herself.

Okay, okay, I know it's important! I realize my life's on the line here! Back off!

The phantom herb didn't pay attention, but then, it never did. Slate turned in place, trying to get a better fix on it.

She was grateful that this sort of thing didn't generally happen more than once or twice a year. It was always dreadfully annoying when it did, as if she were some kind of botanical bloodhound, following a scent that wasn't really there.

It was hard to get a fix on any particular direction without wandering around with her nose in the air. She'd learned not to do that. People tended to look at you funny.

She sighed again. Maybe she'd be lucky, and it'd be one of the murderers. Then she could take him and get out of here, without any complications.

Beyond the current complications, which are already complicated enough, thank you.

"They're ready, ma'am," said the warder, leaning past the heavy wooden door.

Slate stepped over the threshold and into the hallway leading past the cells. Someone put his hands through the bars, then jerked them back when the warder made a move in his direction. Another prisoner laughed at him.

The men behind the bars were a sorry lot. The prison was progressive as such things went—they changed the straw regularly and gave everyone meals and fresh water—but there wasn't much anyone could do about the lice or the smell or the despair.

Slate swept her eyes over the half-dozen men, frowning.

None of them were anything she'd want to take back to her partner. Most of them had the dull, sullen look of men who had fallen into violence for lack of any other option.

There was one near the end who had shoulders like an ox. He didn't look very bright, but maybe he'd be good at hitting things.

At this point, that may be the best you can hope for. Who knew prison scum were so...unpromising?

The smart ones had talked or bought their way out, the truly dangerous ones had been hanged already—what was left were the dregs. She couldn't see trusting any of these men, even on a suicide mission.

And none of them smelled of rosemary.

Women were rare enough down here that some of the prisoners watched her avidly, crowding against the bars, even as nondescript a little thing as she was. She tried hard to be nondescript; it was one of her great assets. Short, drab, brown hair, brown skin, eyes of no particular color set in a face of no particular beauty—these were tools as useful in their way as grappling hooks and forger's pens.

Still, even a nondescript woman was more than they usually saw in the dungeons. There were one or two catcalls and much grabbing of crotches, but no scent of rosemary.

The warder made as if to stop the men's behavior, but something—probably Slate's total indifference—dissuaded him. "Ma'am?"

"No," she said. "None of these will do, I don't think." She sighed, glanced over the big one—*I suppose if there's no one else, he'll have to do*—then grimaced again. "I suppose we'd better look at the murderers, god help us all."

"Are you sure? One of 'em's in for arson too, and he's a bad one."

She touched the courier pouch slung at her waist, with its papers. "I'm given my pick of the prisons, by the Dowager's orders."

And it's only by her grace—and this mad notion of hers—that I'm not in a cell myself. I don't think you know that. I don't think you need to know that.

"I know, but…"

The warder, Slate suspected, was a decent man, and would obey orders without question, but his sensibilities were deeply offended by the notion of a woman coming in and possibly releasing a murderer. Slate wasn't exactly keen on the idea herself. She didn't mind traveling with murderers—she'd slit a throat or two in her time, and Brenner's entire career was founded on other people's corpses—but arsonists were something else again, and did not make for comfortable traveling companions.

Then again, the gods knew, she and Brenner couldn't undertake this mad venture entirely on their own.

She patted the warder absently on the shoulder. "I don't much like it either, but orders are orders. Let's see them."

The warder sighed and went to go roust the murderers.

It wasn't impossible that there was something in the keep itself that was setting off Slate's rosemary sense. People said that the Dowager's keep was built on the ruins of an older building. People said that there were rooms no one had opened in a thousand years, filled with old wonders from civilizations dead and gone.

People said a lot of stupid things.

Slate had, in her line of work, fenced several objects supposedly from that distant past. At least two had been fakes, but an artificer she trusted had sworn that one was real. None of them had smelled of rosemary and none of them had done anything particularly magical. She'd forged the certificates of authenticity and sent it on its way and that was that.

The warder opened the door and beckoned her down to the line of murderers.

Perhaps fortunately, none of them smelt of rosemary either. Two were vague, silent creatures, and the third was a ratty young man whose eyes moved over her body like insect feet. She met his gaze and he looked away immediately, then back at her, then at the warder. No question which one was in here for starting lethal fires.

Definitely not. This one was a mad dog—he wouldn't fear her, and fear of Brenner's knives wouldn't hold him for long. They'd have to kill him within hours, and what good would that do anybody?

I don't mind if he kills me, but I'd as soon skip the preliminaries...

"No." Slate left the cell block and went back out into the main room. The rosemary had to be coming from somewhere. One of the wardens? *God, how will I explain that?*

The rosemary flooded her nostrils again.

Slate glanced at the door. The warder was still inside, settling the prisoners, and couldn't see her doing anything...odd.

She closed her eyes, tilted her head back, and sniffed.

By turning her head and taking several blind steps, she got a brief sense of direction from the smell. Assuming she wasn't deluding herself, it seemed stronger from one side of the room. She navigated that way with eyes closed, took a step, then another—definitely getting stronger—took a third step and banged her thigh on the warden's corner desk.

"Bugger!" She glanced around, rubbing her leg, didn't see the warden, and went back to sniffing. Ah—almost—no—*there!*

"Ma'am?" said the warden, behind her.

The elusive rosemary fled. Slate opened her eyes, and found her nose inches from another door.

"Who's behind here?"

"Oh," said the warden. "Oh—ma'am, you don't want that one. He's bad. I mean, they're all bad, but he's—you *really* don't want that one."

"Unfortunately, I think I might," she said with a sigh. "Open the door, please."

The warder gave her a long look, but the Dowager's orders were stronger than his sense of propriety. He fumbled a key out of his key ring and opened the door.

The walkway was shorter than the one through the murderer's row, the cells smaller. All of them were empty. Slate stepped into the hall, feeling the flagstones cold and slippery underfoot.

She walked to the end, to the single occupied cell, and turned to look at the prisoner.

Rosemary hit her so strongly that she nearly choked. Slate had to throw her sleeve across her suddenly dripping nose. If it had smelled like crushed leaves before, now it was as if someone had poured purest rosemary oil directly into her nasal passages.

She choked on a sneeze. Bad things happened in the back of her throat.

Fine. Fine. I get it.

It was a very small cell with no windows.

The prisoner was a tall, dark-haired man with a shaggy growth of beard. His age was indeterminate, but she wouldn't put him over forty, probably less. The beard didn't help, and he was far back in the shadows.

He was sitting with his back against the wall, watching her with unreadable eyes.

Slate tried to say, "Excuse me," snuffled, and sneezed twice.

An eyebrow went up, but he didn't say anything.

I suppose "Bless you," is a little much to ask under the circumstances.

12

"Are you—damn—*urrrggghhkk*—" Her tongue pressed itself to the roof of her mouth as rosemary stormed the castle of her sinuses. There were no survivors.

She sneezed until she could sneeze no more. Her eyelids ached. She put her hands over her face.

"I'd offer you a handkerchief, but I'm fresh out," the prisoner said. He had a dry, abrasive voice. "I'm sorry if the smell offends you."

"It's not—" she waved a hand, still scrubbing at her traitorous nose and watering eyes. "It's—*snorgggk*—allergies. Sorry."

The other eyebrow went up, whether at the allergies or the apology. Slate wondered if it mattered which one. He didn't say anything.

She got herself under control, sniffled a few times, and put one hand on the bars. "What are you in for?"

The prisoner looked away contemptuously.

"He killed eight nuns and two guards," said the warden behind her. She could hear the glower without turning around.

"In fairness," said the prisoner, holding up a finger, "it was three nuns and five novices. And I *was* possessed at the time."

"Possessed?" she repeated, barely registering the word. He looked intelligent enough, at least compared to the alternatives, and the odds of their success hinging on his ability to, say, do long division in his head seemed unlikely. *I've got that bit covered anyway.* There was muscle enough on his frame for her purposes, but there was a slight hunch to his shoulders that worried her.

She moved suddenly, experimentally, and he flinched. Only a fraction, barely noticeable, but she'd been watching for it.

He's not broken, but he's got something. Shock, maybe. Definitely damaged goods. Could just be from being locked in here for a while, though. Hmm.

Still, I'm only asking him to die, not reintegrate with society, so maybe that won't matter. I suppose being possessed could be problematic.

Unless it helps.

The rosemary smacked her again. She turned away from the cell, groping for a handkerchief that, at this point, provided only emotional support.

"Snerrrghghk..."

"Generally, the gawkers actually know who they're looking at," the prisoner said. "If the temple is sending women to minister to me in my hour of need, they might consider screening them better."

The warden grunted. Slate flapped a hand at the prisoner irritably, face buried in the damp handkerchief.

Eight nuns and novices and two guards. Would you do that if the bars weren't there?

Oh, probably.

"Wait—" she said, as it finally dawned on her. Possibly the sneezing had knocked some stray memory loose. "Possessed? Eight nuns?" She turned to look at the warder, who nodded glumly. "Lord *Caliban?*"

It had been a nine-day wonder through the capitol—the madness of Lord Caliban, the Dreaming God's knight-champion, paladin and demonslayer, who had been taken by a demon himself and run mad, killing half the priestesses in his god's temple in one single bloody morning.

She stared at him.

He inclined his head. "*Sir* Caliban, actually. They stripped me of my title, although they were forced to leave me the knighthood. At your service, I'm sure."

"I thought they'd hung you!"

This was perhaps not the most tactful thing that Slate had ever said. Judging by the angle of his eyebrows, it was not the most tactful thing he'd ever heard, either.

He rose to his feet. He moved well enough, for a tall man in a box barely six paces wide. He lacked Brenner's dangerous grace, but knights were in a different line of work than assassins, at least technically.

Same line of work, different approach, I suppose.

"Indeed," said Sir Caliban. "It was judged that since I was possessed, I was not exactly responsible for my actions, and so I was given…mercy." He sketched the lines of the small cell with one hand.

"Did they exorcise your demon?"

"The demon is dead."

"But if you were possessed, why did they lock you up at all?"

He exhaled, a sound a little short of a sigh but rather longer than a snort. "Must I go into it?"

"Do you have anything *else* to do today?"

"Fair enough." He gave her a small, mocking salute, perhaps in acknowledgement. "Well. Questions of guilt have always been difficult with demons. It was determined that a soul such as mine must have been guilty of…something…to allow the demon entrance. And so…" Again, that quick sketching gesture, marking the boundaries of a severely limited world.

"Were you guilty?"

His eyes glittered, but he didn't say anything. Slate hadn't really expected an answer.

She leaned against the bars, moving more slowly. The warder started to say something, and she waved him off.

Moving equally slowly, like a strange cat meeting another in an alley, Caliban approached the bars.

"You're not from the temple. For a gawker, you're singularly ill-informed. And you're standing much too close to the bars for anyone with sense."

If he expected her to recoil in horror, he was disappointed. He stopped a foot or two away. Slate was fairly sure that she could get an arm through the bars and around her throat if he chose, and equally sure that she could get out of the way if he tried, as long as the warden didn't do anything stupid, like rush to her defense.

She wondered briefly if she'd even *try* to get out of the way. It seemed a matter of academic interest only.

He'd have to make it a quick death, he'll hardly have time for a long one...

Her hands were wrapped around two of the iron bars. He looked down and very deliberately gripped the bars to either side.

Her fingers were small and scarred and nimble, darkened with ink and spattered with the pale marks of engraver's acid. Her fingernails were somewhat chewed—a vile habit, but she didn't expect to live with it much longer.

His hands were much larger but also scarred, old cuts forming a raised and random pattern across the backs. The sleeves of the prisoner's tunic were too short for him, and when she followed his wrists upward, she could see the thick band of muscle across each forearm.

Swordsman, then. God's teeth and toenails, I believe it actually is Lord Caliban.

She could smell unwashed flesh and old straw and rankness, but over that, pungently, hung the scent of rosemary.

Great. I'm paying attention. Now what? Do I offer him the job, or am I supposed to stay as far away from him as possible?

As usual, her erratic gift offered no advice.

She squared her shoulders and met the man's eyes. They were dark and brown and held hers. One eyebrow had an ironic tilt, but behind his eyes, Slate could smell despair.

There were a great many things she had prepared to say—vague explanations, stripped of any facts that could be dangerous, mentions of the Dowager's name, promises of amnesty in the unlikely event any of them survived. She considered them all and rejected them one by one.

"Would you like to go on a suicide mission?" she asked instead.

He smiled. It was the first genuine smile she'd seen all day.

"I would be honored," he said.

CHAPTER 2

The warden was not thrilled by the notion of letting a mass murderer go, particularly not a famous one. Slate wasn't sure if he was making money by taking visitors to gawk at the prisoner, or if he actually expected Sir Caliban to fall on her like a starving wolf the minute he was out of the cell.

He hadn't looked much like a wolf when the warden had herded her back to the guard room. The way he'd looked down the hallway after them, face schooled to immobility, had reminded her more of a dog lost and wondering where its home had gone.

Let's not get sappy. Your puppy made chew toys out of ten people.

"I don't like this, missy," said the warden. He leaned forward in his chair, his fingers splayed over her documents.

Slate wondered if going from "ma'am" to "missy" was a bad sign. *Probably.* "Look, I have signed orders from the Dowager allowing me take any of the prisoners that I feel will be useful. I have the authority to do this."

Please, god, I hope I have the authority to do this.

The Dowager Queen's exact words had been, "Take anyone from the prisons you feel will be useful. They may have a pardon, in the event any of them survive." And then she'd gestured with a hand covered in rings, and Slate had been hustled out of the audience chamber, feeling like a mule had kicked her in the gut.

Clear enough. Slate had a feeling that "anyone" probably hadn't included Sir Caliban. Perhaps the Dowager had forgotten he was down here.

Still, the rosemary had been unmistakable.

Unless it was trying to warn me of danger, and he really is going to kill me as soon as he gets out of the cell.

Oh well, now or later, it's all the same, I suppose…

"Find him some clothes," said Slate, after the warden had puzzled over her papers long enough. "I'm in a hurry."

"Are you sure you wouldn't like some nice murderers instead?" he asked plaintively.

"Quite sure, thanks."

"We've got some likely lads being transferred in for robbery next shift—"

"Just the knight."

"That one—ma'am—you gotta understand, he's bad crazy. *Demon* crazy. It's not just like he hit somebody a little too hard on accident—he carved up those women like chickens. And he says things at night that aren't canny."

Back to ma'am again. I must be winning.

"Then you'll be glad not to have to listen to him any more." Slate reached over and plucked her papers off the table.

I suppose we'll have to get him a sword.

Well, that's a quick death, too, if he's any good.

The warden gave her a last look of entreaty. "Ma'am—"

"The Dowager is not to be kept waiting," she snapped, and turned her back on him.

I am too old for this. Thirty is much too old to be rousting around prisons any more. If I weren't going to die, I'd think seriously about retiring.

She heard the chair scrape back against the stone, and the sound of grumbling. A door opened, and closed. Slate exhaled.

Now let's hope he's getting clothes and not the Captain of the Guard.

The Captain would back her up. Probably. He'd been pleasant enough to her before, if not to Brenner.

The warden's spare keys were on his desk. Slate put out a hand, thought better of it, and then picked them up anyway. She pushed the door open and walked down the hallway.

Caliban was still standing by the bars. He did not look surprised to see her—it had only been five minutes, after all, and he could undoubtedly hear the arguing from the guard room—but his eyebrows shot up when he saw the keys.

Slate bit her lip, looked at him, had second thoughts and shot them down. She slid the key into the lock.

"Are you sure you want to do that?" he asked. His voice was still light and dry, not as deep as she'd expect from a man his size.

"Nope." She turned the key, hearing the clunk, and pulled it out again.

They both looked at the cell door for a moment.

What—does he need me to invite him over the threshold like an unquiet ghost? Should I back up? Is he afraid I'll bite?

He reached out a hand and pushed the door, very lightly. It swung open with a long creak of metal that hung in the air like a crow's caw.

Slate had made peace with her god several times over in the last few days, but she commended her soul to heaven again just in case.

A tremor went through Caliban, barely there, but Slate's eye for detail was finer than most. She looked away, because unlike Brenner, she had never liked the sight of pain.

Caliban took several steps, and then a final one over the threshold. He swallowed, and seemed briefly at a loss for something to say.

Slate nodded at nothing in particular. It had been four or five months since Lord Caliban had enjoyed his notoriety as a murderer through the capitol. She didn't know how long trials for this sort of thing took, but he must have spent at least a season in that cell.

"Well," he said, rubbing his palms down his thighs. "I suppose I should ask what you want of me, madam."

"You should probably have asked that first," said Slate. *I wonder where "madam" rates compared to "ma'am" and "missy." Hmm.* "But there's little enough I can tell you before certain—assurances."

He raised his eyes from the floor to her face. "Will you require me to swear an oath, then?"

"An oath!" It startled a laugh out of her. *God, he really is a knight. Brenner will have a litter of kittens.*

"I am told that the oath of a killer of nuns and novices isn't worth much," he said, eyes hooded.

"Nobody's oath is worth much," Slate said. "It's nothing personal." She waved a hand. "Anyway it's a suicide mission. You—and I, and a…coupla other people…will be going somewhere, and doing…err…something. Which is probably impossible, and we'll likely all die."

He gazed at her levelly. She had no idea what he was thinking.

She wracked her brain for some detail she could give, something he could mull over, without giving enough information to be dangerous if he turned her down and gossiped to one of the wardens. "We're going to Anuket City," she said finally. That seemed innocuous enough—there were plenty of opportunities to do something suicidal on the way to the city-state of Anuket City, let alone once you actually arrived. And the fact that the Dowager's kingdom was at war with them was about as far from a state secret as one could get.

"Ah." Caliban leaned against the stone wall at the end of the hallway.

Slate stared at her feet and wiggled her toes. Caliban's feet were bare. She hoped the warden would bring sandals.

It was stupid, this staring at her feet. There was a murderer an armslength away.

Strangling wasn't as quick a death as she'd like, but it still only took a few minutes. *I'll probably thrash rather embarrassingly. Still, could be worse. I do hope he doesn't try to bludgeon me to death.*

"The Dowager knows something about the Clockwork Boys," said Caliban.

Sonofabitch…

Slate threw her hands in the air, turning away. "God's teeth! Why do we even *bother* with secrecy, if men in goddamn solitary confinement can figure that out!?"

Damn. I should have kept my mouth shut. I forgot he was a knight—he might even have encountered the Clockwork Boys at some point. I suppose it doesn't take a genius to put "Anuket City" and "Dowager" and "suicide" all together.

"Answer the question," he said, directly behind her.

"You didn't ask one," she snapped, turning around.

He was closer than she'd expected. He loomed quite effectively in the narrow corridor, particularly since he had nearly a foot of height on her. He reached out and caught her arm in his scarred fingers.

She considered flinching and didn't. *A snapped neck would probably be the best to hope for, but I suppose beggars can't be choosers. I wonder if he takes requests?*

"She knows something," the former knight said again. "Doesn't she?"

"Not nearly enough," she said, meeting his eyes. "Not how they're made, or where they come from. That's half our job. The other half is to try and stop them."

"That *is* a suicide mission," he said.

"Mmm, quite." She dropped her gaze to his hand. His skin was very white against hers. Probably he had always been pale, but months of captivity had turned his skin the color of wax.

He was holding her wrist. Why did men always grab your wrist? There were any number of ways to break that grip, of course, but it was mildly infuriating nonetheless.

He released her, looking oddly embarrassed. *Was he trying to scare me? Poor man.* "Did you think I was exaggerating?"

"The thought had crossed my mind."

"Assuming you live through it, there's a full pardon offered. I don't know if that would include reinstating your title or not."

"We won't live through it."

"No, I shouldn't expect we will."

"Even *getting* to Anuket City right now is a fool's errand."

"Good thing we're fools, huh?"

"And what—" he began, but the door at the end of the hall banged open, and the warden gasped.

"You shouldn't have let him out, ma'am!" He hurried down the hall and shouldered past Slate to stand between them, bristling like a paunchy bulldog.

"Why not? You were going to." Slate reached out and plucked the folded clothes from his arms. She shook them out. Tunic and trousers, neither of them new, but clean enough and neatly patched. "Hmm. It'll do, I suppose, and—yes, excellent, sandals." She passed them both to Caliban.

There was a brief, awkward silence.

"Come *on*," said Slate irritably. "Our inevitable deaths aren't going to happen by themselves."

Caliban rolled his eyes up at the ceiling.

Damn, he's having second thoughts. But he guessed too much, and I told him too much, I can't let him stay here. Damn.

"Don't tell me you're having second thoughts—" she began.

It was the warden who touched her shoulder and said "Should leave a man privacy to change, missy."

"Oh. *Oh.* Right. I'll…err…be in the guard room."

She and the warden retired to the central room. Slate returned his keys. He glared. She pretended not to notice.

The silence got uncomfortable. The muffled sounds of prisoners talking and moving around in the other rooms didn't help. Slate dug for another handkerchief, didn't find one, and tried to locate an unobtrusive patch of sleeve.

The warden cleared his throat. "It's not too late to put him back."

The door opened, and Caliban came through. He looked considerably better in the clean clothes, which were too large rather than too small. He was still dirty and bedraggled and his beard was truly unfortunate, but now he only looked very bad instead of like death warmed over.

A decent bath and a shave, and we might aspire to "human." Or, err, demon. Something.

He can't still be possessed. They wouldn't put him in a regular prison if he had a demon in him. He'd be so loaded down with spells and irons that he couldn't sneeze without banishing himself.

Well, assuming he was even possessed in the first place. He might just be mad, after all.

He seems sane enough at the moment, except for the twitchiness. 'Course, if I was in a cell for a season, I'd likely be twitchy myself.

Slate was probably the only one who noticed the way Caliban paused before stepping through the doorway, as if he still could not quite believe that there were such things as open doors before him.

"Right!" said Slate brightly, turning to the warden. "I assume you have something for me to sign?"

"What? Err...yes..." The warden rummaged through a stack of papers on his desk, then in a desk drawer. Slate read a few, upside down, and picked one out.

"This it?"

"Oh, yes, err..."

She signed it with a flourish. Paperwork, at least, Slate under-stood. "And a copy for me, and one for you, and…excellent!" She folded hers up, saluted with the corner, and strolled out of the guardroom.

Her heart was pounding. It usually pounded when she offered people documents, but generally that was because she had forged them and was waiting to see if she'd get caught. It was interesting to learn that being on the correct side of legality didn't help much.

The warden didn't stop them. Slate hadn't expected him to. Once papers were signed, people seemed to give up. It was a strange sort of magic.

The door led to a hallway, which led to another hallway, and then to a flight of stairs with a pair of guards. Sir Caliban fell into step behind her, a pace back and to her left, a practiced distance. *He's probably been an honor guard more times than I can count.* Slate's lips twitched.

What the guards might have thought of the small, drab woman and her grim escort was anyone's guess. She wondered if they even recognized that he was a famous mass murderer. Guards tended to rotate regularly—prison duty was a punishment, not a reward—and many of them might not even recognize him on this side of the bars.

Of course, anyone with an ounce of sense ought to recognize that a grimy man in ill-fitted clothes, who paced like a bodyguard, was not in the normal run of events. But that was bureaucracy for you. Get past the first layer of guards, present official-looking paperwork, and nobody asked questions.

They swept by the guards unchallenged. Slate felt a small bubble of triumph, or possibly hysteria.

There were more corridors and more halls and more guards. None of them challenged her, even when they left the prison and entered a corridor more suited to a palace.

"This really is foolishness," said Caliban in an undertone behind her. "The warden should have given you guards—an escort—*something*. Letting a woman walk out of here with a murderer—I'd have his skin if he were serving under me."

He sounded genuinely outraged. Slate had to laugh.

"Relax, mister murderer, you're not getting off that lightly."

She turned her head as she spoke, in time to catch his grimace.

"Sorry. *Sir* Murderer, should I say?"

"Whatever you like, madam," he said, not meeting her eyes.

Still raw. He can say it, but he doesn't like it when I do. Interesting. Not surprising, but the way he speaks, you'd think he'd hide it better. Ah, well.

"Here we are." She turned down another, narrower hallway, and knocked on a door at the bottom of a shallow step. Caliban stood behind her, feet apart, his hands folded behind him.

Good lord, is that parade rest? I think it is.

Brenner is going to have a field day.

She knocked on the door again, a bit louder.

"Enter," said a voice from inside.

The room was small and cluttered and full of papers. The Captain of the Guard, an iron-haired, iron-eyed man, looked up when she entered.

"I beg your—oh, it's you. Do you have a report, Mistress Slate?"

"Sir. Uh." What was the proper military form for this sort of report?

To hell with it, I'm a civilian, even if they've drafted me into this lunacy. They can bloody well deal with it. "I...err...found one."

The Captain nodded. "Very well, then."

Caliban hung back at the doorway for just a moment, then stepped into the room as hesitantly as if it were cold water.

"God's balls!"

"A pleasure to see you as well, Captain," said Caliban, inclining his head. One hand went to his side, as if to touch a non-existent sword-hilt, then dropped.

Slate was pretty sure that no one in the room missed that. She waited for the captain to turn to her and demand an explanation, or demand that Caliban be sent back to his cell or—well, something.

After a minute, while the two men continued to stare at each other like two tigers in a very small cage, Slate stopped holding her breath.

Can't they yell at each other or have a manly hug or something and get it over with?

She read some of the papers upside down on the Captain's desk while she waited. Most of them had to do with duty rosters. There was an interesting one about a sweep of the gutterside slums. Apparently unlicensed prostitution was up. She hadn't known that.

"My god, Caliban, you look like *hell*."

Slate glanced up, and saw the Captain staring at the former knight with an expression less of horror than chagrin.

Hmm, they really do know each other. I suppose there's no reason a Captain of the Guard wouldn't know a famous temple knight. Maybe they worked together doing…knight…stuff…

"I've been possessed, arrested, exorcised, and locked in a cell for four months. There's a dead demon rotting somewhere in the back of my soul. What do you *expect?*"

That does sound unpleasant. Hmm, I wonder what a rotting demon's like? Maybe he smells it the way I smell rosemary.

God, that'd be awful. Poor bastard.

Slate went back to reading. It looked like the Stone Bitches were about to get arrested. That was a shame, really: they'd hired her a time or two to produce false bills of sale. Decent people. Understood craftsmanship.

"Ah. Yes." The Captain actually seemed to be at a bit of a loss. He glanced over at Slate, cleared his throat, and gathered up his papers. "I didn't expect—are you *sure* you want—?"

"Yes," said Slate.

"Yes," said Caliban.

There was an awkward silence. Slate wondered which one of them he'd actually been talking to.

Deprived of other people's mail to read, she studied her feet again.

"Well." The Captain dropped his papers and ran a hand through his hair. "You realize, Lord—*Sir* Caliban, you would be answering to Mistress Slate here. She is nominally in charge of your mission, by the Dowager's order. You'd—ah—support and render aid. And so forth."

Caliban made a small, ironic bow in her direction. "Madam."

Slate glanced at the Captain, wondering if he'd hoped that would be a deal breaker. Apparently it wasn't. The Captain sighed.

"Sit down. I'll call for the...ah...*hell*."

With this fragmentary statement, the Captain swept out of the room. Caliban looked after him. Slate wondered if he'd noticed himself flinching back from the man's movement.

"Hmm," the paladin said.

"If you make a run for it, you could probably get out of the palace," she said by way of conversation. "I don't know if you can kill the front guards barehanded, but it's probably worth a shot. I'd leave the city right away, mind you."

He looked at her, his eyes widening.

"Just a thought." She sat down on the edge of the desk and began reading the warrants for the Stone Bitches again.

"You're a very odd woman," he said.

"You don't know the half of it."

The door opened again. The Captain ushered a heavyset man inside. He was bald, with the variegated pattern of shine indicating that he was probably shaving his head to avoid showing how badly his hair was thinning. His thick fingers were wrapped around the handle of a large leather case.

"Sit," the Captain ordered Caliban. And: "Stop reading my mail."

Caliban quirked an eyebrow and sat. The bald man knelt next to the chair and rolled up the sleeve of the knight's tunic. Slate stopped reading the Captain's mail, put one heel up on the desk and hugged her knee to her chest.

The bald man opened his case, and took out a set of needles and a jar of black ink. A wave of rosemary welled up and smacked Slate across the nose.

Gods, I go months without this happening, and now this. Dammit, Grandma, if they hadn't burned you at the stake, I'd light you myself.

"I'm getting a tattoo," said Caliban evenly. "Why?"

The Captain pinched the bridge of his nose with his fingers. "Let me start at the beginning. You know that we're losing the war with Anuket City, I assume?"

Caliban smiled sourly. "They weren't admitting that when I got locked up, but most of us suspected."

"We're still not admitting it, but yes, we are. The problem is the Anuket troops—the Clockwork Boys, as they call 'em. As fast as the army cuts them down—which frankly isn't very fast—more show up. They're not human. We don't know how to stop them except sheer brute dismemberment."

Slate could feel her eyes watering. She snuffled.

"Here." The Captain dug through papers and came up with a hunk of debris. It looked like a cross between the inside of a clock and a piece of driftwood. Tiny gears and cogwheels encrusted the sides like barnacles.

The knight took the object and turned it over in his fingers. "What is this?"

"Part of a Clockwork Boy. It used to move, but we boiled it for a few hours and it finally stopped."

"Are these made of bone?"

"We don't know. The alchemists are still fighting over it. Half of them think it's organic, and the other half think someone carved each little piece. They use a lot of words that I don't think even they understand."

"Hmm." Caliban handed the piece back to the Captain, and wiped his hand on his pant leg.

"Anyway." The Captain set it down on his desk. "They've got to be making them somewhere—or building them, or breeding them, or summoning them, or the Dreaming God knows what."

Caliban might have said something, but the tattoo artist sank a needle into his bicep, and he winced.

"Anyway. Your—ah—group will be traveling to Anuket City to attempt to infiltrate and learn how this is happening. And if possible, to stop it."

"*Snrrrgghghk…*" Slate pinched the bridge of her nose and tilted her head back miserably.

"You don't have spies there already?" asked Caliban.

The Captain shook his head. "Not any more. All the ones we did have wound up going missing." He reached into a pocket and pulled out a handkerchief, which he dropped in Slate's lap without comment. "Our spies in Anuket had been largely diplomatic corps, frankly—they're supposed to watch the politics, not break in and steal state secrets. And now they're presumed dead anyway. So we're trying a more brute force solution."

The bald man's fingers moved with surprising deftness over the pale skin of Caliban's upper arm, leaving dark lines behind. Slate retired to a corner and blew her nose.

"And we're the best you could come up with?" said Caliban.

"No," said the Captain. "You're not the Dowager's first choice, or even the second, I'm afraid. But those people are also presumed dead now, so here we are."

"And that's all you know?"

"That's all we know. A scholar will be accompanying you. He's made something of a study of arcane machinery—it's possible that his expertise may help. In theory he has a counterpart in Anuket City that should know more, but that other scholar has vanished."

"Lucky him," muttered Slate.

"You can't expect this to work," said Caliban, shifting in his seat. The bald man made a wordless, irritable noise, like a man with a restless horse. Caliban settled. "Even getting to Anuket City at this point is madness…unless things have changed since I went in the cell, there's a no man's land between us and them."

"Things have changed, all right," said the Captain. "The no man's land is about twice as big, for one thing."

Caliban shook his head in disbelief.

"You note we're using prisoners, not soldiers, and not just for deniability. The Dowager's grasping at straws, if you ask me. But if you live through it, there's a full pardon." The Captain sounded unconvinced.

"What's to keep me from leaving with the lady here and simply riding off?"

"Aww," said Slate.

"Well, your word would be nice," said the Captain. (Slate snorted.) "But failing that, the thing on your arm should do it."

"What?" Caliban looked down at his arm.

Crudely rendered in black ink, a small toothy creature was portrayed with its teeth sunk into the flesh of Caliban's arm. As art went, it was barely above a child's drawing, but it had a primitive, scowling menace.

"What's that supposed to be?"

"I haven't any idea." The Captain sighed. "But if you betray us, the tattoo will eat you."

Caliban stared at him, then laughed. "You're kidding. You can't possibly be serious."

"Oh, yes."

"And they called *me* mad?"

He stood up.

"I wouldn't—" Slate began.

Caliban yelped and slapped at his shoulder, like a man stung by a biting insect. His hand came away bloody, and not just from the freshly inked tattoo. Red beaded under the black ink teeth.

"Gods—hells—it *bit* me!"

"They do that," said Slate tiredly. "I saw one eat a man once. He eventually cut his arm off, and it showed up on the stump a few days later. Don't ask me to explain how it works."

Caliban opened his mouth and said something, in a guttural sing-song that sounded like, *"Ngha! Ngha'ha, ha, halihalikaliha!"*

There was a brief, appalled silence.

"Ooookaaay..." said Slate, and sneezed explosively.

Shit. He is *mad. Shit. The rosemary was trying to warn me off. Shit.*

Maybe Brenner can kill him and dump him in an alley.

"Good god, you weren't kidding, were you?" said the Captain.

The bald man laughed, revealing a stump of a missing tongue. Slate looked away, grimacing.

"That's enough, Boran," said the Captain. "Leave us."

The tattoo artist packed his case away, and waved his fingers at Caliban and Slate, eyes twinkling. Neither of them returned his wave. He left, humming to himself.

Slate wondered vaguely where they'd found him. Minor wonderworkers were common enough, often possessing very specific talents. Still, what kind of turns did a life have to take before you discovered that your personal gift from the universe was making carnivorous tattoos?

Caliban sat down again, clearing his throat and glaring daggers at the Captain. When he spoke, he seemed to test the words first to make sure they were coming out correctly. "I can't believe you'd do this to me. Particularly after I saved your—"

"Yes, well. Times change. People change."

"Apparently so."

Somebody's pretty self-righteous for a nun-killer. This may be a long trip.

"I'm sending you off to die, anyway," said the Captain, not meeting his eyes. "Do the job as best you can. You'll probably be dead long before the tattoo gets any ideas—and if you do live, we'll take it off you."

Caliban turned his head away. Slate watched him fight himself visibly under control and decided to intervene.

"Great pep talk, Captain," she said. "I know *I'm* inspired. Are you quite done? Can I take him away now?"

"You sure this is the only one you want?" the Captain asked her. "The Dowager said the prisons were opened, god help us all."

Slate shrugged. "If you thought numbers would help, you'd send the army. He'll do. I hope."

"Sir Caliban?"

The knight opened his eyes and looked at them levelly. "My word would have been enough," he said.

The Captain shrugged. "Then you've got nothing to worry about." And when Caliban simply gazed at him, he added, "Look, I don't like this either. But the Clockwork Boys have to be stopped, and soon. We just don't have the men to hold them off forever. If this works—well, the gods can call me to account for it on the other side."

Caliban transferred his gaze to Slate. "That's why you told me to run for it," he said.

She nodded.

The Captain's eyes flicked from one to the other, but he didn't say anything.

"Why are *you* doing this?"

Slate pushed one of her sleeves up to the shoulder. Her own tattoo looked larger, perhaps because she was so much smaller. Jagged black teeth formed a semicircle halfway around the arm. The ink was not a great deal darker than her skin, but there was raw pink flesh under the creature's teeth.

"Ah."

When the tongueless wonderworker had given her the tattoo, the smell of rosemary had been so overpowering that the Captain and one of his men had to hold her steady while she sneezed and jerked. It had been humiliating. Her nose had bled by the end of it, and her head had felt as if it were packed to the seams with wool.

The Captain had been apologetic. She'd ruined two of his handkerchiefs. Whatever he thought of himself, it did not involve holding down twitching women while tongueless wonderworkers etched curses into their flesh. Even if they *were* criminals.

"When is the scholar due to arrive?" Slate asked.

"He is supposed to arrive tomorrow or the next day. We expected you to leave in three to four days—are you sure you won't stay at the palace?"

"No need, is there?" Slate smiled, because otherwise she thought she might cry. She slid off the desk. "Three days, then. You know where to find us."

She led the way out the door, with the knight walking a single pace behind her.

CHAPTER 3

The road out of the keep led down a cobbled way, into a broad square full of merchant stalls and food carts and jostling people.

They got about two blocks down, nearly to the edge of the market, and Caliban had to stop.

It was too much. There were too many people, too many colors, moving too quickly. The sky was too large. He felt dizzy, as if he might fall upward into empty space.

He tried to keep up with the woman—Slate—but his head spun and he staggered. She was moving too quickly, outpacing him as he shied like a nervous horse at the loud voices and flapping cloth.

"I'm sorry," he said, his voice high and hoarse. "I—wait—*please*—"

She turned, startled, and he put his hands over his face to block out the world.

"Hey now—hey—" Her voice was sympathetic but wary, as if she wasn't sure whether to console him or slap him. "Hey, now, you knew it was a suicide mission, don't go to pieces on me, the tattoo won't eat you as long as you're trying—"

"It's not that," he said. "It's the *sky*. There's too much of it."

Now that's *a sensible thing to say. Perhaps you really are mad.*

"Oh. *Oh.*"

Her fingers touched his sleeve, then she curled her hand around his arm and tugged him forward. "It's okay. Keep your eyes closed, here—come on—just through here—"

He followed, keeping one hand over his eyes. The sounds of the city were still overwhelming, but they ran together into a muted roar, and he could ignore it.

To think that a season ago, he'd walked or ridden through these streets without thinking them strange at all. He'd moved like a fish through a darting, multicolored sea.

"Come on—step down—you're doin' good—"

Such a great champion you are, now, being led blind by a woman half your size. Demons must tremble...

His own particular demon muttered down in the dark, ragged ends of syllables with no earthly meaning. Death hadn't silenced it completely. It was a more familiar sound than the city, now, but not a comfortable one.

"Here. It's an alley—this is the best I can do—"

He cracked his fingers cautiously, and saw stone between them. It was indeed an alley, the corners thick with trash, the walls close and comforting. The sky was a narrow crack of blue overhead. A shudder of relief wracked him.

"I'm sorry," he said. "I didn't expect—this is foolish of me—"

"It's really not that uncommon," she said. She was still holding his arm, and patted it absently, as if he were a skittish horse. "A lot of people get out and get a touch of agoraphobia at first. It'll pass off in a day or two. I shouldn't have taken you straight into the marketplace, I wasn't thinking."

"You sound as if you've known a number of prisoners," he said dryly.

"Oh, yes."

She released his arm and retreated the few feet to the other side of the alley, leaning against the wall near the mouth. He tried to look out into the market again, found it a dizzying whirl, and looked away.

He looked at Slate instead. She was a small-boned woman, her eyes grey and glittering, like flawed quartz. She had dark brown hair in a thick braid down her back, and a long, mobile face. Her skin was a few shades lighter than her hair and her clothes were loosely cut and nondescript. Mouse brown, sparrow brown—some creature that relied on being small and drab and getting out of the way of predators.

She scowled out at the marketplace as if it had personally offended her.

Caliban was vaguely aware that he would not have looked twice at her in the days when he was a god's champion. Beautiful women had strewn themselves in his path like rose petals.

And that morning, after you were done with the sword, they were strewn in your path again. Although not many roses are that exact shade of red, and they were not so beautiful any more.

Shut up. You're out of the cell. Quit wallowing. You've told hundreds of people they weren't responsible for what the demon did with their body. Take your own damn medicine.

It was embarrassing that he'd spoken with the demon voice in the Captain's office. He hadn't meant to. It must have been the tattoo, or the tattoo artist. Magic made the corpse stir, as if something were walking past it and kicking up the flies. It took them a while to buzz and settle down again.

Such a lovely metaphor.

The tattoo itched. He wanted to scratch it, but he was afraid it might scratch him back.

My mind hasn't been my own, and now my flesh isn't either. At least they're a matched set.

Slate was peering out the mouth of the alley, chewing on her lower lip. Her eyebrows were pulled down. She was not a beautiful woman, he was forced to admit, but she had an expressive face. That was what had struck him, even in the cell, the way each thought passed visibly across her face, like the shadow of clouds moving over a hillside.

Once she'd stopped sneezing, anyway.

Or perhaps she was a perfectly ordinary woman, and he was merely maundering because she was the first one he'd seen in a season. What a thing to wreak on a man—the sky too large, all movements too fast, and all women too interesting.

He risked another glance at the whirl of activity outside the alley. His stomach churned a bit, but it wasn't quite as dizzying.

"If I called us a carriage," said Slate thoughtfully, "can you make it to the street? It's—oh, half a block, I'd say."

"I think I can make it," he said, although his stomach knotted at the thought.

The sky, the sky, I'll fall into the sky...

She gave him a concerned look. "I could blindfold you if you like."

Caliban had little enough pride left, but the thought at first horrified, then amused him. What a pair they'd make—a short little criminal leading a blind, shambling wreck of paladin. The Dreaming God wasn't known for his sense of humor, but sometimes you had to wonder.

"As entertaining as that would be for the locals, no. I can make it. Just...don't walk too fast."

She nodded, and stepped out of the alley.

They went at a walk. Caliban fastened his eyes on her back. She was wearing a completely unmemorable skirt and tunic, in dull grey-brown. If he lost sight of her, he was going to have a hell of a time finding her again. The seam at her left shoulder was starting to come loose. He could see each individual thread working free.

Well, she was visiting a prison, not going out dancing.

I wonder what she did to earn a death sentence?

The thought was startling. He glanced aside, caught a glimpse of the market swirling around him, and bore it for as long as he could before returning his gaze to Slate's back. She turned to glance at him, and he gave her a nod. She nodded in return and plunged forward.

The Dowager's city didn't give death sentences for most crimes. The Dowager preferred money and hard labor, in that order, and dead men are notoriously bad at either.

He doubted she was a murderer. Her stained, elegant hands looked like a scribe or an alchemist. A thief, possibly, which conjured up all sorts of images of daring midnight burglaries, and escapes across the rooftops.

Caliban almost snorted at the thought. Did anyone really *do* that? Pickpocketing perhaps, banditry certainly, but that sort of genteel thievery seemed more like a romantic fiction than an actual profession.

Would they really sentence you to death for it?

A spy? A traitor? Would they send a traitor out on a job like this?

Would they put her in charge?

The cursed tattoo throbbed on his shoulder and he grimaced. It was, he had to admit, an excellent piece of insurance.

They passed a fishmonger's stall, and a man carrying several wrapped, dripping packages ran into Caliban's shoulder. He staggered back, more from the unexpected contact than the force.

"Hey, watch where you're going! Are you drunk?"

"No, I—sorry—" He plunged after Slate, suddenly terrified of losing her in this jumble. She was an unlikely safety, and yet without her—would the tattoo begin chewing at his arm? Would he fall into the sky?

The man cursed after him, brandishing a fish. Slate glanced back, saw Caliban following, and nodded.

He was watching her so intently that when she pulled up short, he nearly ran into her, and then she backed up into him anyway, cursing.

He looked over her head. A space was clearing in the crowd in front of them, as people drew away. He watched a woman trip and fall down, and still keep scuttling backwards with a look of fear and disgust on her face.

"Shit," Slate muttered. "Another blighter."

In the center of the circle was the prone body of a man. He was well-dressed, but there was something badly wrong with his skin. It peeled away as if he'd been badly burned, revealing bloody grey and yellow shadows beneath it. As the knight watched, one arm ratcheted upward, pawed at the air, then fell back down.

"That man's hurt," he said, starting forward.

Slate grabbed his arm. "Are you nuts? Stay back!"

"But that man needs help!" The sky retreated. The dying man in the middle of the pavement took all his attention. "Why isn't anyone helping?"

"You're insane! He's beyond help!"

The crowd was very quiet. The sound of the man's breathing rattled against the stones. He pawed at the air again jerkily, running down.

"Damnit, let me go, maybe I can—"

Slate turned into him, rammed a shoulder into his chest, and threw her full weight against it, like a woman trying to brace up a wall. Since he probably weighed twice what she did, this was spectacularly ineffective, but it did at least convince him that she was serious.

"Don't make me use a knife," she growled.

My god, I believe she would... "What's going on?"

"Where have you been for the past—no, never mind, stupid question." Slate put a hand to her head. "It's blight."

"Blight? Here? In the capitol?" Caliban frowned over her head. "There were some rumors that it had been seen in the outer cities, but no one thought it would reach the capitol."

"Yeah, well, they were wrong. Showed up right at the beginning of the year. The guards should—here we go."

A grim-faced guard appeared from the direction of the keep, pushing gawkers back with the shaft of his pike. "Get back, get back, you've all seen it already…"

He hardly needed to say that. The circle around the body was a good twenty feet in diameter. No one was taking any chances with blight.

A few moments later, the bone-pickers arrived. They wore grey gauze wrapped over every inch, even a thin veil of gauze over the eyes. Two of them leapt down from their cart and produced long poles, lifting the still-twitching body of the blighted man on the ends and ferrying him to the cart.

One of the grey figures dumped a bucket of water out across the stones. You could track its drainage by watching the ripple as the crowd skittered aside.

"And that's that," muttered Slate. "If you see another one, for god's sake, don't touch it. They don't know how it spreads, but they're pretty sure skin contact is a bad idea."

"I'll be careful," said Caliban. His head felt hollow, and the light was giving him a headache.

Slate plunged back into the crowd, giving the bone-pickers a wide berth.

She stopped at last on the edge of the street, waving for a cab. Caliban put a hand over his face again. He was horrified to discover that he was on the edge of tears.

It was too much all at once. The sky, the tattoo, freedom, a suicide mission, the blight victim—too much. He'd spent four months in a cell, four months of changeless days and changeless walls, of praying for something, anything, to happen.

And now it had. He did not know if he was grateful, but he knew he was overwhelmed.

Has the god answered my prayers at last, or is this another punishment for my sins?

It seemed unlikely that it was the god. The Dreaming God's presence was heat and light and rock-hard certainty. Caliban had not felt it in a very long time, and he no longer felt certain of anything at all.

Wheels rattled. Slate took his arm again. "Come on, the carriage is here."

He climbed into it obediently, and sagged back against the wooden seat when the door closed. The inside was a safely bounded world, the proper size. The knot in his stomach loosened.

"Seven Crows," Slate told the driver, leaning out the window.

"That's two blocks from here," the driver said, disgusted. "You could walk it faster than I can drive you."

"Just do it," said Slate. "My friend's sick."

"Drunk, more like…" muttered the driver, but he snapped the reins and called "Heeee-yup!" to the horses. They plodded off. The wheels creaked.

"I'm sorry," said Caliban again, resting his hands on his thighs. "You must be regretting your choice."

She smiled briefly and patted his knee. "No. This'll pass in a day or two, and you'll be fine. Or at least no worse off than the rest of us. Or you'll kill us all. Either way, really." She leaned back and closed her eyes. Her face, when there was nothing passing across it, looked tired.

And that was another odd thing. She touched him without fear, but he hadn't seen any interest in her eyes. Caliban wasn't used to that. Women usually noticed him. Some men, too. He was the god's own champion, a great demonslayer, and by all accounts a very handsome man.

Is she a woman for other women, then? He hadn't gotten that impression.

There was a strange scar on the ring finger of her right hand. It looked like a wedding ring in reverse, two ridges of blotchy scar tissue around a smooth band of unmarred flesh.

Caliban looked down at his own hands, at the dirty fingernails and grime between them, and almost snorted at his own arrogance.

You haven't bathed or shaved in a season. A woman hardly has to prefer her own sex not to find you attractive. You're not exactly the elite Knight-Champion of the Dreaming God any more, if you haven't noticed.

Perhaps she's simply not attracted to mass murderers.

The carriage rumbled to a halt. "Just a little farther," said Slate apologetically.

The last leg of the journey passed without notice. There was an inn, a blur of empty tables, a flight of blessedly enclosed stairs. Slate opened the door to a suite, and ushered him inside.

"He's a *knight?*"

The man who spoke was a wiry, compact fellow with heavy eyebrows and shoulder-length hair. He had been slouching with his booted feet over the arm of a chair.

He had not actually been flipping a knife, because hardly anyone really did that, but he looked like the knife-flipping type. A pile of cigarette ends in the ashtray showed what he'd been doing instead.

When Slate informed him of their new acquaintance's identity, he sat bolt upright. "Have you lost your mind? The pick of the Dowager's prisons—the finest cutthroats and criminals in the kingdom—and you bring us a *knight?*"

"They're not the finest," she said, "or they wouldn't have gotten caught. Yes, I picked him. His name is Sir Caliban. Caliban, this is Brenner. He's an assassin."

He could be at that, Caliban decided, looking Brenner over. The man moved with more strength than grace, and yet, despite pacing wildly back and forth across the room (as he leapt up and began to do) his feet made no sound. He wore dusty black clothing, and his boots were very fine.

It was funny in a way, that a man who could forget how huge the world was could still recognize good boots.

The inn was not so good as the boots, but it could still have been a lot worse—a suite of rooms, one narrow window, chairs and a fireplace in the sitting room. Someone was paying rather a lot of money for it.

The fireplace had a smoldering fire in it. Caliban stumbled to it, feeling the warmth on the backs of his legs. He had not warmed himself at a fire in a long time.

"Good god, a knight? Why not bring some watchmen along too?"

"They had some," said Slate. "I didn't much care for their looks."

"Yes, but—gods! I thought you were going to get us a half-dozen thugs, some muscle for the trip, not a *knight*." Brenner stopped in front of Caliban, raking his eyes up and down. His eyebrows moved like angry caterpillars.

A season or a lifetime ago, Caliban would have drawn his sword and shown the man muscle. He might be an assassin, but few assassins were terribly good at a straight assault. The way this one moved said that he was probably a more-than-competent knife fighter—he had that unconscious tendency to present only a profile to the enemy—but a sword gave you a good bit of advantage in reach, although not as much as one might think.

A straightforward attack, then, right down the middle, butchery rather than swordplay. It would have the advantage of surprise. If the man got a knife out, he could adjust tactics accordingly.

Caliban did none of these things. He had not held a sword for months. He could not even think of a response to the man's words, and his wits were generally the last thing to desert him. Possibly they'd fallen into the sky.

Ngha, ngha, hggahnmama halikalikali... muttered the demon.

His hands were shaking. Caliban put them behind him. He looked up and met Brenner's eyes, which were blue, with pale rings around the pupil, and knew the man had seen him trembling.

Of course. Assassins were an observant lot, or they didn't last very long. Little things like trip wires and the changing of the guard could really put a damper on one's career.

"He's a complete wreck," said Brenner, displaying his grasp of the obvious. The caterpillars slammed together over his nose.

"Shut up, Brenner," said Slate tiredly. "And sit down, too. The poor man's been in a cell for months, he's hardly at his best. You know how people get when they've been on the inside for too long. Some rest and decent food, and he'll be fine."

"I just don't see *why*," said Brenner. "Do you have some kind of armor fetish you never mentioned before?"

A whining assassin. Caliban had seen everything now.

"I had a feeling, okay?"

Brenner turned away from his quarry and toward Slate. Caliban felt a shameful flush of relief that the man was leaving him alone, and an immediate twinge of guilt. The assassin looked half again as large as Slate, and he descended on her like a stooping hawk.

Caliban took a step forward, despite himself. He had thought that he had slaughtered chivalry on that red morning four months ago, but perhaps there was a little left after all.

Slate seemed unimpressed. She waved Brenner off with a back-handed gesture, a slap at the air, and stalked over to the room's narrow window. "Relax, Brenner."

"Tell me why!"

"I told you! I had a feeling!"

"If you think I'm traipsing over half the countryside with a bloody *knight-errant* based on some kind of woman's intuition—"

She growled, turned around, and planted a hand in the middle of the assassin's chest. She pushed. He fell back a step, probably out of courtesy. "A *feeling*, you idiot!"

Brenner opened his mouth, shut it again, and said, in a rather different tone, "Oh."

"Yes."

"Like that one time—"

"Yes."

"With the sneezing—"

"*Yes.*"

He folded his arms and leaned against the wall, looking deflated. "You should've said."

"I thought I did!"

There was some shared knowledge here that was lost on Caliban. He found that he didn't care. The world was starting to spin again. He looked around for another chair, found one in front of the fire, and sat down. The world slowed, jerking rather than spinning. He put his face in his hands.

"All right," said Brenner, behind him, "if that's the way it is. I still think—well, never mind."

"I'm not a knight-errant," someone said. Caliban realized after a moment that it had been him. He dropped his hands.

"What?" Brenner turned around.

"I'm not a knight-errant. Errants are questing knights. I don't. Didn't." He cleared his throat.

Brenner's eyebrows didn't know whether to pull down in a scowl or go up in astonishment. The caterpillars did a complicated jig across his forehead instead.

"I was a paladin, actually. A holy champion of the Dreaming God. I killed demons. No questing." It sounded strange to say it. It seemed so unlikely now. He had once kept vigils in white marble halls, his nostrils full of the scent of incense and holiness. It was a long way from this small, cramped room over an inn, and the only thing he could smell were cheap candles and his own sweat.

He ran a hand through his hair. "It's a minor theological difference, I grant you."

The assassin stared at him then swung around and stared at Slate, who spread her hands helplessly.

There was a silence, except for the rustling of cloth as the other two shifted their feet. Then a loud bark of male laughter rang by his ear.

"Good lord," said Brenner. "You're kidding. Is this *Lord* Caliban?"

"Yes," said Slate.

"The one who—"

"Yes."

"With the guards and the nuns—"

"*Yes.*"

Brenner grinned hugely. He had excellent teeth. "I take back everything I said, Slate, darlin'."

"Shut *up*, Brenner," said Slate, a well-polished phrase if Caliban had ever heard one. He wondered if they were lovers. They seemed more like siblings who did not entirely care for one another.

"Lord Caliban! Ha! You've got quite a set, girl. I always said." A heavy hand fell on Caliban's shoulder. The knight controlled a flinch.

"*Sir* Caliban, actually," he said. And when Brenner whooped again, "Or just Caliban."

"You planning on killing our Slate some night on the road, *Sir* Caliban?"

The knight smiled sourly. "Not if you're closer."

Apparently this was the right response. Brenner slapped him on the back and went back to his chair. "Excellent! At least we'll all go to hell in good company."

Caliban traded a brief, ironic glance with Slate. The question of why she was the one in charge of their little jaunt into death's jaws had been answered.

She turned toward the door. "You can use my room. I'll have them draw you a bath."

The door closed behind her.

Silence filled up the room, broken by Brenner snickering to himself.

"What did she do?" asked Caliban, when he couldn't take it any more.

"Do?" Brenner slung his legs over the arm of the chair again.

"You know. What crime…?" His hand moved toward the tattoo on his arm.

"Oh!" Brenner grinned again. "She works in documents, our Slate."

"Documents?"

"Making them, taking them…She steals paperwork, and changes it."

Caliban frowned. "Is there money in that?"

Brenner laughed, apparently at his ignorance. "A lot more than in jewels and murder, my good knight." He leaned forward. "Say you're a merchant with a rival, and you get wind that he's about to get audited. You hire our dear Slate, and she goes in, takes their account books, makes some numbers dance up and down, puts them back, and presto! Your rival's dragged up before the courts, you pay Slate a sizeable amount of money, and no one ever knows."

"There's a lot of that going on?"

Brenner shrugged. "There's enough. Thieves with cutthroat accounting skills aren't exactly common. Me, I just cut throats and skip the accounting bit."

"How nice for you."

"She steals other things, too. Land deeds, proofs of annulment—very popular with the nobility, annulments—quite a busy girl, our Slate. Seen her walk past jewelry boxes, straight for the filing cabinet every time. Quite a set, and I don't say that lightly." He grinned. "'Course you know that. Ha! Sent her to get some dumb muscle, and she comes back with Lord Caliban, the mass murderer."

I don't think I like this man very much.

I don't think he's half so dumb as he pretends to be, either.

There was no question why Brenner was along, at least—Caliban would bet diamonds to road apples that there was a tattoo on the man's shoulder with its teeth sunk into his flesh.

"Why didn't they hang you, anyway?" the assassin asked, dropping into the chair opposite him. The caterpillars spasmed.

"I was possessed."

"*Sure* you were."

What Caliban might have said to this—and he had no idea himself—was cut off by the door opening. Slate emerged, balancing a bundle of papers topped with an inkwell. She jerked her head toward one of the adjoining doors. "Bath's ready. Brenner, make yourself useful and go find the man some decent clothes and a sword."

Brenner executed a mocking salute and slithered out the door.

"Can we trust him?" asked Caliban.

We. She and I are a we. *When did that happen?*

"Brenner? He's got a heart of gold…cold, metallic, and made of money. But the tattoo will keep him in line. More or less."

"I don't like him," said Caliban.

"Who does?" asked Slate.

CHAPTER 4

Evening came. By the time the sounds of splashing from her room had finally stopped, Slate had changed, eaten, and finished writing a letter to the Stone Bitches. The servant boy had gone in and out five times, carrying hot water. She wondered how long it took to wash off a season's worth of grime, or to shave off that much beard.

Brenner had returned after an hour or so, dropping off a pile of clothes. She heard him say something from the next room, and Caliban's sharp response, but couldn't make out anything but the tone. Brenner laughed. The door opened and closed again.

"Baiting him, Brenner?" she asked, bending over her writing.

"I offered to shave him, since he doesn't have a mirror. He said he'd do it himself. Acted like a hot towel was a murder weapon."

"Can't imagine why he wouldn't want you to have a razor near his neck."

"I *know*."

The assassin trailed his fingers over her neck as he passed. She hunched away, annoyed. They'd been lovers once, a few years ago, and although they hadn't resumed the relationship, she got the feeling he hadn't given up hoping.

He didn't press the issue. Instead there was a metallic *clunk*, and she looked up, startled.

Brenner slid a sword across the table in front of her. "For our fine knight."

Her eyebrows went up. "That's a big sword." The blade was wider than her wrist and longer than her arm. It looked like something you'd use to brace a ceiling with, rather than a weapon.

"Now, now, you know it's not the size of the sword—"

"Shut *up*, Brenner."

He grinned, slinging the equally large scabbard across the back of the chair. "Anyway, it's the kind the temple knights carry. I went and looked." Another blade, a long knife, hit the table with a clunk. "And here's the one I think they actually use. I can't imagine you could swing *that* bloody thing indoors without taking out half the building."

"Oh. Good thinking." Brenner knew weaponry, she'd give him that. Slate tried to pick up the sword and grunted. She was fairly strong—people kept their documents in some odd places, and she had to climb walls and rain-pipes more often than not—but her wrists started shaking uncontrollably at the weight. "Good lord. They actually swing this thing?"

"Oh, yes. Our dear paladin could probably chop a bull in half with that sword."

"I suppose that'll come in handy if we need any bulls chopped."

Brenner sat down on the edge of the table. Slate moved her letter and her inkwell out of the way. "He'll be excellent muscle, I imagine, if he doesn't run mad and chop us up instead."

"It's a quicker death than getting eaten by a tattoo," she pointed out, sprinkling a thin layer of drying sand over the letter

"True enough."

He fell silent after that. It was one of the restful things about assassins; they knew how to be quiet. He lounged in his chair instead, like a big black cat in front of the fire, doing nothing much, thinking his own thoughts behind his pale blue eyes.

They were killer's eyes. Her mother had warned her about men with eyes like that. Granted the line of work her mother had been in, it had been very specific advice: "Get the money up front. They're fine in a brothel, but don't go out to his house, whatever you do."

It was good advice, and her mother would definitely not have approved of her brief liaison with Brenner. Still, despite his many faults, she'd found him reliable. They'd worked together a few times. Unless someone offered him a great deal of money to kill her, he was trustworthy, which made him the closest thing she had to a friend, and how sad was *that?*

But he did know how to be quiet.

She waited until the ink was dry, then folded up the letter and waved it at him. He plucked it neatly from her fingers, but didn't try to read it. Like most people, Brenner was the next best thing to illiterate. *Sad for him, job security for me.*

"Do the Stone Bitches still operate out of that warehouse on Old Slaughterhouse Row?"

"Far as I know, yeah."

"Will you run that by them? They're about to get raided."

"Your wish is my command." He saluted with the folded paper, fingers rising to the tattoo on his shoulder. "Doesn't this count as betraying the crown?"

"I'm still planning on doing everything in my power to stop the Clockwork Boys. Beyond that, I don't think it cares."

"Interesting." Brenner tucked the letter into his belt and strolled out.

Slate slouched down in a chair in front of the fire. It was mid-spring, and the days were warming up, but the evenings were still chilly. She poked up the fire, then curled up in the chair. Her eyelids were heavy.

Long day. I suppose it's probably better for your last days to be long ones, but I think I could stand a short one now and again. For variety.

The door to her room opened. Caliban came out.

She glanced up sleepily, then sat bolt upright. "Good lord!"

The bath hadn't been able to do anything about the dark circles under his eyes, but otherwise, it was hard to imagine that it was the same man.

Freed of the grime, his hair had lightened to a dark honey, and freed of the ragged growth of beard, he had a strong jawline. He'd kept the beard in front, neatly trimmed, but thinned enough that she could make out a broad lower lip. With his hair pulled back, the ironic eyebrows were much more obvious.

Brenner, with his usual eye for detail, had judged the man's size exactly. In decently fitted, well-cut clothes, instead of prison rags, Caliban looked about ten years younger. He looked like—well, like a champion of the gods, in fact, if a pale and sardonic one. *And not a bad looking one. Raowr.*

Down, girl. He's a walking corpse anyway. Quit staring.

He was just an unexpectedly good-looking corpse, that was all.

"I didn't cut my nose off shaving, did I?" he asked.

"No, it's still there. You, uh, look a lot better." She tore her eyes away before she said anything embarrassing.

What, like, "Take me now?"

Mmm. I realize Brenner set a bad precedent, but I'd just as soon get away from men with a body count.

Not that it matters anyway. I'll probably be dead on the road soon, and doubly dead if we ever get to Anuket City. That's one more complication I really, really don't need.

Fortunately, Caliban couldn't hear what she was thinking. "Thank you, madam." He sketched a half-bow in her direction. "I feel much better. It's amazing how four months of dirt drags at you."

This was true. Caliban could hardly believe how much better he felt, now that he'd scrubbed himself clean. It had taken the sweating servant half a dozen trips, lugging clean water in and dirty water out, to remove the stink of the prison. He'd had to cut great tangles ruthlessly out of his hair, and he was surprised at how much was left.

"I'm afraid, madam, I must beg you to leave the servant boy a rather large tip. I have no money, myself."

Slate nodded. "I'll add it to the cost of the room. Our expense account is positively decadent."

Caliban nodded. That explained the clothes, then, although the cut was rather alarming. Not because they didn't fit, but because they fit *exactly*, practically as if tailored. Even the boots were an excellent fit. That the assassin had looked at him so briefly and judged his size so exactly was a trifle alarming.

If he can judge a cut of clothes this fine, I wonder how he can judge a cut of the knife?

It was almost worth it, however, to see the look on Mistress Slate's face when he entered the room. She'd been draped over the chair—apparently both criminals shared a criminal disregard for furniture—looking half asleep, until she'd seen him.

Definitely not a woman only for other women, I think. At least I clean up well.

Gha gha, ngh'aa, ha...

He grimaced as the demon voice slithered up from someplace between the back of his mind and the pit of his stomach. *Stupid. Stupid to be thinking about women at all.*

He did not think he was still dangerous. The demon was dead, even if its corpse was rotting in his brain. He'd realized long ago that the muttering voice was not *alive*, that it was more like a peculiar spiritual stench of decay.

But that didn't matter. The dead novices at his feet had been too large, too irrevocable a thing. He had not been the architect of their deaths, but he had been the instrument, and he could not quite pretend that it had happened to another person, that someone else's muscles had moved and lifted the sword and swung and lifted the sword again—

The shudder worked its way up the back of his spine and he turned his head a little as it struck.

Still. Women should not look at me with anything but revulsion. It is an old habit of thought to think otherwise.

I must forget old habits.

"There's bread and cheese on the table," said Slate, who was looking back at the fire again. What she might have read in his face was anyone's guess. Caliban could barely read his own thoughts. "Someone ought to be up with stew in an hour or so."

"Thank you."

He turned to the table, took a step, and froze.

A naked sword lay across the table, gleaming in the pool of light cast by the oil lamp beside it.

It was a large blade, meant to be used one- or two-handed. Light did not so much gleam on the steel as caress it intimately.

Damn that assassin. His eye had been *perfect*.

Is this a cruelty? Did he know how deeply holding such a sword would cut me?

Was he trying to be friendly?

The last time he'd held such a sword, blood had dulled the edge—blood and bits of other things. His keepers certainly would not have trusted him with a sword again, whether the demon was gone or not. His blood roared in his ears.

If I pick the sword up, and the demon isn't gone—if all that ritual, if the pain and the chanting and the water and the blood wasn't enough—

—so much water—

"Brenner got you a sword," said Slate behind him.

He looked over his shoulder. She'd flopped sideways in the chair, peering at him with her head tilted upside-down over the arm. The long column of her throat could not have been more exposed if she'd been on a chopping block.

If there was still a demon in him, it would take him three strides to cross the room, swinging the blade over his head—the ceilings were high enough that he need turn only a little sideways, rather than straight up—and then down. Necks were harder to cut through than people thought, but with his weight and the weight of the sword, he could hardly fail to cleave through, straight into the overstuffed arm of the chair. The wood and the cloth would probably bind worse than flesh and bone would.

"Is it the right kind? Brenner said it's what the temple knights used…" She yawned, stifled it. "Sorry."

And we'll all go to hell in good company…

Caliban reached out and closed his fingers around the hilt.

Nothing happened.

He exhaled, waiting.

Still nothing.

He lifted the sword. It was a heavy blade, not beautiful, but that was correct. There were beautiful swords for parades and temple services. This was for the butchery of demons. It needed to be strong and sharp and brutal.

His muscles did not fire with alien strength. He did not turn around and paint the walls with Slate's blood.

The exorcism worked. The demon's really dead.

Be damned. Or not.

It occurred to him that his face was wet. He set the sword down, very carefully, and wiped his eyes.

He looked over, and saw that Slate wasn't looking at him, very deliberately, and took that, as perhaps it was intended, as a kindness.

"So tell me about yourself," Caliban said to Slate, the next evening. Brenner had gone off on some unknown errand of his own, seeing to whatever odd supplies an assassin needed, and they were eating a quiet meal together in the common room of the suite.

She paused, her spoon in midair. "Me?"

"We're going to be on the road together for what—two weeks?—and in Anuket City for quite a while after that. I might as well know who I'm traveling with."

She set her spoon down and picked up a piece of bread, chasing the remnants of the soup around her bowl with it. "Um. My name is Slate, I'm thirty, and I have a tattoo that's going to eat me unless I find out how to stop the Clockwork Boys. I've never actually met a Clockwork Boy." She took a bite of bread. "But apparently the only way to stop them is in Anuket City, which no one on this side of the mountains has been able to get to for months. I think those are the important bits."

Caliban sighed, leaning back in his chair. He had gone out earlier, and while he still jumped away from sudden movements, the sky had not been so huge, and the world not quite so incomprehensible. He'd stayed close to the walls and doorways nonetheless.

The sword across his back seemed to anchor him. Perhaps that wasn't a surprise.

He ran his fingers down it now, slung over the back of the chair. "Brenner said you were some kind of...guerrilla accountant."

Her gaze sharpened. "Did he? Damnit."

"Is it true?"

"It was. I suppose I'm not much of one now."

"How do you go from stealing paperwork to a sentence of death?"

She smiled. It was a surprisingly charming smile. "So if you alter the wrong papers, they charge you with aiding and abetting the enemy. Who knew?"

His eyebrows went up. "And they sent you out on this jaunt anyway?"

"It was years ago," she said defensively. "I was young and dumb and didn't know better than to fool around with defense contract paperwork. I haven't done that for years, but some bright young clerk—may his pens leak eternally—managed to trace my handwriting. I hadn't learned to disguise it very well back then." She shrugged. "It wasn't a big deal, really—tampered with some paperwork to make it appear to be under budget, but—well, anyway. With the latest war on, they apparently have people going through all the old contracts, and…you know."

Caliban did indeed know. He would have been very surprised if they'd gotten so far as executing Slate. Skilled forgers were too valuable to waste.

She took another bite of bread. "So anyway, I got charged with a count of treason, and I thought they'd hang me, but the Dowager had this wild idea. I lived in Anuket City for a few years, so I'm supposed to know the lay of the land." She dismissed the land and its lay with a flick of her wrist. "Never mind that I was gone long before the Clockwork Boys were invented…or grown…or discovered…or whatever."

"So they chose you."

"Uh-huh. I think she figures there might be some complicated recipe for making Clockwork Boys, and I might need to steal it."

"Is it likely to be a recipe, do you think?"

She shook her head. "It could be anything. It could also be a person—some kind of sorcerer or wonderworker or something—and we're hoping Brenner can kill him. Or her, or them. It could be an artifact, in which case one of us can probably lift it."

"What if it's a process? Something that a lot of people know?"

Slate shrugged. "Well, then, we try to learn it, and come back and tell the Dowager. Maybe her pet wonderworkers can figure out a weakness. Maybe they'd all melt if you throw live chickens at them or something."

"They're supposed to be eight-foot-tall killing machines. Do you really think chickens would work?"

"I don't know that it's been tried."

Caliban contemplated this for a few moments. "This all assumes we can make it to the city at all, now that there's a war in the way."

"That it does."

"*Can* we make it?"

She grinned, looking almost like Brenner for a moment. "Do you believe in miracles, paladin?"

He grunted.

They ate in silence for a while. Caliban had another glass of wine, and poured her another one too. She frowned at it.

"So how does one get to be a guerilla accountant, anyway? What's your family like?"

Slate stopped frowning at the wine, and frowned at him instead. Caliban almost smiled. Despite a full day, and seeing several other women, the mobility of her face still intrigued him.

Slate took a swallow of wine, as if to fortify herself. "Not much to tell. My mother was a very high-class courtesan who counted her fertile days by the moon. Her beauty was impeccable, her math skills were not." She swept a hand at herself. "And here I am."

"And you became an accountant."

"She could afford very good tutors. Since my beauty was *not* impeccable, I made sure my math skills were above reproach." She took another slug of wine.

There was an old hurt there, Caliban could tell. It wasn't hard to decipher. He wondered if she thought she was hiding it.

"The rest is the usual story," said Slate. "Got married when I was too young to know better. It lasted about six months, and then he went off with a blond from the Weaver's Quarter and I went off to Anuket City. And came back eventually, of course."

"What an idiot," said Caliban, because that was what you said to this sort of thing. "You're well rid of him." Privately he wondered about the wedding-ring scar on her hand. Had she tried to burn the ring off? Slate did not strike him as the sort for impractical romantic gestures, but one never really knew.

"It made things easier," she admitted. "So. That's me, anyway." Slate set the wineglass down. "So what's it like to slay demons?"

He grunted. "Messy. Someone comes into the temple with a report, and you ride out to find it. If it's in an animal, you kill it. Usually it's an animal. If it's in a person, though, you try to convince them to go back to the temple. Usually they're fighting it, and they're happy to go along. Sometimes you have to kill them."

"How do you know if they're possessed, and not just...?" She trailed off and waved a hand to indicate any number of options.

It was a fair question. Caliban stared into his wine. "Most of the time, demons are pretty stupid—they start babbling in no earthly language, or levitating or something. The smart ones are a lot harder, some of them speak the language very well, have experience puppeting a body around, but they're rare, and you get a feeling—they usually have a kind of accent, and they don't move right. But it can be hard. You learn to do it after a few years, but the old ones, the smart ones can still catch you out. And if the human host works with them willingly, which does happen sometimes...well, they're nearly impossible to spot until they make a mistake."

"Not a lot of sword work, then?"

"Enough of it. If they realize what's happening and don't come quietly—or if they get a big animal, like a bull or a boar—well, it gets ugly."

That was putting it mildly. The last bad demon he'd dealt with had taken a draft horse, and had killed two men before they'd sent him out after it. Running around a field with a solid ton of demon in hot pursuit, panting out the ritual of exorcism and trying to cut the thing's legs out from under it one by one...no, "ugly" didn't quite cover it.

"How can you tell if there's one in an animal, if it's a matter of accent?"

"They're generally not good at hiding it. You ever hear a cow speak in tongues?"

She giggled. He hadn't actually been joking, but he'd take the giggle. It was much better than having her frown all the time.

She sobered. "So that voice yesterday, in the Captain's office—"

"Ah. Yes." Now it was his turn to fortify himself with wine. "It talks sometimes. The demon's dead—genuinely dead, the temple certified it—but the body's still in there. If that makes any sense."

Slate frowned. "An *actual* body?"

"More of a metaphorical one, although it's quite real nonetheless. It's hard to explain. It's definitely not alive, it's…ah… decaying, after a fashion, I think. But magic shakes it up, makes the flies come buzzing out, and then I start…err…muttering a bit." He took another swallow of wine. "It doesn't happen that often."

"Hmmm." She pursed her lips for a moment. "You're sure it's dead?"

"Very sure, madam."

She lifted an eyebrow.

"I haven't killed you. Ergo—" He drained the rest of his wineglass.

"Ah. Good enough."

She got up from the table, taking her wine with her. Caliban poured the rest of the bottle into his glass and followed her to the chairs.

They had not been able to find a third room for him at the inn, and neither he nor Brenner had been particularly keen on sharing a room, so the temple knight was sleeping on the floor in the common room. Slate avoided the pile of blankets by the simple expedient of climbing over the back of the chair. Less agile and with a fuller glass, Caliban shoved his bedding aside with his foot and took the other chair.

"It doesn't sound very glamorous, demon hunting," she said.

"It's not. I've killed a lot of possessed cows."

"Then why was *Lord* Caliban so lionized?"

No-longer-Lord Caliban shrugged. "Temple paladins, you know. We dress well, when we're not off killing things. We're polite. We do heroic things that sound interesting—nobody realizes that most demon possessions end with butchering farm animals. Most of us aren't total bastards, since the Dreaming God has certain requirements in his servants. We're uncomplicated and look good in white. You know how it is." He considered for a moment. "We're not sworn to celibacy."

The sexual tension in the room kicked up several notches, rather abruptly. Caliban twitched.

I shouldn't have said that. That was stupid. I should have stopped drinking several glasses ago.

Slate wasn't helping, sprawled bonelessly over the chair like that. He wondered if she even knew *how* to sit in a chair.

Maybe she spends so much time hunched over account books that she can't sit normally the rest of the time.

He was surprised to see that she did actually have a shape underneath her usual layers of clothes. It was more generous than he would have guessed.

Well. One hardly dresses their best to visit a prison.

Stretched over the chair, however…

He took another swallow, vaguely hoping that sobriety would lie at the bottom of the glass.

"Mmm." She eyed him warily. "Uncomplicated and look good in white. Right. So how did a demonslayer get possessed?"

His libido went back to wherever it had briefly emerged from, which was a relief, even if the question wasn't.

"Oh." Caliban set the wineglass down, and stared into the fire, the black logs crazed with fine red cracks. "I'd…as soon not talk about it, if it's all the same to you. It doesn't matter any more anyway."

"It's okay. We're all going to die anyway in a few days. At most in a couple of weeks," she said, with a sort of grim cheer.

He blinked at her. "Is that meant to make me feel better?"

"Sure. You don't have to worry about getting rid of all your problems before they mess up your life anymore." She waved a hand in his direction. "I'm back to biting my fingernails, and Brenner's…well, I don't know what all of Brenner's vices are, and I don't want to. So you don't have to worry about whatever sins temple knights commit that let the demons in, because it's not going to matter."

He weighed this bit of wisdom and came to a conclusion. "You're drunk."

"Well, a little. I generally don't drink very much. Still, since I'm going to die anyway…" She wriggled around until her knees were over the back of the chair and her head was hanging over the seat and she was gazing solemnly at him, upside down. Bits of Caliban's spine cried out in sympathy.

"Fine, I grant you that my life's not worth much at the moment. But what if I'm worried about the afterlife?" He could feel a smile tugging at him, despite the subject—an inverted drunk guerrilla accountant was giving a disgraced temple knight spiritual advice. Possibly the gods had more of a sense of humor than he'd thought.

At the moment, she's probably in better grace with the gods than I am, anyway.

"*Are* you worried about the afterlife?"

"Not really."

"There, you see?" She folded her arms. Her hair brushed the floor under her head.

"Are *you* worried about dying?" he asked. He didn't mean to ask it, hadn't expected to hear himself saying it, and yet there it was—years in a temple got into your head. You provided spiritual comfort, like a reflex. It was even the paladin's voice he was using, the one that was always so effective, soothing and comforting, a little quieter than usual. A brother's voice, a priest's voice, a voice that spoke to the nerves and said: *Trust me.*

People opened up to that voice. If you did it well enough, you hardly ever needed the sword.

He wasn't sure if the fact that he could still do it involuntarily, despite months in a prison cell, demonic possession, murder, and half a bottle of wine was comforting or horrifying.

One of the two, anyway. Possibly both.

"Oh, I'm quite petrified." Slate wrinkled her nose, but there was a timbre in her voice that told him she wasn't entirely joking.

If she'd been right side up, at this point he would have reached out and put a hand on her shoulder. God, he'd held variations of this same conversation at least a dozen times with the newest squires. That there was no difference between an accountant thief and a novice demonslayer was also either comforting or horrifying.

Next it's the long, friendly look, and then they say something—generally doesn't matter what—and the proud ones straighten up, and the healthy ones cry, and the funny ones try to make a joke and choke up halfway through, and you put an arm around them and say something—still doesn't matter what, it's the tone that does it—and wait until they're done and then offer a handkerchief, and then they say something embarrassed, and you tell them that you cried for three nights the first time you actually went out after a demon.

Hmm, with the way she gets sneezing, I should probably offer her the handkerchief a little early—

Ngha, ha, nghaa, the demon said, which might have been an agreement, or a commentary on handkerchiefs.

He'd never seen a possessed person use one, if it came to that. Perhaps they didn't have handkerchiefs in hell.

"On the other hand," Slate said, making a sweeping gesture— Caliban rescued his wineglass—"whenever it starts to bother me, I think the same thing."

Here it comes. He dug in a pocket for his handkerchief.

"Really stupid people die all the time. And if *they* can manage it, I oughta have no problem."

He blinked.

That wasn't in the script…

"Err. You're not going to *cry*, are you?" Slate asked worriedly, eyeing his handkerchief.

"Ah…no." *And that's what I get for thinking I know what I'm doing.*

Kalikalikaliha, n'ha'mah, added the demon, which was arguably also something he'd gotten for thinking he knew what he was doing. And that was the other side of the paladin's voice, and the Dreaming God only knew if he could still manage *that* any longer.

He shoved the square of cloth back in his pocket. "I'm fine. But I think I'm about ready for bed." *Before my delusions run away with me, or I start gibbering in tongues again.*

"Mmm, probably a good idea." She kicked off with her feet and rolled off the chair, landing on her feet. He would have broken his neck if he'd tried that.

She staggered and sat down, hard.

It was not chivalric to snicker. He did it anyway, because if you were going to be thrown out of a religious order on your ear, you took what small comforts you could get.

Slate grumbled at him and slouched off toward her door.

"Madam—" he said, feeling oddly stilted, and then, "Slate—"

She turned and looked at him, one hand on the doorknob.

"Thank you. For—" he searched briefly for the words, "—giving me my death back."

She inclined her head as graciously as the Dowager accepting tribute, and slipped through the door and away.

He watched her go, then spread the bedroll out across the floorboards in front of the fire.

Probably they were all going to die. Still, it was better than life in a cell six paces across.

Caliban wrapped himself up in his blankets and stared at the fire. Unsure whether he was comforted or horrified, he drifted off to sleep, with the demon mumbling curses like a lullaby.

CHAPTER 5

Caliban took the sword out to the yard behind the inn the next morning, to see how much he had lost. The yard was for storing carriages when their owners were staying the night, but there weren't any in residence at the moment. Barrels of lamp oil and the less perishable supplies lined the walls, but there was a broad, empty space in the center. Grass grew up through the bricks.

He set his teeth and stepped out from the comforting closeness of the inn, directly into the emptiness.

Nothing happened. He did not fall into the sky. His stomach stayed quiet.

He exhaled.

Very well, then.

He knelt in the center of the yard, the sword in front of him, and tried to pray.

Dreaming God, who holds us all within His dreams, I thank you for this day you have set before me, for the sword I am given to serve you. I thank you—

And there he stopped, because the next line was *I thank you for my life,* and that seemed an odd mockery. He was a dead man, after all.

He hadn't even meant to pray. He had done it because you started the sword practice with prayer, every time. It was automatic. You drew the sword, you went to your knees, you bowed your head. It was part of the sword practice.

It was useless. The temple had thrown him out. The god had obviously turned away, or the demon would never have gained entrance. He could still feel the hollowness in his soul where the god's presence had once been.

Ngha, maha, kalikalikali...

No. I cannot believe that. I must believe that the gods do not send us trials that we cannot endure.

It would have been easier to believe that if he hadn't seen so many people broken by the trials they had endured.

He'd broken a few in his time. Exorcisms were not gentle things.

He had prayed in the cell for hours. Days. He had kept vigil on his knees, praying. Not for forgiveness, not for mercy—he deserved neither—but simply for a death.

The god had not answered. The hollow place in his soul stayed empty. Weeks had stretched to months, and he had stopped believing that there would ever be an answer. His faith had turned to bitterness and bile.

And then a little brown sparrow of a woman had come to the cell door and begun to sneeze.

The temple had abandoned him. Did the Dreaming God still have a use for him after all? Or had the god, too, washed His hands of His former paladin?

If He was still there, wouldn't I feel Him? Or does what's left of the demon keep even gods away?

Caliban sighed, got up, and drew his sword.

It wasn't as bad as he'd feared. He'd lost a fair bit of tone, but no worse than the time he'd been laid up with a broken leg. The memories were all still there, ground into slow, stupid muscle until it was second nature.

He ran through the sword forms, separately at first, then together in sequence. It was a crisp morning, but even so, within a very few minutes, sweat was dripping off him and his breath was coming fast.

He sheathed the sword and went to dunk his head in the horse trough.

When he came up for air, Brenner was sitting on one of the barrels, watching him. There was a cigarette between his lips.

Caliban saluted him, somewhat ironically, with the sword. "I did not get a chance to thank you. It's an excellent blade."

Brenner nodded. "Are you going to ask where I got it?"

"Should I?"

The assassin grinned. "Perhaps I killed a temple paladin for it."

"Perhaps you did," said Caliban evenly, giving no sign of how his stomach lurched at the thought.

"Ah, you disappoint me." Brenner chuckled. "No, I went to a weaponsmith. He does very fine work, and he occasionally supplies the temples."

"Now you disappoint *me*," said Caliban. "Did you at least steal it?"

"Tchah!" Brenner clucked his tongue. "One does not *steal* from weaponsmiths. They're skilled labor. You do your part to keep them in business. Stealing from them is short-sighted."

Caliban scratched his chin. This was an unexpected social conscience for an assassin.

"Of course, as Mistress Slate reminds me, we're all going to die shortly, so does one have the luxury of being anything but short-sighted?"

"Aww." Brenner slid off the barrel, grinning, grinding the cigarette end out under his heel. "Our Slate is a dear little fatalist, isn't she?"

"I take it you don't share her view," said Caliban, practicing a lunge that took him away from the assassin's grin.

"Nah. The trip's bad enough, mind you, but she's got her own reasons for not wanting to go to Anuket City. And it's different for me, you understand—I expect to die any day, so one more suicide mission isn't any different. Our Slate's in a much lower-risk line of work."

Caliban raised an eyebrow at that. "You're both breaking into people's houses at night, aren't you?"

"Yes, yes, but it's different. You wake up and find a teeny little girl with big eyes like our Slate going through your papers, you call the watch. You wake up and find me standing over you with a knife, and…well, now."

A knife appeared in his hand. He waved it under Caliban's nose, perhaps by way of demonstration. The former knight-champion stood his ground.

I recognize a test when it draws steel on me. He sighed internally. *I wonder how this will go down.*

"It occurs to me…" drawled Brenner, "that if you're going to be watching our backs, it would be nice to know how good you are."

"You've been watching me for a few minutes now, unless I miss my guess," Caliban said.

"Chopping at shadows, while very pretty, is not quite the same thing."

"I suppose not. What do you propose, then?"

Brenner lunged at him, his body unfolding like a preying mantis closing on an insect.

Caliban had been expecting it, practically since the assassin had showed up, and he still barely managed to get out of the way.

Dreaming God, he's fast!

He leapt backwards, swung his sword, saw it going directly at Brenner's head, and pulled the blow with a brutal snap that left his wrists throbbing.

Ow. Ow. Ow.

"You idiot!" he yelled. "This is live steel! You can't—if I hit you—"

"I'd best make sure you don't hit me then," said the assassin cheerfully, circling on the balls of his feet. He was indeed presenting just a profile.

Knife-fighter. Yep. Damn.

"This is *not* a good idea, Brenner!"

"It's a great idea!"

I've got a good bit of reach on him, particularly with the sword, for all the good it does. I know I'm stronger. And it doesn't bloody well matter because whether I cut him or he cuts me, I lose. Damn, damn, damn.

"Put some armor on, at least!"

"Oh, quit whining, paladin. I'm hardly the first person you'll have killed."

"If you're trying to annoy me, you're succeeding."

"Aww."

They closed again. Rather, Brenner closed, and Caliban dodged backward and swung his sword in an easily avoidable arc.

"Surely you can do better than that."

"Yes, but I'd rather leave you both legs."

Brenner was getting bold now, realizing that the knight didn't dare hit him. Caliban gritted his teeth and watched for an opening.

"So which is it for our knight, eh? Do you think you're going to live, like me, or are you waiting for your death, like our Slate?"

Caliban kept his eyes on the man's hands. Another knife had joined the first.

"Hoping for a heroic death to wash away all those sins?"

"Spare me the assassin's psychology," muttered Caliban, practically without hearing himself. There had to be an opening, he knew just what it would look like...

It came. Brenner lunged again, a knife in each hand. Caliban slapped the leading blade away with a blow to his wrist, wished badly for gauntlets—*I'd crush his bloody fingers if I had some decent gauntlets*—and the assassin was coming up beside him now, hip to hip, and that was a bad place for a man with a knife to be, and if he turned, he could take his head right off with the sword, but not before he got a knife in the kidneys—

"What in *hell* are you people doing?" Slate snarled from the doorway.

Both men froze. Since there was quite a lot of momentum going on at the moment, this meant that Brenner, ducking under the sword, actually fell to one knee, arms extended around Caliban's waist in a sort of lethal hug. Caliban tried to pull the sword up short one-handed. His wrist laughed at him. Something went *poing!* inside his arm, and his fingers opened. The sword jerked, wavered, fell, and landed—flat first, thank the gods—on Brenner's shoulder.

"Oof," said the assassin.

"Are you killing him or knighting him?" asked Slate, emerging from the door and pacing around the two of them as if they were a peculiar bit of statuary she'd discovered in the courtyard.

"Um," said Brenner. "We were sparring."

"Yes," said Caliban. "Sparring."

They exchanged a brief look, unified in the face of a common enemy.

"Is *that* what they call it? Do you need to get a room? Do you want me to go away, come back with a bucket of water, maybe?"

"I think we're good," said Caliban, picking his sword off the assassin's shoulder, very carefully.

"I think so," said Brenner, moving his knives delicately away from Caliban's kidneys.

"Good to know." She glared at both of them. "I realize we're all going to die, but I'd just as soon we do it there and not here."

"Awww...."

Caliban saluted her with the sword. She snorted and stalked off.

The men looked at each other.

"Next time, maybe."

"Oh, yes."

As truces went, it wasn't much, but Caliban figured he'd take what he could get.

"I don't suppose you could find some armor as easily as you found a blade?"

"I could probably manage that," said Brenner, and smiled.

"Madam Slate?"

Slate looked up from her work. "You can skip the madam bit. It makes me sound like my mother."

"Was her name also Slate?"

"No, but she was a madame." Slate leaned back in her chair, enjoying the expression that Caliban was trying (and failing) to hide. "What do you need?"

"I wish to attend a service at the temple," he said.

He was standing in parade rest again. The ridiculous demon-killing sword was slung over his back. He looked exceedingly martial and faintly ridiculous standing in the middle of a moderately priced inn room.

"So do it," said Slate. "I know I'm supposed to be in charge, but we haven't gone anywhere yet. Go do whatever you want. Get drunk, get laid…go to the temple…err…whatever it is paladins do for fun."

He took a deep breath, held it for a moment, and then said, very patiently, "I cannot go to the temple of the Dreaming God."

"Oh?" And then, as realization dawned, "*Oh!* Right. They know you there, don't they?"

He nodded.

"You, uh…" Slate started to make a hand gesture, realized that there was absolutely no way to express, *You kinda murdered a bunch of people there, didn't you?* that would not come out as horrible, and let her hand drop. "Right."

"I know that you are skilled in…ah…clandestine work. I was hoping that you might be able to assist me. A disguise of some sort, perhaps."

A disguise. Right. Slate looked up at him. *Six feet tall and some change, face the sort they stamped on coins, could probably model for a statue of the god of justice or courage or hitting things with swords. A disguise. Yeah.*

"I could dress you up as a really big leper," she said. "Or put you in a packing crate and arrange for delivery during a service. That's about as much as I've got in the way of disguises."

"I thought…perhaps a large hat…"

Dear god, he's serious.

"It's gonna take more than a hat," said Slate. "Look, I'll see what I can arrange."

He bowed his head. "Thank you."

"Yeah, well. Don't thank me yet."

She came back two hours later, tossed him an oilcloth cloak, and said "Get ready for the evening service."

He looked up at her, astonished. "Truly? So quickly?"

"I'm talented."

"I have never doubted."

Slate fought back a sigh. She knew he had a sense of humor, sometimes even a particularly sardonic one, but it seemed to manifest very erratically. She was pretty sure that right at this moment, he was entirely serious.

They stepped outside the inn together and into a downpour.

"Here's your disguise," said Slate, pulling her own hood up over her head.

"…I see." Caliban glanced at the sky. He looked as if he was rethinking his assessment of her talent. "Convenient. Do we simply not remove our cloaks at the temple?"

"We can do better than that."

He fell immediately into guard position behind her. She felt like she had a very large dog at heel. People were probably giving them odd looks, but everyone caught out in the downpour were wearing cloaks and heavy hoods or broad brimmed hats of their own, so she couldn't tell.

She hailed a carriage, tried to climb in, had Caliban attempt to hand her in, gave him a look that practically steamed the rainwater off him, and settled herself inside without further incident.

"Sorry," he said, sitting opposite. "Were you a nun, courtesy would dictate...never mind."

"I am *not* a nun," said Slate. "Incidentally, that's the first time I've ever had to tell anyone that."

Caliban smiled briefly. "I was largely raised by them," he said. "Please believe me that it is no insult."

"Mmm."

The carriage rattled to the temple square. Four temples stood opposite each other, one in each cardinal direction. The Dreaming God's temple stood on the eastern side, pillars sheathed in marble, glinting even in the evening rain.

Slate paid the driver. Caliban stood next to the door, looking slightly lost.

"Fine," muttered Slate, giving him her hand. "Don't tell Brenner."

He gravely assisted her down onto the wet cobblestones. Slate wondered if treating her like a nun boded well for their working relationship.

He did murder several of them, of course.

Yes, well. People are complicated.

She strode out across the square toward the temple, only pausing when she realized that her guard dog was apparently no longer at heel. Slate turned her head.

He stood staring at the temple. It was too dark to see through the shadow of the hood, but he had an edge of his cloak in his hands and was wringing it with such force that she almost feared for the oilcloth.

"Come on," she said, walking back to him. "If you stand here, people are going to notice."

"I was a fool to think I could come here," he said hoarsely. "I can't go in there."

"Well, I already paid the bribe and I hate to waste money."

He blinked at her. She wondered if anything else she said would have gotten through to him. "Bribe? You *bribed* someone?"

"Seat in the choir loft. I told him we're wealthy donors looking to check out the acoustics, but he's pretty sure we're actually going to be screwing. Come on, you can have a breakdown once we're out of the rain."

That got him moving. "One of the temple servants took money? But we could be possessed! Or—or—this is a threat to the security of the temple!"

"Good thing it's us, huh?"

He stalked beside her all the way to the temple steps. The doors were open, revealing a glimpse of vaulted ceilings. Slate started up the steps, didn't hear footsteps, turned and looked again.

"Do we need to keep doing this?"

Caliban shook his head. "I'm sorry," he said, pulling the hood lower over his face.

"Good. Let me do the talking."

They went through the doors. Slate heard Caliban draw in a sharp breath, as if he'd been struck. She put her own hood back and went up to the short, pleasant-faced man standing at the door.

"It's me," she said.

"Lady!" he said. "Of course—yes—follow me." He looked curiously at Caliban but asked no questions. "When you are finished, you may leave by these stairs. Please lock the door behind you. The loft is not open for evening services, but of course, in this case, an exception…"

Caliban rumbled something wordless and angry.

The temple servant looked doubtful for a moment. Slate took his hand, pressed a coin firmly into it, and said "Thank you for your assistance. I predict great things for so helpful an individual as yourself."

"Yes, of course…" He glanced at the coin in his palm and the doubt smoothed away completely. "Anything that I can do to be of assistance, of course!"

"How much did you give him?" whispered Caliban, after the servant had closed the door behind them."

"Enough to buy two or three rounds of drinks."

"He sold out the temple's security for so *little?*" For a moment, Slate was afraid that Caliban might charge out the loft and after the hapless young man.

"Yes. Because if I'd given him too much, he'd know something was afoot. Too much money is as dangerous as too little; it means you want it too bad. Now sit down and commune or whatever it is you do. We have to leave before the service ends, if we want to be safe."

The choir loft ran the width of the temple, well above the level of most seating. There were wooden seats, all empty, and the lamps were unlit. Evening services did not require a full choir, merely a few singers down at ground level, behind the altar.

The statue of the Dreaming God was almost at eye level with them, across the temple. It was smiling remotely, eyes closed. In one hand, it held a book and in the other a familiar-looking sword.

Slate peered over the railing. The seats below were mostly empty and Slate thought the priestess standing beside the altar had a distinctly harried look.

None of this seemed to matter to Caliban. He sank down on his knees at the railing, eyes fixed on the distant figure in white, and seemed to become a statue himself.

They had only a few moments to wait until the service began. A few more seats filled up, but not many. The Dreaming God's church was wealthy because people were usually very, very grateful to have demons dealt with, but this did not always translate to attendance at their services.

Slate, never much inclined to kneel, sat on a seat and tried not to fidget. *Not that it matters. I suspect I could bounce a brick off Caliban's head and he wouldn't notice right now.*

She wished Brenner were here so that she could say something sarcastic to an appreciative audience. On the other hand, Brenner would have had so much to say about the situation that it was probably for the best. She didn't want Caliban to try to strangle the assassin before they even got on the road.

She shifted uncomfortably on the wooden seat and thought *I should have brought a book.*

Caliban would probably have noticed a brick to the head. In fact, he might have welcomed it.

As the priestess's voice swelled out around them—Sister Dominique, an uninspired speaker but rock solid on theology—Caliban felt the presence of his god.

The Dreaming God was there. He was in His temple. He was looking down at His faithful. Caliban knew it. He *believed* it, not as an article of faith, but as he believed in sunrise and sunset and the turn of the seasons.

He could feel the god. Words and incense and holy fire. Strength and certainty and the sword.

He wanted that. He wanted that surety and that strength, that feeling of being in exactly the correct place. He wanted it more than he had ever wanted food or drink or a woman's body, more than he had wanted freedom in his filthy little cell. He wanted to be *whole*.

He had never minded the grim, hard, dirty work of demon-slaying. He dealt with the sorrow and the pain and the atrocities that demons worked and the atrocities that paladins wrought trying to stop them. He had been a sword in the hand of his god, and that was all that he had ever asked to be.

And here he was.

And here the god was.

And the hollow place in his soul did not fill up.

The god was all around him and Caliban stood in the center of holiness and was not touched.

His lips moved in time with Sister Dominique's, saying the litany that he knew by heart, and *nothing happened*.

One moment, he begged his god. *One touch. One word. Please. I will never ask again. Just let me know that You have not forgotten me. I beg of You. Please.*

There was no answer. Only the demon, rotting down at the bottom of his soul.

Perhaps there would never be an answer again. The god had made His choice. And Caliban, now, would have to live with it, for as long as he was able.

He rose to his feet.

"All right," he said to Slate. "I had to know. Thank you."

She nodded. She asked no questions. He pulled the hood of his cloak up over his face and left the temple of the Dreaming God for the last time.

CHAPTER 6

The scholar turned up the next day. The meeting at the guardkeep was not precisely auspicious.

Caliban, Brenner, and Slate walked to the guardkeep. Caliban was pleased that he could do so without a halt in his step. The flap of tarps in the marketplace elicited no more than a twitch.

He was pretty sure that Brenner still saw the twitch, mind you.

What Slate saw was anyone's guess.

The guards, who had looked through him the last time, saw a Knight-Champion this time—out of armor, but carrying the sword. They saluted. Brenner snickered. Caliban discovered that his jaw was aching and had to consciously stop gritting his teeth.

The Captain of the Guard's office was overcrowded, holding all three of them, the Captain, and the scholar.

The scholar was a young man with an open, thoughtful face. His current disagreeable expression did not sit well on it.

"Why are we bringing a woman?" he asked, peering down his nose at Slate. "I will not travel with one of their sex."

Slate's jaw dropped. The Captain put a hand over his eyes.

"I *beg* your pardon?" said Slate, clearly unable to believe what she had just heard.

"It is granted," said the scholar, flicking his fingers outward in an abbreviated gesture of blessing. "Go forth and sin no more. Captain?" He turned away. "I believe I asked—"

Caliban and Brenner, acting with rare unity, reached out and grabbed one of Slate's arms each, before anyone could learn what her sudden lunge in the scholar's direction might mean.

"Let me go," she hissed. "I'll kill him. The tattoo can only eat me once."

They exchanged looks over her head. Three days had not been enough for the men to establish more than an uneasy truce—the sparring had helped, but not much—but it seemed they'd just found another bit of common ground. Neither one let go.

"Err," said the Captain. "Learned Edmund, this is Mistress Slate. She will be in charge of your mission."

"What?" said the Learned Edmund, turning to look at Slate.

"Learned Edmund is a dedicate of the Many-Armed God," said the Captain, making furious little head-jerk gestures at the man in question.

Ah. Of course. Caliban stifled a groan. The Many-Armed God was portrayed carrying six pens, one in each right hand, and six books, one in each left. His scholars lived rigidly monastic lives, copying out ancient libraries. They were breathtakingly brilliant men, one and all—the Many-Armed God simply didn't take anyone who wasn't a genius.

The key word, though, was *men.*

Unfortunately, their rigid lifestyles tended to leave them xenophobic, misogynistic, and anything else one could care to name—but very, very brilliant.

The sad thing, thought Caliban, *is that he's probably exactly the sort of scholar we need to get to the bottom of this. Not that it may matter...*

Learned Edmund stared at Slate. Slate stared at Learned Edmund.

"Why am I not to lead this mission?" asked the dedicate, turning back to the Captain.

"The Dowager has placed Mistress Slate in charge, on the understanding that she is the most knowledgeable at orchestrating such...clandestine operations."

Brenner's probably at least as good, but I can't imagine the Dowager spending thirty seconds in his presence. There's me, of course, but what I know about breaking and entering can fit in a thimble.

"I am not comfortable with a member of the distaff sex leading us," said Learned Edmund.

Slate's arm twitched in Caliban's grip. He was surprised her feet were still on the floor, and more surprised that people still used the phrase, "distaff sex."

"And I don't see why I am not in charge," the scholar continued, oblivious. "These three are, after all, criminals, are they not?"

"I'm an assassin!" said Brenner brightly.

Caliban put his free hand over his mouth. The Captain suffered a sudden coughing fit.

"Indeed," said Learned Edmund, giving Brenner a dismissive look. Apparently subtlety was lost on him.

Brenner gave Caliban another look, which clearly said, *I tried. Your turn.*

The paladin sighed. "I am Knight-Champion Caliban, of the Temple of the Dreaming God." He cleared his throat, the immensity of the falsehood nearly choking him. "*Former* Knight-Champion, I should say."

Learned Edmund seemed to loosen a bit. "Oh. A spiritual brother—I see." He offered a hand.

Caliban flicked a glance at Brenner, who casually slid his foot between Slate's ankles.

It'd have to do. Caliban dropped her arm, clasped the scholar's hand, and bowed.

"It is an honor to serve beside a dedicate of the Many-Armed God," he said.

Brenner rolled his eyes. Slate got herself back under control and shook the assassin off. She was absolutely expressionless, except for a certain tightness around the lips.

"Yes—an honor, but still—"

"Are you from the monastery in northern Ghaston, Learned Edmund?"

"I—yes—"

"I traveled there once, some years ago. A lovely area."

"Yes, very. And you're changing the subject, Knight-Champion. I am *still* not comfortable traveling with a woman on such an important mission!"

Damn. Well, I tried...

"I promise, we'll keep her from ravishing you in the night," said Brenner.

The dedicate flushed. Slate said, "Shut *up,* Brenner." The Captain had his hand over his eyes again.

Into this dreadful moment, the knock on the door fell like a stone into still water.

Everybody looked at the door. Finally the Captain called, "Come in."

It was a guardsman: young, looking a little grey.

"We have a situation out there, Captain."

"I've got a situation in *here* at the moment—nevermind. What is it?"

"Another case of blight, Captain."

The Captain frowned. "We've got procedures. Keep people away from the body, and call the bonepickers. They've got orders to burn them—"

"Captain, it's a kid. The mother won't leave it. She's been holding it for a couple of hours, and there's no way we can get her away from the body without one of us getting exposed."

The Captain's face went a little grey himself. Caliban felt a shudder lurking at the base of his spine. *Ah, gods, sometimes there are no right answers...*

"Several hours?" said the Captain quietly.

"Yes, sir."

"Then she's already exposed." His voice was very flat. "Go over to the crossbowmen and have them draw straws—"

"I'll do it," said Brenner.

The Captain stared at the assassin. "You?"

Brenner shrugged. "Yeah, I'm scum. But none of your boys will shoot half as straight, and there's nothing I don't know about quick and clean."

"He's very, very good with a crossbow, Captain," said Slate, almost inaudibly.

The Captain's nostrils flared. For a moment, Caliban thought he would throw the proffered help back in Brenner's face, and small blame if he did. *What a deal with the devil that is...*

Then: "Very well. Smithkin, get this man a crossbow and take him to the scene."

Smithkin looked even greyer.

Brenner paused on the threshold, not meeting anyone's eyes. "If the blight gets worse, you'll want to get a sharpshooter. Probably a couple of them."

The Captain nodded slowly.

The door shut behind them.

There was a long, brittle moment. Caliban waited for Slate to either catch it or smash it into a million sharp-edged pieces.

Slate drew herself up to her full height, which put her only a little below the scholar's eye-level. "I believe, honored dedicate, that we have gotten off on the wrong foot."

Learned Edmund opened his mouth, and Slate lifted a hand to forestall him. "Believe me, I realize that this is not an ideal way to proceed, for any of us. Had we the choice, we'd perhaps choose differently. Nevertheless, we're what you've got to work with. Now, I am certain that we all share the same desire, do we not?"

"Do we?" asked Learned Edmund skeptically.

"We do. The defense of the Dowager's kingdom against the Clockwork Boys is uppermost in our minds, believe me."

That's true, anyway. After a fashion.

Learned Edmund nodded. "My temple has charged me to assist in this matter. And, if I may, to ascertain whether Brother Amadai still lives."

"Brother Amadai?" said Caliban.

"The scholar in Anuket City," said Slate.

Ah. The one who had gone missing. Caliban vaguely remembered something about that, although he'd been distracted by the tattoo being inflicted on him.

Learned Edmund clearly did not like agreeing with Slate, but said "If he is still there, yes."

"I believe that our goals align, then," said Slate. "We all wish to reach Anuket City swiftly and as safely as we can."

The dedicate narrowed his eyes. "I do not wish to deal with unseemly displays of emotion on the road," he warned.

"I'll attempt to keep my weeping and vapors to a minimum."

It was probably a good thing Brenner had left. Caliban wondered how long it had been since the Learned Edmund had exchanged words with a woman at all. He was guessing a good decade.

The dedicate swung around and looked at Caliban. "And you have no objections to placing yourself under this woman's command, Knight-Champion?"

The Knight-Champion doesn't think it'll matter a pig's eye who thinks they're in charge, Caliban thought, but aloud he only said "None whatsoever, Learned Edmund."

If we get out of the city gates without killing each other, the gods will have granted us a miracle.

"Very well, then," said Learned Edmund. "If we must."

The Captain pried his hands away from his eyes, and looked over the group. "*Well* now," he said, with false heartiness, "now that *that's* all settled. We've arranged horses—I believe you've seen to your own supplies. I've gone over your planned route and I have papers so that you can cross the border at Archenhold…

assuming you can get there." He favored Slate with an ironic smile. "Not that you couldn't have seen to your own papers, I'm sure, Mistress."

She smiled faintly and inclined her head. "I'll let you know if I think of any improvements on yours."

"The army is expecting you. They are under orders to render all reasonable aid."

Caliban wondered what "reasonable aid" would look like, and if it would make walking into the teeth of the Clockwork Boys any less suicidal.

"You leave tomorrow, then."

They all nodded. Slate walked out the door, her back ramrod straight.

"Sir Caliban—" The Captain held out a hand to stall his leaving, eyes flicking over the hilt of the sword across his back. "Are you sure? I've been thinking—you're a knight, after all, and it might not be too late—"

"It's much too late, I think," said Caliban, and let the door fall shut behind him.

They spent the last night in the capitol the way they'd spent the previous few. Brenner went out on some errand of his own, Caliban sliced at shadows in the courtyard, and Slate forged every document she could think of that might possibly make their lives easier down the road.

Dinner had come around, and Caliban had returned and taken another bath. The man bathed more than a cat. Slate supposed she couldn't blame him—in his shoes, she'd probably be trying to make up for lost time too. Still, it seemed like every time she saw him, he was soggy.

He was sitting in front of the fire, eating and steaming slightly, when someone knocked on the door. Slate pushed her chair back to get it, but he got up instead, sword in hand, which would have been more menacing if he hadn't also had a towel over his shoulders.

"Paranoid much?" she asked.

"The servants already brought dinner, and Brenner never bothers to knock." He opened the door.

"Excuse me, sir," said one of the servant boys, "but—errr—" His eyes crossed on the blade.

The knight put it away. "Yes?"

"Package for the lady."

"Thank you." He took it. The boy fled, not waiting for a tip.

Slate hefted the package, baffled. There was a faint gurgle. *Ink? I didn't order any more ink...* She found her letter opener and slit it open, then laughed aloud.

A bottle of very old whiskey sat nestled inside, along with a tiny soapstone carving of a dog. There was no note and no return address, but she hadn't expected one.

"What is it?"

"A thank-you from the Stone Bitches. A fine group of women, one and all." She sat the bottle on the table. "Although if I try to drink very much of this, I'll be under the table."

"I'll help," he said, sitting down opposite.

She peered at him over the top of the bottle. "Are paladins allowed to drink stolen whiskey?"

"This one is."

"Excellent."

She poured two glasses, raised hers. "To...err..."

"To dying well," Caliban said, clinking his glass with hers.

"Hear, hear."

Four seconds later, Slate remembered why she didn't drink whiskey. The drink burned her tongue and her throat and her belly and the fumes went roaring through her nasal passages and made her choke, which made her sneeze, which went dreadfully wrong.

Caliban reached out and plucked the glass from her fingers. Slate said, "*Gnnnrghh...* Thank you." She sneezed again.

He reached into a pocket and pulled out a handkerchief.

"Thanks."

"Don't mention it." He poured himself another shot. "You weren't kidding about the allergies, eh?"

"I am allergic to everything," said Slate, with a certain grim pride.

"Including prisons, as I recall."

"Oh, that. No, that was a family thing." She propped herself up on her elbows, her eyes watering. "My grandmother was a wonderworker from down south. Every time there's magic or danger or just something I'm supposed to pay attention to, I get this horrible blast of rosemary."

"Rosemary?"

"Yeah." She blinked blearily at him. "You reeked of it. S'why I asked you."

"Did I? Hmm."

"Yeah, apparently I was supposed to pay attention to you."

The words hung in the air between them for a little too long. Slate looked away from his eyes and searched for something else to say. "You want to look at our route?"

"Will it help?"

She gazed into the bottom of the whiskey. "Realistically, no. But I suppose anything's possible."

He helped her unroll the map, and pinned one corner down with the bottle.

"Hand me the dog," said Slate. Their hands touched fleetingly as he dropped the soapstone figure into it. His skin was much warmer than hers.

Must be all those baths. The man doesn't have time to get cold.

"Right," said Slate. "So we're the dog here, in the Dowager's city. Nice and surrounded by mountains, very defensible, all the ore you could want. Even a good bit of pastureland, if you don't mind mutton three meals a day. They're not gonna starve us out. Only problem is that the only way out is along the river, here." She traced the blue squiggle of the Falsefall River as it wended its way through the mountains.

"Where the Clockwork Boys are coming in," said Caliban. "When I...ah...stopped getting regular news, they were afraid that the Clockwork Boys would bottle up the opening to the river valley."

"Yeah, that happened last month. Jammed into the mouth of the valley like a cork in a bottle." She gazed at the soapstone dog's position glumly. "I wish that wasn't such a good metaphor. We're all stuck in the bottle and the Captain expects the lot of us to wiggle our way out around the cork."

"Lovely."

"The army is theoretically holding them at a ford about there." She stabbed a finger into the map.

Caliban stared at the map. "That's nearly a third of the valley lost!"

"Oh, more than that. There's reports that a couple columns of the Boys got through and they're raiding along the trade road."

The paladin sat down opposite her and rested his forehead against his fist, studying the map. "And we need to get past the... cork, as it were...to reach Anuket City."

"Yep." Slate made the dog walk the length of the valley and hop to the point where the Falsefall joined up to another, larger river from the north. At the Y-shaped intersection, she set the dog down. "Anuket City."

Caliban shook his head. "That's a lot of war zone in the way," he admitted.

"Exciting, huh?"

"Not the word I would have chosen."

"Well, hopefully we'll fare better than the last group that went that way…"

He blinked at her. Slate realized that their faces were rather too close together and sat back.

"The *last* group?"

"What?" said Slate, with studied nonchalance. "You think we're the first ones they've sent out? They had two proper groups before us. Actual military and artificers and everything."

Caliban picked up the bottle and poured them both another drink.

"There's a reason they're down to prison scum now. First batch got squashed by a clocktaur column. In full sight of the military outpost, I'm told."

Caliban winced. "And the second group?"

"Oh, this is the fun one."

"…Fun."

"Well, for a value of fun." Slate picked up the dog again. "See, the Captain would really like it if we could find the second group…or what's left of them."

"Would he, now."

"Yeah, the Captain would like a lot of things." Slate snorted. "They think they checked in at the army outpost here, although we should probably double-check on that. Fog of war and all. After that, they lose track of them completely."

Caliban tilted his head, eyes narrowing, and said, "I gather from your expression there's more to it than running afoul of a Clockwork Boy."

"Oh, I have no idea how they died," said Slate. "It might be exactly that. What matters is what they had with them. Brother Amadai's journal."

She sat back with an expression of triumph. Caliban looked blank.

"The scholar from Anuket City," said Slate. "The one our extremely obnoxious dedicate is hoping to track down. The reason the Many-Armed God people are involved in this at all."

"I was a little distracted when he was talking," said Caliban. "I was hoping you wouldn't go for his throat."

"Well, it was a near thing."

Caliban gazed into his drink, clearly fighting back a smile.

"Right," said Slate. "So Amadai is some kind of genius and he went off to Anuket City ages ago because that's where the best artificers live. Anyway, the spies that are mostly dead now? One of them got a package out before they got caught, which was this journal from Brother Amadai. That's part of how we know he's involved. And the journal had drawings of the Clockwork Boys in it, although Amadai's handwriting was abysmal and a lot of bits seemed nonsensical. So they sent the journal along with the second group, who were supposed to be meeting up with our *dear* friend Learned Edmund here on the *other* side of the blockade, in hopes that Learned Edmund could decipher more of it. The spy couldn't include any kind of notes with it, but they're hoping it might have a key to stopping the Clockwork Boys."

"What happened?"

"Nothing happened. I'm told the Captain got a rather plaintive homing pigeon message two weeks after the meeting time, asking where they were."

"So they didn't make it," said Caliban thoughtfully. "And the journal?"

"Presumably with their bodies, assuming they weren't murdered by bandits who tossed it on the fire."

"Did no one think to make a copy?"

"Oh, *yes*." Slate's lip curled. "And if I meet them, they'll throw me in the dungeons for murder instead of forgery. That useless, motherless, talentless son of a goat!"

Caliban's eyebrows went up and he silently topped off her glass.

"*Paraphrased,*" said Slate angrily. "And corrected spellings and left out margin notes about the weather and whatnot, because they were clearly unimportant."

"I take it they weren't unimportant?" asked Caliban.

"It was code," said Slate, gulping whiskey and stifling her cough with the back of her hand. "A cascading code, which is a thing the Many-Armed God people do sometimes when they want to prove they're smarter than anyone else. But without all the supposedly unimportant bits, and without the misspellings, we don't know where to start or what the keys are. The temple sent back a nice note saying that it was now gibberish and did they still have the original? Which they'd sent off with the second group of idiots. I was so mad when the Captain told me about that that I could spit."

"So we need to find this journal," said Caliban.

Slate sighed, her anger fleeing as rapidly as it had come. "Maybe. And maybe we do and Learned Edmund finally translates it, and it's mostly recipes for boiled cabbage. I can see why you wouldn't write, "To Break Clockwork Boy, Hit Here" if you're in Anuket City, mind you, but just because something's in a complicated code with scary pictures doesn't mean it's going to be any good."

Caliban stared into the bottle.

After a moment, he set it aside and picked up the stone dog.

"So which way are *we* going, then?"

Slate scratched her chin. "I figure we'll follow the trade road to the army blockade and see what they can tell us. Possibly we'll find out something about the second group on the way. The Captain's sent word to expect us. It's possible they'll know a route through, or be able to clear us one. At the very least, they'll have more up to date intelligence than we will."

"And then?"

"We wing it."

Caliban put up an eyebrow. He was watching her face in a way that made Slate vaguely uncomfortable. *Well, I did just outline a plan that's nothing less than suicide...*

Any further conversation was drowned out by a loud thumping on the door. Caliban got up and drew his sword again. Slate sighed.

It was Brenner, with his arms full of metal. Caliban pulled the door open just as he had lifted a foot to kick at it again.

"Where'd you get *that?*" said Slate, quite astonished, as the assassin dumped a pile of armor in the middle of the room with an unholy clatter.

"I mugged a paladin."

"You did *not.*"

"Fine, but it would have been easier. Took days to find this stuff. I was afraid it wasn't going to come in before we left."

Caliban reached down into the pile and tugged a piece loose. It was a shoulder guard, embossed with the stylized closed eye of the Dreaming God. He turned it over in his hands, his expression unreadable.

"This is temple armor," he said.

Brenner grinned. It wasn't a kind expression.

That was meant to be a painful gift. Damn Brenner, anyway. Slate stifled a sigh. *Oh, well, they can work it out themselves. I suppose it doesn't matter if they kill us or we kill us, at this point.*

"I am not allowed to wear this any more," the paladin said, almost to himself.

"Well, I'm not going out again," said Brenner, pouring himself a shot of the whiskey. "Hey, this is the good stuff!"

"Gift from the Stone Bitches."

"Bless their vicious little hearts." He clinked his glass against Slate's.

Caliban crouched in the pile of armor, picking each piece up and setting it down carefully, his fingers lingering over the metal. It didn't look as heavy as Slate had expected—chain and leather, rather than shiny metal plate. *Perhaps that's just the ceremonial armor. Hmm.*

There was a heavy chain with a silver disc on the end. The closed eye gazed out sightlessly from the center.

"It's stolen, if that makes you feel any better," said Brenner cheerfully.

Caliban snorted, running the chain through his fingers. "That seems about right...*gha, ha, ngha...*" He coughed, and covered his mouth with his hand.

"Try it on," said Brenner, his eyes bright with malice. "See if it fits."

"I'm sure it does. You got the clothing well enough." His lips twitched. "Have you ever considered giving up killing people and becoming a tailor?"

"Oh, yes."

"And?"

"I don't like people unless I'm stabbing them."

Slate snorted and kicked him under the table. Brenner grinned and took another shot.

The knight glanced at them with ill-concealed contempt. Slate huffed. *Fine, if you're going to be like that, see if I feel sorry for you.*

He started pulling on the armor. It took longer than Slate would have expected. Her mother used to dress the same way, one piece at a time, layered for battle.

Slate herself had traded skirts for trousers, since they were going to be on the road. It had taken her probably a tenth the time to get dressed as it took Caliban to get his armor on.

"This is a lot easier with a squire," he said, trying to get a recalcitrant buckle across his back.

Slate and Brenner, acting as one, leaned back in their chairs and crossed their legs.

"Fine," he muttered.

Brenner poured out another shot and drained it, then pushed a package toward Caliban with his foot. "Got you a cloak, too."

"Thanks."

"It's white."

"Of course it is."

Caliban got the last piece on. His back was so straight she could have ruled a column of figures with it.

He held up the tabard. It had the sigil of the temple on it.

He looked at it for what seemed like a long time, and then he folded it reverently and set it aside. Slate did not know that she had ever had a lover touch her with as much tenderness as the disgraced knight handled the cloth.

"This I can no longer wear," he said simply.

"Oh, come on—" Brenner began, and Slate kicked him hard under the table.

"It looks good," she said. *Not a* useful *observation, but what the hell do I know about armor?* It did look good though. He looked more like a heroic statue than an actual human. She could see why the temple knights never lacked for female company. "You look great. A regular ladykiller."

Brenner blew whiskey out of his nose, yelped in pain, and clapped his hands over his face.

Caliban stared at her, his brown eyes draining of warmth until they were the color of cold liver.

Oh...my...god. Did I just say that? Slate put a hand out as if she could grab the words back. "I didn't—ah, crap, I can't believe—I didn't mean—"

I'm drunk. Oh god, I'm drunk, and I actually forgot...

He picked up his sword, and walked out the door without looking back.

"I can't believe I said that," said Slate into her palm.

Brenner finally stopped choking and howled like a hyena instead. "I can't believe you did either!"

"Shut *up*, Brenner," said Slate.

"Oh, relax. It's not like the stick up his ass can get any stickier."

There wasn't anything much she could say to that. Slate got up and went to her room.

She paused by the window, which overlooked the yard behind the inn. There was an armored figure below, taking cuts at his shadow in the moonlight.

She thought of going down and apologizing, then thought better of it. *At this point, I'll just make it worse.*

Oh, well. We probably won't make it to Anuket City, and even if we do, then we're all going to die anyway…

CHAPTER 7

They gathered in the courtyard outside the guardkeep just after dawn. There was a horse for each of them. The Learned Edmund had two mules in addition to his horse, laden with obscure, lumpy baggage, and there was an extra pack mule with supplies. Caliban was wearing the white cloak.

"You really don't have to wear that," Slate murmured. "Brenner's just being an ass."

He shrugged. "It'll be grey by the time we're out of the city anyway."

The Captain of the Guard had come out to see them off, probably fearing that if he didn't, he'd come out later to find one of them standing atop the corpses of the other three. Possibly brandishing a severed head in each hand.

Not that that's an unreasonable fear, mind you. I'll put my money on Brenner, with Caliban at an outside chance. I just hope I get a shot at the Learned Edmund first.

She eyed a spot between the scholar's shoulder blades longingly. He'd apparently decided that the knight was the only person he was going to talk to. Brenner found this a relief. Slate just found it obnoxious.

A groom handed her the reins to a horse, and vanished before she could say something like, "What the hell am I supposed to do with this?"

Caliban went over and spoke to the Captain quietly for a moment. They both vanished inside the building.

Slate looked at her horse. It was large and brown and had a black nose. It glanced at her, then gazed off in the distance in resignation.

Her mother had arranged for riding lessons for her approximately a thousand years ago, because courtesans catering to the nobility were catering to the *mounted* nobility, and sometimes you needed to go out for a ride with a patron. Whatever her faults, Slate's mother had certainly done her best to groom her daughter for a better life, which had involved endless rounds of lessons. As a result, Slate could dance reasonably well, read beautifully, and play the harp badly.

And ride.

Theoretically.

It didn't come up a lot in the city. You called carriages, or you walked, but you never *rode* anywhere. When she left the city, she went by stage. She hadn't actually been on a horse since she was eleven.

Slate rubbed her damp palms on her trousers and gazed up.

There was certainly a *lot* of horse there.

Slate had remembered that horses had been very, very large when she was a girl, but she had secretly hoped that this was because she had been so small by comparison. Unfortunately, either horses had grown or she hadn't.

Caliban re-emerged, wearing an undyed tabard over his armor. There was no device on it. The Captain of the Guard was behind him, looking more unhappy than usual, and judging by the way the paladin was stalking away, the Captain had managed to offend him somehow.

Granted, that's not a hard thing to do. I'm amazed he's even talking to me after last night.

Slate tried to get a foot into the stirrup, just about managed it, and then realized immediately that the stirrups were so long that it was only going to get her partway up the horse, and she'd have to scrabble at the thing's back like she was climbing a wall.

Would it stand for that? How patient was a horse, anyway?

She tried again. The horse took a step to the side once she had a foot in the stirrup, sending her hopping after it with her legs at an angle that she hadn't achieved in recent memory.

God, I hate being short.

She looked around to see how everyone else was doing. Caliban, naturally, was sitting on his horse, looking ready to pose for an illuminated manuscript. Brenner, who had never been on a horse in his life, had taken out his dagger and was showing it meaningfully to his mount. The horse did not look impressed.

Learned Edmund was checking the packs on his mules. He looked over at her and then away. Slate gritted her teeth and reached for the saddle. She'd bloody well climb the horse with a grappling hook if that's what it took.

This would be much easier if horses came with rain gutters. You give me a good rain gutter, I can be in the window in under a minute.

Horses did not come with windows either.

Before she could make another abortive attempt at mounting, Caliban dismounted and appeared on the other side of the horse, doing something to the complicated welter of snaps and buckles that she vaguely recalled was "tack." Slate figured that it was probably too much to hope that he was lowering a ladder.

He came around the other side, ducking under the horse's head with a murmured word, and did the same thing on this side. Glory be, it seemed to involve shortening the stirrups.

While that will undoubtedly be much more comfortable once I'm on the horse, I still don't know how I'm going to get up there in the first place...

The knight finished what he was doing, turned to her, and dropped to one knee as if he was offering fealty. Slate recoiled, then saw that he was actually offering her his interlaced hands as a mounting block.

"Ohthankyougod," she said, stepping into his hands.

"Not a god, just a paladin," he muttered, then belied his irritated tone by waiting patiently while she used his shoulder as a stepladder and ascended the heights of Mt. Equine.

Slate might have been inclined to suspect something other than chivalry—after all, a lot of men might enjoy being climbed on by a woman—but he then went over and did the exact same thing for Brenner.

This was quite a sight. Learned Edmund stopped even pretending to pay attention to the mules.

The assassin eventually got into the saddle, and Caliban—looking distinctly the worse for wear, and with boot prints crossing his new tabard—went back to his own horse.

"Is the circus ready to leave town, then?" asked Learned Edmund.

They rode out.

Twelve hours later, Slate was praying for the sweet release of death.

Her legs felt like…like…possibly there weren't words in the language for what they felt like.

They had been riding for hours. They left the city, the suburbs, the fields. They crossed several bridges. They passed more fields. Trees swept in from the sides and swept out again. Farmers went past in carts. Brenner clung to his mare like grim death, and with much the same expression.

Caliban tried to talk to her once or twice, either to tell her that he'd forgiven her for what she'd said last night, or to tell her that he'd never forgive her for what she'd said last night. Slate bounced along in the saddle, sneezing, and had to ask him to repeat himself so many times that he gave up. The knight-champion rode ahead and talked to Learned Edmund instead. Apparently the two religious types had found something in common.

Well, the one hates women in general and the other one hates me in particular. Maybe that's a conversation starter.

This would have annoyed Slate, but she had other things to worry about, like whether her legs were going to fall off.

Fortunately, her horse seemed inclined to follow the other horses, or steering would have been an issue.

She was covered in sweat. Dust stuck to the sweat and made a thin layer of grey grime that covered her from head to toe. Everyone else was also the same vague dust color. Caliban's cloak had gone dingy grey practically before they were out of the courtyard.

She would have found that amusing if she'd had the strength.

She discovered that whoever had packed her horse had thoughtfully included a waterskin. She aimed a stream of water into her mouth. It tasted like ambrosia.

How would you know? You've never had ambrosia.

It couldn't be better than this.

Hours passed, like a kidney stone.

Slate stopped thinking, stopped feeling anything. It was easier to do that. If she wasn't there, she wasn't feeling the horrible chafe against her thighs, the ache in her hip joints, the dryness of her eyes and nose and tongue. She went away inside her head for a while, in a kind of meditative misery.

There was nothing but the horse. There had never been anything but the horse. Possibly she had been born on a horse. She was undoubtedly going to die on one.

When she came back, it was because Caliban was tapping her on the knee and saying, "You going to get down, or are you posing for an equestrian statue?"

"Huh?" She looked around. They were at a ferry station on one side of the Highmelt River, a little town of a few small houses, a tradehouse, and a stable. Judging by the light, it was early evening. They seemed to be in the stable yard of the trade-house. "Are we crossing?"

"Not tonight. We're stopping here."

"Oh."

He waited. She looked at him. *Surely he's not waiting for me to get down from this thing.*

Learned Edmund appeared out of the gloom, his arms full of saddlebags. "They've got two rooms. There's enough stable space, though. Barely."

The fact that he was addressing Caliban and not her was not lost on Slate, but she really didn't care at the moment. Her hip joints appeared to have locked in place like blocks of cement.

"Excellent," said the paladin, nodding. He turned back up to Slate. "Madam?"

"Get him out of here," she hissed under her breath.

His eyebrows arched.

"*Do it.*"

Brenner bounced by, stiffly, an expression of frozen horror on his face. He hadn't been able to get down, either, and apparently any attempt to control his horse had failed utterly. The mare smelled food, and was roaming the yard looking for it.

Learned Edmund looked at Brenner. Brenner smiled horribly at him. His mare made another circuit of the yard.

Slate's horse sidled as the mare passed. Caliban put his fingers around the stirrup to hold it in place—Slate noticed with mild interest that she couldn't feel her ankles, and was wretchedly grateful—and turned back to the scholar. "Perhaps, Learned Edmund, you could bespeak us a meal and see when the ferry first runs tomorrow morning?"

The dedicate gave all three of them a suspicious glance, as if expecting them to be plotting behind his back, then inclined his head and went inside.

Caliban waited until he was gone, then dove for Brenner's reins, and managed to catch them. The horse brought up short, and Brenner lurched in the saddle and let out a sound that was just sort of a sob.

"I'll kill the beast," the assassin rasped. "I'd cut his throat right now, but I don't think I can get off if he falls down."

"It's a her," said Caliban.

"You think that'll stop me, god-boy?"

"Horses are expensive," said Slate, who knew to the penny how much it cost to house and feed a horse, although she had only a vague notion of what they actually ate.

"Oh. Hmm. Damn."

The knight got both sets of reins together, and led the horses to a rail, where he tied them up. He turned back, hands on hips. Brenner and Slate stared down at him glumly.

"When did you two learn to ride?" he asked.

"Nineteen years ago."

"This morning."

Caliban put his hands over his face. "We're going to die." His voice was surprisingly calm, but it had a hysterical edge to it.

"I've been *telling* you," said Slate, much aggrieved.

He raked his hands through his hair and muttered something under his breath. Slate wouldn't swear that it hadn't been, "*Ngha, ha, ngha...*"

"Okay. Neither of you can get down?"

"No."

"Not if I don't get to kill the horse."

Caliban stared upward and uttered a particularly vile curse to no one in particular.

"I didn't think they knew words like that in the temple," said Brenner, sounding rather pleased despite it all.

The paladin ignored him, squared his shoulders, and walked to the side of Slate's horse. He reached up and caught her around the waist. "Put your arms around my neck."

She obeyed, and he dragged her off the horse and set her on her feet. Her knees buckled immediately, but he'd apparently expected that, and held her up by main force.

Slate found her face pressed into his chest, which smelled very strongly of dust and metal and horse. Chain clinked. She got a powerful whiff of rosemary and sneezed wretchedly.

He sighed—she felt it more than heard it—held her up with one hand, and dug out a handkerchief with the other.

Her knees grudgingly admitted that they could probably hold up on their own now, and she stepped away, clutching the handkerchief. "Thangkks."

"Don't mention it."

"Do *I* get to do that?" asked Brenner snidely from horseback.

"Yes, actually," said Caliban, coming around the side of Brenner's horse.

Slate found that she still had the strength to snicker.

"Aww," said Brenner, putting his arms around the knight's neck. "I didn't know you cared."

"I really don't."

The assassin's knees also buckled when he hit the ground. The knight also held him upright. Slate wondered if he'd worn the same expression of stoic martyrdom when she'd been clinging to him.

Oh, probably.

He herded them both into the inn, like a sheepdog with a pair of bitter, bow-legged sheep. *Twelve hours in the saddle and he's not even limping. That* bastard.

Brenner, fortunately, looked as if he might be permanently damaged. Slate approved of that. If she was miserable, someone else ought to be, too. She felt as if she had been...no, the only metaphors that came to mind were mostly sexual and too disgusting to contemplate. *Still.*

They passed through the common room. Slate didn't really see it. The sheepdog was still herding.

He stopped at last at the foot of the stairs, and gestured to his sheep. "Go up to your rooms, you two. I'll have them send up trays."

Slate looked up the stairs. There were quite a lot of them.

I could ask him to carry me. No, that'd be humiliating, and then he'd have to carry Brenner, too.

Actually, that'd almost be worth it. I wonder if he'd do it.

Behind her, the assassin turned away from the stairs and locked his fingers on the edges of the knight's tabard. Caliban stared down at him, lip curled in something between pity and disgust.

"Send...*beer*..." Brenner rasped.

The knight pried his fingers loose. "I'll see what I can do."

They ascended the stairs like a pair of mountaineers tackling a cliff face.

"My legs will never close again," she muttered.

"That would be music to my ears if I wasn't dying," said Brenner, a step below her.

"Do you think we'll make it to Anuket City?"

"I don't think I'll make it to my *room*."

Eventually, of course, they did make it. They got halfway down the hallway,

realized they didn't know which rooms were theirs, and sagged together against the wall. Slate's ankles, heretofore numb, started to make their presence known. She didn't dare sit down, or she'd never stand up again.

"I think I hate him," said Brenner, leaning against the wall next to her.

No need to ask who he was talking about. "I'm gettin' there," said Slate.

"I could kill him. He's got to sleep sometime."

"Then who'd get us off the horses tomorrow?"

"Good point."

Someone came up the hall. It was Learned Edmund, carrying a pack. He stared at them both down his nose.

"Are you two *drunk?*"

"Not yet," said Brenner, "but soon enough."

"Do you know which rooms are ours?" asked Slate.

He pointed his thumbs at two opposite doors. Slate pushed herself away from the wall and picked one.

It was tiny. The tradehouse knew they had the monopoly on people waiting overnight for the ferry, and apparently had decided to capitalize on the fact. It held a bed big enough for one person, assuming they slept in fetal position. It also had a basin, a window the size of an arrow slit, and a strip of floor. The bed was ancient, sagging, and would have required a team of skilled carpenters to achieve "decrepit."

It looked *wonderful.*

Slate stepped inside, shut the door behind her—whatever Learned Edmund had to say, she didn't want to hear it—and crawled onto the bed. Then she arranged her legs by picking her thighs up with her hands and dropping them into position. Then she leaned back against the headboard and whimpered for a few minutes.

A few minutes later, the door opened. Caliban dropped her bags on the floor, said "I hope you realize I'm a knight, not a valet," and left. She made an obscene gesture at his back.

Give the man a high horse and he thinks he can ride around on it. I should've left him in the cell.

The door opened again. It was Learned Edmund, who was trying not to look at her.

"The innkeeper wants money."

Slate located her moneypurse and flung it at the scholar's head. "Give him whatever he wants."

"Your…friend…wants beer."

"Give him whatever *he* wants, too."

"Quite." The scholar curled his lip and took himself off. The door shut.

A quarter of an hour later, someone knocked. *Ah. They're polite. That lets out anyone in our little band.* "Come in," Slate called.

A serving girl came in, dipped a little curtsy without disturbing anything on her tray, and handed her a wooden bowl of stew and a spoon.

Slate gabbled out something about undying love and large tips, and barely restrained herself from planting her face directly into the stew.

The serving girl smiled, curtsied again, and slipped out.

Slate applied herself to the stew. A minute later the door banged open again, and she set the spoon aside and sighed.

It was Caliban again. He was carrying a single glass of wine. Slate's eyes locked on it like a vulture spotting a carcass.

"With Brenner's compliments," he said dryly, handing it into the room. "He put something into it."

"Was it poison?" she asked hopefully.

"I don't think so."

"Damn."

She took a sip, detected the faint machine-oil-and-flowers taste of poppy milk, and took a much larger sip. "Tell Brenner he can have my firstborn."

"I'm sure he'll be thrilled." The door shut again.

Slate applied herself to wine and the stew. By the time she'd finished, the poppy milk and the alcohol were starting to take effect. Her legs still hurt, but she just didn't give a damn. They were miles away, clear down at the other end of her body. Who needed 'em, anyway?

Bless Brenner's black little heart.

Maybe she wouldn't bother to undress. Maybe she wouldn't bother with her shoes. Maybe she'd go to sleep, right here...

The door crashed open again. "Just leave it open, for god's sake," she groused, glaring at the ceiling. "I don't know why I even *have* a door."

It was Caliban, yet again. He dropped a bedroll on the floor.

"What're you doing?" she asked, sitting up. She was pleased to see that her hip joints worked again, although not without complaint.

"I'm sleeping in here."

"What?"

"The other room's the same size as this one. We couldn't fit two people on the floor unless we stacked them. The stables are full, Brenner's threatening to put a dagger in the eye of anyone who tries to get him off the bed—and I believe him—and Learned Edmund is apparently afraid that if he sleeps on your floor, your feminine exhalations will cause his genitals to wither and his bowels to turn to water. That's a direct quote, by the way."

Slate discovered that she was giggling helplessly into her hands and stopped immediately. It had to be the poppy milk.

"That leaves me. If you need to get up in the middle of the night, try not to step on my head."

"I suppose we could flip a coin for the bed," she said, trying to be fair.

He gave her a withering look. "I realize, madam, that you do not think much of my knighthood, but chivalry is not *that* dead."

"Suit yourself," she said, annoyed.

Back to "madam" again. Swear to god, the man's pricklier than a cactus with a rash.

In the time it took him to strip off his armor, she managed to get a boot off. *One* boot. The act of bending knee and hip joints to get her foot within range was torture, even with the poppy standing between her and the pain. She pulled the boot off, panted, and dropped it on the floor.

Her other foot was impossibly far away. Possibly this was a task better carried out by homing pigeons.

Caliban dumped his armor in the corner. He reached out, grabbed her foot and yanked.

Hard.

The other boot came off. She yelped.

"Ahhh*bugger!*"

"I'd like to get to bed sometime tonight," he said testily. Her toes felt skinned.

"I thought you said temple paladins weren't total bastards."

"I said most of us weren't."

"I *see.*"

Slate shrugged out of her coat, decided to leave the rest of her clothes on—hell if he was getting any thrills if he was going to be like that—and got under the covers. He dropped out of sight below the foot of the bed. A minute later, the candle went out.

"You better not snore," she grumbled into the dark.

"I don't snore."

"Good."

"I gibber in demonic tongues."

"You're kidding."

"No."

"*Shit.*"

About an hour later, some night-blooming weed opened up and she woke herself up sneezing.

She checked her pockets under the blankets. She knew for a fact that Caliban had handed her a handkerchief earlier. She couldn't find it. Maybe it was in her coat, which was…somewhere in a pile of armor and saddlebags. *Bugger.*

In her bleaker moments, Slate wondered if her talent for smelling rosemary had been balanced out by a curse that prevented her from staying in possession of anything to blow her nose on.

"Ah…ah…ACHOOAAAUGH!"

There are many sensations worse than waking up in the night with your nose overflowing and your sinuses walled up like brick, but she couldn't think of any at the moment. Slate clutched at her traitorous nose and moaned.

There was a rustle at the foot of the bed.

"Sneerrggghhhk!"

Something hit her in the face.

It was lightweight, and bounced off her hands. Slate flailed, dropped it, found it again, unfolded it, and discovered it was a small square of cotton fabric.

He'd thrown a handkerchief at her head.

"Thangghks," she muttered. He grunted.

Well, it's an odd sort of chivalry, I suppose, but maybe it's not completely dead at that.

At some point a few hours after *that*, when the night was bleakest and blackest, Slate woke up because something by her feet was gibbering in demonic tongues.

I'm dead, she thought, staring at the ceiling. *I'm dead and in hell.*

"Ngha, ha, ngh'aa, halikalihali, kalaak-ngha…"

Oh my god, he really wasn't *kidding.*

She sat up, feeling her hip bones grate in their sockets, and crawled to the edge of the bed.

It was Caliban, all right, or his decaying demon. She didn't know why she was surprised.

He was lying on his side, head pillowed on his arm, muttering into his elbow. His voice was low and guttural and had a nasty bite to it.

"Nghaa…Kai! Kai! Kalaak-ghaa…"

"Hey. Err. Wake up, man."

"Nghaaaa?"

"You're speaking in tongues in your sleep."

"Gha, kamama…"

"It's really creepy."

He didn't stop. She looked around for something to poke him with.

The only thing close at hand was his sword, which he'd hung over the foot of the bed, in easy reach. Slate grabbed the scabbard in both hands and nudged him with it awkwardly.

He twitched a bit. *"Nghaa! Kalikalikaliha!"*

Oh god, I hope I'm not making it mad.

"Come on, wake up!" She gave him a good whack in the elbow with the side of the scabbard.

He opened his eyes, caught the sword in both hands and shoved upward, hard. Only the fact that she was marginally more awake than he was, and already jumpy from the demon's voice, let her jerk back out of the way. The pommel shot past her chin.

As it was, her hands stung from the leather ripping through them. She yelped, fell backward, and blew on them.

"What? What is it? *Nghaah!*" He cursed, jumped up, and knocked over the candle. She heard steel being drawn, followed by a thud and another yelp, and the clatter of said steel hitting the floor.

You really can't draw a sword that size in a room this size, m'boy.

Slate rolled quietly off the bed on the other side—there was about a handsbreadth between the bed and the wall, and she slid down into it—and dug around on the floor until she found the candle.

There was another thud from somewhere overhead and a curse.

She dug in her pocket for matches. Matches she always had, even if she usually didn't have a handkerchief.

Light flared under her hands. She was half under the bed, but that seemed to be the safest spot at the moment.

Caliban was standing, looking down at her. His sword gleamed on the floor between them. There was a large dent in the plaster where he'd hit it with the pommel, trying to draw in the miniscule room.

"So I guess I shouldn't poke you when you're speaking in tongues," she said.

"Apparently not," he said, pulling her to her feet.

"Shall we try to get back to sleep again?"

"They say third time's the charm."

Whoever 'they' were, they were right, because there were no more allergies, no more demonic voices, and Slate slept clear on through morning.

CHAPTER 8

The next few days passed in much the same fashion.

The second day was worse than the first, even though they stopped much more frequently and went much more slowly. The inn had bigger rooms, however, and Slate got to sleep in a bed without a paladin sulking on the floor.

They did not ride for so long each day as they did the first. Learned Edmund chafed at the delay. Slate and Brenner merely chafed.

Caliban found them some kind of herbal gunk. It was full of comfrey, and stank to high heaven, but supposedly it healed saddle sores.

This was a difficult bit of self-medication, but Slate would have cut her own throat before asking Caliban for help—chivalry be drawn and quartered, there were limits—and Brenner would get entirely the wrong idea. She had to barricade herself in her room and engage in a series of unfortunate pantless contortions to get the stuff on.

She never asked Brenner how he managed. She was afraid he'd tell her.

The third day was really bad. Slate and Brenner took to slugging poppy milk straight out of the bottle, which meant that they alternated giggling and whimpering. After about an hour of this, Caliban took the reins away from them and tied them in a string to his saddlebow. They found this amusing.

"If you keep drinking that stuff, you're going to wind up addicted to it," he warned them, as he watched the small glass bottle make the rounds again.

"Oh, yeah, I'm real worried," said Brenner. "Remind me again, what were we on? Some kind of suicide mission, was it?" Slate snickered.

He stopped talking to them.

The scenery was not interesting enough to be distracting. It was all farm fields. Slate's mother had come from farming stock and had been determined never to go back.

Once or twice, Slate had missed having a larger extended family to belong to, but looking at the fields and the people working them with hoes and spades, she offered up silent thanks. *I'll light a candle for you, Mother. Two candles.* Ten *candles. I bet these people have to deal with horses* constantly.

Slate and Brenner sang rounds of dirty songs together. Brenner had a surprisingly good voice. Slate didn't. She did get to enjoy watching Learned Edmund twitch when she went for the high notes.

Caliban was trying to pretend he didn't know them, which was tricky when he was the one leading their horses.

At the inn that night, they sat propped up against the wall, shoulder to shoulder, while Caliban looked at them with irritation and Learned Edmund didn't look at them at all.

"I could kill both of them," said Brenner. "We could get to Anuket City on our own."

He said it rather louder than he intended. Learned Edmund's eyes widened. Caliban simply shoved trencher bread in front of the assassin and said "You'd have to walk. The Clockwork Boys are raiding up and down the southern trade roads. No caravans unless you want to go to a completely different city-state and work your way down from there."

Brenner looked at Slate. Slate said "He's probably right," and picked at her bread. Poppy-milk killed your appetite, but she knew she should probably eat anyway.

"I could kill them just a *little*."

"No."

"I will never understand," said Learned Edmund, apparently to Caliban, "why I was not placed in charge of this expedition."

"Because you look about twelve," said Slate, too tired to be diplomatic. "Do you even have to shave yet?"

The dedicate flushed scarlet. "I am nineteen!"

"I am thirty-seven," said Caliban, "and if I can accept Mistress Slate's leadership, so can you."

"She hasn't been leading!" said Learned Edmund. "She's been drinking poppy and falling off her horse! You're the one finding the inns and choosing the route."

Caliban locked eyes with Slate. "She has delegated," he said, his voice a low rumble, in sharp contrast to Learned Edmund's. "Mistress Slate's talents lie elsewhere. I assure you, they are considerable."

"Damn straight they are," said Brenner, snickering.

"Shut *up,* Brenner."

Learned Edmund got up from the table and walked away without speaking.

Slate groaned and dropped back against the wall again. "*Why* did they send him on this trip? He hasn't got a tattoo eating his arm off."

"He volunteered," said Caliban.

Slate blinked. So did Brenner.

"Among dedicates of the Many-Armed God, he is considered very…compassionate," said Caliban.

"Dear god!"

Brenner whistled softly.

"How did you find that out?" asked Slate.

"I asked the Captain of the Guard." He looked down at his hands with a small, ironic smile. "The Many-Armed God's temple were very keen to find their missing scholar in Anuket City, or, if he is dead, to find out what he was working on when he died. They wanted his journal translated very badly. And when Learned Edmund learned that those who accompanied the dedicate were expected to die, his heart was moved by pity at our fate. He offered to go, both to find this scholar and because he knew that he was to be the designated survivor who would bring the information we gathered to the Dowager and the Many Armed God."

"Didn't realize a woman would be in charge, I take it," said Slate. Her head was clear, but she didn't have to like it.

Caliban inclined his head. "He is young and not worldly. I truly do not think it occurred to him or his superiors."

"Did he know they expected us all to die before we even got to the city?"

The paladin sighed. "I believe he was told that it was dangerous. But he is very young, and the young always believe that they are immortal."

"Ugh." Slate rubbed her shoulder and hissed with the pain.

"It should improve soon," said Caliban.

"What, Learned Edmund?"

"No, the pain. Your body adapts to riding the way it adapts to practicing the sword."

"I don't do *that* either."

He helped them both upstairs. Brenner fell into his room cursing. Slate eased herself onto the bed as if into hot water. Each individual muscle was still furious.

Without being asked, Caliban reached down and pulled her boots off.

"Gaaahh!…thanks." *Command. I am in command. Dammit, that child was right. I've been letting Caliban do it all. I should have interrogated the Captain of the Guard about Learned Edmund myself, and instead I was maundering around wallowing in my upcoming horrible death.*

Dammit. And now I'm going to ask for even more.

No. Delegating. I'm delegating.

"Will you speak to Learned Edmund? Tell him…whatever." She waved a hand vaguely. "Smooth it over."

"I will do my best." He stood at the foot of the bed in parade rest, apparently waiting to be dismissed.

"Use the voice on him," muttered Slate.

The Knight-Champion looked startled for just a moment, and then he gave her a genuine smile. "You noticed?"

"Hard not to. If I could sound that trustworthy, I'd be rich."

Well, maybe. Probably it only works if you're six feet tall and look like a war-god.

"Most likely not," he said, sounding a trifle apologetic. "I am afraid it only works if you believe what you're saying."

"You mean you can't *lie?*"

"Normally? Of course I can, though I'm afraid it was never my strong suit. But if you are trying to make people trust you, you must trust your own word first. That's why it works."

"What awful con men you'd make."

"That *is* the general idea."

"What if you're one of those loons who believe every word they're saying?"

His smile faded. "People like that are dangerous," he said. "We try to kill them quickly." He shut the door behind him, and left Slate alone in the room.

Maybe Caliban had been right about adapting. Maybe it was the awful herbal gunk. Whatever it was, after the third day, it started to get better. Muscles either learned how to grip or stopped trying. Joints loosened up. Slate could get out of the saddle at the end of the day, although she never could get back up into it without a mounting block.

Caliban took to sleeping in the stable whenever possible, presumably so that his demonic mutterings would bother no one but the horses. Slate got up early one morning—or rather, her allergies to the mold in the room drove her out of bed before she suffocated—and she found the knight in the stable yard, chopping down shadows.

Slate melted into the shadows of a staircase and sat down. She pulled her knees up to her chin and watched him.

Forehand…backhand…turn…forehand…sweep…

It was a repetitive set of motions, oddly hypnotic. The arms moved, the sword swung, the shadows fell back.

The paladin was a pleasure to watch, she'd admit that. He was not wearing the shell of armor, and it would have taken a better woman than Slate not to admire the play of muscles under his skin. The thin cotton shirt didn't leave much to the imagination.

The black ink across his arm was an ugly blotch beneath the fabric. It wriggled with each chop of the sword. Slate stifled a sigh.

Oh, well. We're all damaged goods here, I suppose.

At the end of the sequence, Caliban dropped gracefully to his knees, a practiced move, and clasped both hands on the hilt of the upright sword. He bent his head, forehead pressed against the backs of his hands, and closed his eyes.

And there he stayed.

Long minutes slid by, and Slate's ankles ached with sympathy. Inside his boots, his feet had to be white and bloodless. *Unless the temple teaches knight-champions how to do that sort of thing…*

Slate had not ever seen much point to prayer, but the intensity of that silent vigil was painful to watch. It seemed cruel that any god could hear such prayers and not respond at once.

She slid to her feet and slipped away before he saw her and she could ask what, if anything, he was praying for.

"I've never met an assassin before," said Learned Edmund to Brenner, after they had been several days on the road.

"Speaking on behalf of assassins everywhere, we were perfectly happy with that."

They'd dismounted to lead the horses up a long, winding hill. Brenner plodded along with his eyes forward, apparently hoping that had ended the conversation.

No such luck.

"Do you enjoy killing people? If I may ask?"

Brenner sighed and glanced at Caliban, possibly hoping for rescue. Caliban shrugged. He had little enough chivalry left, he wasn't going to waste it on Brenner.

"If I say yes, will you stop asking?"

"I'm trying to understand what you do, Mister Brenner," said Learned Edmund stiffly. "I do not believe in judging a man before I know him, and I do not know you well."

Brenner gazed up at the sky, apparently looking for divine intervention, or at least rain. Neither was forthcoming. Clouds drifted by in a sky as blue and airy as a butterfly's wing.

"I enjoy *hunting* people," he said. "I'm good at it."

"And the act of killing?"

"That's just the bit that happens at the end. Look, why don't you go bother the paladin? He's killed at least as many people as I have, and got paid a lot less."

"Dig your own grave, Brenner," said Caliban. "I'm not helping."

"I am quite clear on the motivations of Knight-Champions," said Learned Edmund. "I'm asking about yours."

Caliban stifled a sigh. *Bet you're not half as clear as you think you are. Hell, these days, I'm not even clear on my motivations most of the time...*

Brenner apparently agreed with him. "*My* motives? I kill people who have managed to piss somebody else off. I bear them no ill will; it's strictly business. *He* goes and persuades poor stupid peasants who think they're possessed to come back to the temple to have demons tortured out of them. And *I'm* the bad one?"

Caliban discovered that his hand was on the hilt of his sword. He looked at it as if it didn't belong to him, and carefully pried the fingers away.

"The work of the Knight-Champions is generally recognized as a noble calling—" said Learned Edmund nervously, and licked his lips.

"Ask him if he enjoys it."

The statement made a little silence around itself. Learned Edmund looked back and forth worriedly.

"Did you enjoy killing that woman with the blighted child?" Caliban asked quietly.

There was another little silence, while Brenner stared at him.

"That's *sick*," the assassin said finally.

"You volunteered to do it," said Caliban, still gazing straight ahead, to where Slate's horse was kicking up little puffs of dust from the roadway.

"Somebody had to! They were going to shoot her anyway, and those idiot butchers in the guard would have made a bloody mess of it!"

Swish went the horse's tail ahead of them.

Caliban nodded. "Exactly."

"Exactly *what?*"

"Downhill from here," Slate called back.

In more ways than one...

"Pardon me, gentlemen," said Caliban, lengthening his stride. He stopped beside Slate, knelt, and offered her a hand up into the saddle. She gave him one of her crooked smiles as she mounted.

He was pretty sure she hadn't heard the conversation behind her.

Probably that was just as well.

Another day passed, then two. They passed through miles of carefully tended fields, where some crops were just starting to pull their way up from the soil. It was humble but prosperous land, full of humble but honest people. Slate felt like a fish not just out of water but twenty miles from the nearest puddle.

No one's evacuating. No one's leaving. I suppose you still have to plant seeds even if there's a war going on, but this seems utterly mad...

One night there were no inns, and they stayed at a farmhouse, or more accurately, in the barn.

"I am surprised you did not take the offer of their bed," said Caliban, as they walked back to the barn, carrying provisions.

Slate shrugged. "Safer not to. If we have to run in the middle of the night, less chance of being split up."

"That hardly seems likely out here, with these people."

"I have gotten out of the habit of trusting people," said Slate. "No matter how harmless they appear."

The sun was setting and dyeing the fields crimson. Caliban raised his eyebrows. "That seems a difficult way to live."

"You note that I'm still alive, though. At least for another few days."

"An unassailable argument. At least until we get to the war zone."

She slept that night at one end of the barn, far enough away that Learned Edmund need not fear her feminine exhalations. Caliban took the stall beside her. She woke in the night to hear the demon muttering, and rolled over and went back to sleep.

"I cannot get used to this," said Brenner, looking up the road. They had dismounted and were leading the horses. "That's an army outpost."

"A minor one, yes," said Learned Edmund.

"And we're just walking right up to it."

Caliban laughed softly to himself.

"Something funny, god-boy?"

"Yes."

The assassin's eyes narrowed. "Be a shame if someone slipped up and dropped your name, *Lord* Caliban."

Caliban controlled his expression as tightly as he could, but he knew that Brenner saw his eyes flicker. "They are expecting criminals. As you enjoy reminding me, I, too, am a criminal."

"Damn straight. Try acting like one."

Slate turned her head and looked back at them. There was no mistaking her expression. Annoyance crossed her face like clouds casting shadows on a hillside. "I swear to god, if you two don't stop, I'll tell the army to give you forty lashes for insubordination."

"Can they do that?" asked Brenner.

"They can," said Caliban. "Though time in the stockade is more usual."

"I've never had forty lashes. Actually, I've never had even one lash."

"I have," said Caliban.

Slate had turned back around, but missed a step at that. "What?"

He shrugged. "The demon had a whip."

"And?"

"I had a sword."

"Who won?" asked Brenner.

122

"We're having this conversation, so I did."

"Ah."

Slate waved them to silence, and handed Caliban the reins of her horse. A soldier in dusty blue motioned her toward the guard post. She mounted the steps into the small building, already reaching for the document case at her side.

Caliban looked over the outpost. A wall of sharpened posts ran around the outside. From what he knew of them, a Clockwork Boy would go through that in about five seconds flat.

They had taken the precaution of digging a moat around the exterior. The guard post stood at one end of a narrow bridge. If the enemy did arrive, they could destroy the bridges and let the Clockwork Boys fall into the ditch around the palisade. It wouldn't destroy them, but would at least give the soldiers the ability to attack from above, without being trampled.

Siege tactics were not part of a Knight-Champion's training. Caliban couldn't say if the precautions were brilliant or foolish. Presumably it was the best that could be done with what resources were available.

Just like we are.

The sheer awfulness of *that* thought made him flick his fingers across his eyes in a warding gesture.

Brenner started to say something, but Slate's footsteps stopped him. "All right," she said, coming down the board steps again. "Our papers are in order."

"They're authentic, you mean?" asked Caliban.

She snorted. "They're *better* than authentic, I'll have you know."

They stabled the horses outside the walls, and crossed the bridge to the inside. It was held up with ropes, easily cut. He looked up and saw archers stationed in towers on either side.

"Will archers stop the Clockwork Boys, do you think?" he murmured.

"From what I understand, not a chance in hell," said Slate.

Learned Edmund made a small distressed sound, and pulled his robes more tightly around himself.

The commander of the outpost was a woman with long silver hair tied back into a bun. She looked over the four of them with a dour expression. Slate actually heard Caliban's spine crackle as he snapped to attention.

Didn't think the man's spine could get any straighter. She probably reminds him of a nun.

Slate didn't bother to pretend that she was military. She dropped her papers on the commander's table with a flourish. Brenner was slouching aggressively. Learned Edmund was looking at a female military commander with the expression of a man having an internal crisis.

The Commander looked at the papers. She read them. She looked up at Slate.

"You're in charge, I take it."

"Same as you," said Slate. The woman snorted.

"You're the next batch, then."

"Yep," said Slate.

"Heard the first ones didn't do so well."

"Yeah, I heard that too."

"You run into a column of Clockwork Boys, they're not sending the army to haul you out." She steepled her fingers and put her elbows on the desk. "They *can't* haul you out, you understand? Those things are walking siege engines."

"We're aware," said Slate, not looking at her companions. Brenner and Caliban were aware. Learned Edmund...well. Was it even possible to tell a sheltered nineteen-year-old boy that he was going to die and make him believe it?

The Commander sighed and reached for a stamp. "You're headed to the front, then?"

"Nowhere else to go," said Slate. She was lying through her teeth, but she was pretty sure that she was the only one who knew that.

Brenner can probably tell, but Brenner will go along with it...

The Commander stamped the bottom of the document. "See the Quartermaster for anything you require. We don't have much, but the capital says you're welcome to what we've got." Her expression indicated what she thought about this.

"Cigarettes and poppy milk," muttered Brenner.

The Commander's lip curled, but she handed back the paper. Her eyes scanned over the three men, lingering the longest on Caliban. Slate was pretty sure it wasn't because the paladin was good-looking.

"Did they ever find the second group?" she asked, as Slate turned to go.

"No," said Slate, keeping her voice dead even. "Did they make it this far?"

The Commander's scowl deepened. "They did. They asked for two of my men as escorts," she said.

"Ah," Slate said.

"That was nine weeks ago," said the Commander. "They went north into the hills. They had pigeons with them. One came back the first week. After that, nothing."

"The hills can be treacherous in late winter," said Slate.

The Commander stared into her eyes. Slate stared back.

You may be sharp, ma'am, but you can't read minds. All my papers are in order and that's all you need to know.

In the end, the Commander's contempt for civilians won over anything else. "We'll send word to the front to expect you, but I wouldn't count on that."

"Believe me," said Slate, "I'm not counting on anything right now."

125

CHAPTER 9

"The village up ahead is supposed to have a very nice inn," said Learned Edmund, consulting his map across the bow of his saddle. "Hot baths, good food, and we can pick up supplies for the horses."

"From your lips to the gods' ears, priest," said Brenner.

Unfortunately, as Slate had begun to suspect long ago, the gods did not seem to be listening.

They were nearly to the first row of houses when a man hurried out to meet them, waving his hands frantically.

"Some sort of trouble," Caliban murmured, looking past him.

Brenner slid a hand down to his daggers. "Yeah. Either that's a dead body in the middle of town, or somebody picked an awful strange place for a nap."

The stranger was middle-aged, dressed like a farmer, his muscles stringy rather than powerful. Thin brown hair hung down in disarray. "Go back!" the stranger shouted, as soon as he was within earshot. "Turn around, go back!"

"Is there some trouble here?" asked Caliban, resting a hand on the hilt of his sword. "Can we help?"

Brenner rolled his eyes.

"He is right," said Learned Edmund, not sounding terribly sure of himself. "If they are in need of aid, it is our duty to render it…"

Brenner looked at Slate for appeal. Slate grimaced. *If Caliban takes it in his head to help them anyway, my illusion of authority won't be worth beans.* "Let's see what they want…" she muttered.

"Help?" said the man, and laughed. His voice was high and hacking. "There's no help. It's the blight. You can't help the blight."

"Blight?" Slate sat up straighter in the saddle.

The man looked up at her with faded eyes, as if unable to quite understand the question. "Blight? Yes...yes. It's the blight. People got it—we thought it was contained—then they pulled a body out of the well."

Caliban drew in a sharp breath. Learned Edmund traced a protective sign across his breast.

"It wasn't human. I don't know what it was. Some kind of animal, maybe. But we've all got it now, you see. The whole village—the well water—everyone must have it. They're starting to drop. You have to get away. Tell anyone you see on the road to stay away."

"Is there anything we can do to help?" asked Caliban. There was a flat, fatal note in his voice.

"No." The stranger looked away. "We can kill ourselves well enough. Just go away."

"May the gods keep you," said Learned Edmund, sketching a benediction in the air.

Useless, Slate thought tiredly. *Better the gods grant them a quick death and a strong hand on the knife.* She cleared her throat.

"Is there a way around the village?"

The stranger barely looked at her. "Around the far fields. There's an ox-road, just down the road behind you. Don't touch anyone. Don't let anyone touch you."

Slate nodded.

She thought of all the things she could say, and they all became flat and meaningless on her tongue. She lifted a hand in salute, and then turned her horse.

The others followed. No one said anything.

The ox-road was rough and bumpy, but it did indeed swing in a wide circle around the fields. Tan dust rose in a cloud behind them, turning the mules a vague beige. The village in the distance looked like a bruise.

They passed a farmhouse off to the right. The empty windows stared at them. Slate watched it, fearing that someone might come out, fearing what she might have to do if someone did.

Brenner reached back into his pack, swung his crossbow forward, and slapped a bolt into it. The sounds seemed very loud, even over the clipping of the horses' hooves. *Click. Click. Tap.* Slate would have bet that every ear in the party was riveted on it.

Click. Skreeeeek.

Click.

Brenner will shoot anyone who tries to approach us. And I will let him do it.

No one came out of the farmhouse. There were crows perched on the fence railing, and she could hear them croaking behind the house. A whole murder's worth, by the sound.

Eating something.

Could just be a dead farm animal.

She was careful not to look back, when the ox-road swung wide, in case she might find out what they were eating.

A long time later, they returned to the main road. Slate felt a painful clutch of relief when they rode up onto it, as if somehow the presence of the wider road might protect them.

It seemed to be a cue to speak again. Learned Edmund sighed. "Those poor people."

"Nothing we could do, priest." Brenner reached out and slapped him on the shoulder. Learned Edmund started, and then offered him a tentative smile.

"I don't know why we even bother having wars," muttered Slate. "The world's trying to kill us fast enough as it is."

Caliban gazed between his horse's ears, and said nothing at all.

That night they stayed at a posting-house several hours farther on. They had to ride most of the evening to get there, but there was a unanimous feeling that a bath at the end would be worth the time. Slate's skin felt faintly sticky, as if the death in the village had clung to her like mist.

Word of the plague had already reached the posting-house. Slate had to explain twice, and then Caliban had to explain again that they hadn't touched anyone, they hadn't even ridden through the village, they hadn't come anywhere near anyone with the blight. The innkeeper finally believed them, probably because Brenner was glowering and even Caliban was starting to look inclined to violence. Slate wondered if he had simply decided that blight would be a less sure death than having his throat slit by large men in desperate need of hot water.

There was only one copper tub. They drew lots.

By the time Slate's turn came around—Caliban offered her his place, out of chivalry, and Slate shot him down out of irritation—it was near midnight. Learned Edmund and Brenner had already gone to sleep, and she could hear Caliban removing his armor in the next room.

She would have preferred a soak, but a savage scrubbing with pumice and hot water seemed to remove the stink of death from her skin, even if it left her raw afterward.

A body in the well, they said. Some kind of animal. And an entire village rotting away in hours, or killing themselves to save themselves the trouble.

"Learned Edmund," she said, the next morning. "Will you write a message to the Captain of the Guard and tell him what has happened to the village? I assume that he will have received reports already, but I want to be sure. We'll leave it for the innkeeper to give to the next courier that comes through."

Learned Edmund nodded. "Yes," he said. "Yes, that's a very good idea."

"They'll have been dead for days before anyone gets that message," said Brenner, when the dedicate was out of earshot.

"I know," said Slate. "I know."

On the seventh day, they joined up to the trade road and traffic began to stream past them. It was all going the other way.

"Refugees," said Caliban. He watched a cart go by, dragged by a single elderly ox, piled high with all a family's worldly goods, followed by more and more carts. Those who did not have ox-carts walked. A strapping young woman, taller than Caliban, walked past with an ancient woman clinging to her back.

Caliban dismounted and handed his reins to Learned Edmund. He caught up to the tall woman and her...

"Great-grandmother," the tall woman informed him. "The rest of the family's gone."

"Fools," growled the ancient woman. "I told them. I told them to run. We ran before, you know, when I was a girl, and the ones who didn't died. Stubborn fools. No one ever learns. But I'm not dead yet."

"I learned," said the tall woman. "As soon as we heard the Clockwork Boys were coming, we ran. We got off the main road only just in time."

"They'll chase you if they see you," said the ancient woman. "Like terriers with a rat. But if you hide in the woods, sometimes they miss you. Not in houses, though. They'll get you in a house every time."

"Where is your village, may I ask?"

She gave him the name of a village six days away on a horse. She had been walking a long time, it seemed.

"Thank you," said Caliban. He held out a coin, and the young woman hitched her shoulder down a little. The old woman's hand shot out like a bird's claw and snatched the coin away.

"Paladin, eh?" she said. She grinned, revealing a distinct lack of teeth. "Must be. They don't make many farmers that pretty. Hope the god appreciates it."

"Please forgive Gran," said the tall woman, in almost exactly the same tone that Slate said, *Shut up, Brenner.*

"There is nothing to forgive," said Caliban, and bowed to the old woman with exaggerated deference.

"Ha! Come find me sometime, pretty paladin. I'm not dead yet."

"I fear that you would be too much for me, madam," he said, and took himself back to the others. When he related the conversation, he left that part out. Brenner would have enjoyed it entirely too much.

"South of here," said Learned Edmund, looking up the village on the map. "Well south and east, it seems. But I thought the army was holding on the far side of that village."

"We'll find out when we get there," said Caliban. "Correct, Mistress Slate?"

"Hmm?"

"The army outpost."

"Oh, them. Yeah. Let's get moving."

The inns were full with people streaming west. There was no traffic going their way. Refugees looked at them with bafflement and tried to warn them off.

Well…they tried to warn Caliban off, anyway, and occasionally Learned Edmund. Brenner, they gave a wide berth to. They didn't seem to notice Slate at all. She found this amusing.

When they stopped at a farmhouse for the night, it was empty. The livestock were gone. Learned Edmund got a bedroom. Slate and the other two men threw bedrolls on the floor in the main room, though they deeded her the place closest to the fire.

There wasn't much food, but Caliban insisted on leaving coins to pay for what they took. Slate glanced at Brenner, gave a quarter of a nod, and he pocketed the coins when the paladin wasn't looking.

They aren't coming back for a long, long time. If they're smart, they'll run and keep running, to listen to the refugees tell it.

Two days after that, they found a village destroyed by the Clockwork Boys.

It was decimated. The houses had been smashed as if a tornado had gone through. Doorframes hung like kindling. Walls had been ripped open to get at the occupants. Even wooden floors had great holes torn in them.

At first, she thought perhaps it *had* been a tornado, but the trees around the village were untouched. And tornados did not generally leave human bodies looking so…trampled.

A fire had broken out in one building, and half the village was burned in addition to being smashed. The ashes were still faintly warm.

The bodies were not.

"My god," said Learned Edmund, almost to himself. "My god, my god, my god. These poor people." He signed a benediction, over and over, his fingers flickering so quickly it was hard to follow. *The prayer is quicker than the eye. Nothing up my sleeve…*

Slate had a hysterical urge to giggle. She knew all about reactions to shock, and she also knew that Learned Edmund would never understand.

She nudged her horse forward and rode slowly down the middle of the ruined town, bent over so far that her horse's mane washed over her face like tears.

"We should look for survivors," said Caliban.

"Do it," she said.

There weren't any. She hadn't expected there to be. The carnage was probably at least a day old—fires could burn for a long time—and any survivors had either stopped surviving or gotten the hell out of there.

Caliban checked every building anyway. He came out of each doorway with his face grown grimmer and grimmer, his eyes more deeply shadowed, until she had to look away.

Brenner vanished for a while, and then reappeared, climbing back into the saddle with no grace at all. It was not in Brenner to look sad, but he looked tired and older than Slate had ever seen him look.

The center of the town had a market square. There were ox-carts arranged around it, as if people had been packing up to leave when the Clockwork Boys came.

Both people and oxen were still there, but you could no longer tell one from the other.

She heard the sound behind her of Learned Edmund being sick. A few moments later, she could hear Caliban talking to him in his gentlest voice, low and kind. She could not make out the words, but the tone said: *This will pass. Trust me.*

Slate grimaced. *I wish someone would say that to me, in a voice I couldn't help but believe.*

Her horse was restless at the stench, shying away. It was a relief to concentrate on that, to go to a world where the only thing that mattered was the reins and the bit and the space between the horse's ears.

By unspoken agreement, she and Brenner rode to the far side of the town, upwind, and stopped just outside of the shadow of the houses. Slate took a deep breath, and then another. Brenner spat in the dirt, his jaw working like a disgusted cat's.

Knight and dedicate caught up to them. Learned Edmund's skin was ashen. Caliban was on foot, leading both horses and the mules.

"Well," said Learned Edmund, looking directly at Slate for the first time in a week. "What are your orders?"

She would have suspected him of some malice—who wouldn't be at a total loss in the face of this?—but then she met his eyes and saw that they were full of tears.

It struck her suddenly, how young he was. *Nineteen. Chosen for his compassion.* He looked much younger.

She'd killed a man at nineteen. She hadn't been able to sleep or keep food down for days afterward, and that had been one man, who had richly deserved it, not a whole village mowed down like wheat.

What are my orders?

Slate folded her hands neatly over her saddlebow. Perhaps if she arranged them just right, perfectly symmetrically, she wouldn't have to look up and see the destruction around her.

Perhaps she would not have to decide.

Caliban appeared at her stirrup, and set a hand on her leg. She looked down and met his eyes for a long moment.

"What will you have us do?"

If I ask, he will take command. He has seen carnage before. He will know what he is doing, and he will know that I am out of my depth, and I do not believe he will think less of me for it.

I will not ask.

"I thought the battles were farther south and east. The army's supposed to be holding them." She heard her own voice, sounding angry and betrayed. *I knew they were supposed to be raiding, I knew it, they told me, but the army was supposed to* stop *them. My plan hinged on the army not screwing up.* She took a deep breath. "I did not expect them to be raiding this far down the trade road," she said. "If we travel past this point, we might be a week or more, through territory held by the enemy."

Caliban nodded. "I thought so as well."

"So." Slate drew up the reins. "We cannot continue this way, then. We'll have to backtrack."

"Where are we backtracking to?" asked Learned Edmund.

"For now, the last village." It had been mostly empty, but if anyone was left, they would need to be warned. "After that—well, Brenner, do you think we can figure out where we can join up to the smuggler's road?"

He looked up from where he had been rolling a cigarette, the paper dangling in his hand. "Are you sure that's a good idea, darlin'?"

"No, but I don't see what other choice we have."

He rubbed at his neck. "Yeah, maybe. Somewhere around Six Ells, isn't it? I've never been on it, but if you give me a map, I can probably work it out, assuming they haven't gone and changed the whole thing."

"There's a smuggler's road that goes through the mountains," Slate told the other two. "It's narrow and in bad repair, but it bypasses the valley. The end comes out just over the Archonhold border, maybe fifty miles from Anuket City. I can't imagine anyone would send troops down it, so perhaps if we can get on it, we can get to Anuket City without…" She trailed off, gesturing at the destruction around her.

"I would like to bury the dead," said Caliban. "Or at least burn them."

She looked down at him, startled. He seemed to be addressing her boot, his eyes downcast.

He knows I'm going to say no. We don't have time.

Slate sighed, and learned something else about command.

If he was in charge, he'd say no, but because he isn't, he gets to ask.

"I wish we could," she told him. "But you know we don't have time. I'm sorry."

He nodded stiffly, and released her stirrup. Slate went back to staring at her hands, and listened to the sounds of creaking leather as the paladin mounted his horse.

They had gotten perhaps a dozen lengths down the road, barely into the trees, when the smell of rosemary reared up and hit Slate full in the face.

This was no elusive hint of magic, no subtle warning. This was an assault on the senses. Slate felt like she was drowning in a violent, if herbal, sea.

She dropped her reins, gagging. Her throat burned and her eyes watered. She knew that she was breathing, because she could hear the horrible gasping noises she kept making, but there did not seem to be any air in her lungs.

"What's wrong? What's wrong?" Caliban's horse banged into hers and her leg got pinned between them, but that was a minor concern. The paladin reached across and grabbed her shoulder. "Slate! Slate, my god, what's wrong?" He shook her, which didn't much help matters.

"Got to get off the road," she rasped, through a throat gone thick and bubbling. "Get off the road! Now!"

"What foolishness is this?" demanded Learned Edmund.

"Do it!" Brenner said, turning his horse awkwardly and riding for the cover of the trees.

Caliban, to his credit, did not ask questions. He grabbed Slate's reins and brought both horses to the edge of the road, then slid off to lead them into the woods. It was a good thing, because Slate was in no condition to lead anybody anywhere. She wrapped her arms around her head, wracked with coughing, while that godawful overpowering reek of rosemary sank into her bones.

They were deep in the trees, set far back from the road, when Slate slid off her horse. She staggered, nearly falling. Something held her up—a tree trunk, a paladin, she couldn't tell and it didn't matter. She could not stop coughing, and danger was coming, down the road, stinking of magic.

"Shut—me—up—" she managed to choke out.

Caliban stared at her. "What?"

"Too much—noise—stop—" She rolled her eyes up at Brenner in mute appeal.

He didn't fail her. The assassin pounced, knocking her down, and curled himself around her head. She choked helplessly into his midsection, pounding weakly on the forest floor and his shoulder with her fists.

"What are you doing? Are you mad?" Caliban hauled at Brenner's arm.

"Get down!" the assassin growled.

"You'll smother her!"

"If I have to, yes! *Get down!*"

"But—"

Slate gathered the very last shreds of air in her lungs and gasped "Down—quiet—*that's an order!*"

Obedience was a habit that prison and possession had not broken. Caliban sank to his knees, one hand still on Brenner's elbow.

Down the road, three abreast, a column of Clockwork Boys came marching.

They were huge. They were horrible.

There were a great many of them.

The basic shape was centaur-like. Some had four legs, some had six. They stood between eight and ten feet tall.

Slate had seen drawings before, but she hadn't known how much faith to put in them. The drawings were all strangely geometric, depicting enormous creatures made out of slabs and blocks, like nothing Slate had ever seen.

The brief glance she got, in the space between Brenner's arm and ribcage, showed that the artists had not been so far wrong after all.

The Clockwork Boys were the color of old ivory. Their heads—if it was anything so normal as a head—were blunt wedges, like a squared-off horse head. Slate caught a glimpse of what looked like inlay—carving—something.

Gears. They're covered in gears, like barnacles. It's how they move, somehow—but it doesn't make sense. *They're alive, but they're a made thing, but nobody could have* made *that, surely—*

She understood now why the artificers were tying themselves in knots.

The creatures could not exist, but they did. And they could smash apart a building or an army column with equal ease.

How did the army ever kill even one of them? I suppose you could take it apart with hammers, like a stone wall, but it would take hours…

They have to be stopped.

They expect us *to stop them.*

If she had not been about to choke to death, the sheer insanity of it all would have made her laugh. Or cry. Possibly both.

Impossible, uncaring, the Clockwork Boys slammed down the road. Their feet pounded the ground like hammers.

They were abreast of the trees now. Brenner curled more tightly around her, blocking her view.

Slate was going to suffocate. She was going to die with her face jammed into Brenner's ribcage, which was not a way she'd ever wanted to go. She thrashed weakly, involuntarily, despite every nerve screaming at her to lay still, lay still, let the danger pass, don't make a sound…

A black-gloved hand covered her throat. He didn't squeeze—yet—but Slate could feel his fingers like bars of iron, ready to close the moment she began coughing again.

Panic seized her, and under it, relief. *Good old ruthless Brenner. He won't let me kill us all. He'll kill me first.*

Slate had to admit that dying with Brenner's hands locked around her windpipe *was* a death she'd seen coming. *Could be a lot worse.* Brenner was a very efficient killer, even if he couldn't ride a horse.

"It's okay, darlin'…" he whispered into her hair, "I've got you."

His voice was really quite soothing, given that they were talking about her impending death. She would have laughed if she had enough air.

She could not keep track of time. She breathed through her teeth and Brenner's shirt for eternity and he said things to her that he had never said when they were lovers.

"It's okay. I've got you. It's okay."

Possibly if he'd said those things when they were lovers, things would have turned out differently… *Yes. Because strangling on your own spit while monsters walk the roads is the perfect time to re-litigate old relationships.*

"I won't let go."

Don't, she willed him. *Don't. I'll kill us all. Don't let go.*

He didn't let go.

The end of the column passed.

A long time later, the scent of rosemary faded.

A little time after that, Brenner released her throat.

Slate took a deep breath, coughed it out, took another, and that one went down normally. She could smell other things, which in this case was mostly Brenner. He smelled like leather and cigarettes, and that was wonderful, because it wasn't rosemary.

The assassin helped her politely to her feet.

"She knew," said Learned Edmund, staring at her. He was holding the horses' reins bunched together. Slate wondered if the horses had been too stupid to run or if the scholar had somehow soothed them. "How did she know?"

"Word of advice," said Brenner, slapping leaf-litter off Slate's back. "If our Slate starts choking and sneezing and tells you to do something, *do it.* Don't ask questions."

Caliban was staring at them. His expression was indescribable.

"What?" asked Slate, wiping at her nose.

"You two," said the paladin slowly, "have a *very* odd relationship."

"Oh, come on, if your friends aren't willing to strangle you, what kind of friends are they?" asked Brenner.

Caliban turned away, shaking his head.

"So those are the Clockwork Boys..." said Learned Edmund, almost to himself.

"Big ugly bastards, aren't they?" said Brenner.

"I should have been better prepared," said the dedicate. "The last correspondence that we received from Brother Amadai included a drawing of one. But I could not picture the scale. I thought perhaps they were the size of a man, no more..."

Slate shuddered. She'd only caught a glimpse through Brenner's arms of the creatures, and it had been enough to give her nightmares. She snuffled into her sleeve.

When she got back to her horse, there was a handkerchief draped across the saddle.

CHAPTER 10

They struck out north, through the woods, looking for the smuggler's road. It was a stupid idea—they didn't know how far it was, or what it would look like—but the other two alternatives were to go back, behind a marching column of Clockwork Boys, or forward, through territory that the Clockwork Boys were raiding, and there was just no way.

Slate had been entertaining a faint illusion that between the three of them—Caliban, Brenner and herself—they might be a match for a Clockwork Boy. She'd never seen one, after all, and she had a lot more faith in Brenner's knives than a soldier's sword. The sight of the column had squashed that flat. It would be like trying to kill an elephant made out of stone.

She had a persistent vision, though, of Caliban standing before one of the gear-riddled monoliths, his sword held upright before him, like a hero out of an old story. It bothered her, not least because Caliban had *been* just such a hero. She could see him meeting his death that way again, on his feet, with his sword before him.

Getting maudlin. Getting sentimental in my old age. I shouldn't care how any of us die anyway—we're all just looking for ways to fall down. If we even make it to Anuket City, I'll be impressed, and if we do, I'll be dogmeat as soon as I walk through the gate.

All this time, Slate had been expecting to die in Anuket City. She had personal history there that wasn't going to lie quiet.

They'll be so very glad to see me. One more loose end to tie off. Messily.

For all her fatalism, it had not truly occurred to her that the Clockwork Boys might get her beforehand.

Heh. What everybody told me was *the great threat actually* is *the great threat. Who knew?*

"How the hell do we fight something like that?" asked Brenner.

Nobody had to ask what he meant.

"You don't," said Caliban. "You run, unless you have an army with you."

"They do not float," offered Learned Edmund. "Most of those who escape, I am told, have been able to get into deep water. They walk along the bottom unharmed, but they cannot reach you if you swim."

"That won't work for me," said Caliban, sounding more clipped than usual.

"You can't swim?" asked Slate, bemused.

He did not meet her eyes, which was strange. "I do not do well with deep water."

"An exorcist afraid of drowning," said Brenner. "There's irony for you." Caliban ignored him.

"I said, it's ironic that an exor—"

"I heard you."

"You two stop bickering or I'll scream bloody murder and call the whole lot of them down to put me out of my misery."

"That seems excessive," said Learned Edmund.

"Does it? Does it really?"

Learned Edmund fiddled with the reins in front of him and said nothing, which was the way that Slate liked it.

For Caliban, the Clockwork Boys had been less revelation than confirmation. He was a temple knight, not a soldier, but he had seen siege engines before. The Clockwork Boys were living siege engines. Monstrous, like no construct of wood and metal that he had ever seen, but not profoundly shocking.

What had shocked him far more was Slate and Brenner.

If the Clockwork Boys had not come down the road when they did, he would have probably pulled his sword on the assassin. The man's gloved hands had literally been around Slate's neck.

And then she had ordered Caliban to stand down and the Clockwork Boys had gone stomping by and he had realized that the forger and the assassin shared some knowledge he didn't.

If it had been left up to Caliban, they would all be crushed under clockwork by now.

Slate knew that. Slate called on the assassin to help her, not me.

Because she had trusted Brenner to do what needed to be done, and not Caliban. And she had been right to do so.

In his heart of hearts, he had been feeling superior to the two of them. Not just because they could not ride horses worth a damn, but because he was a knight and they were criminals. Slate was in command, but Caliban had always known that if she floundered, he could step in and lead.

And if I had just then, I would have killed us all.

Worse, even as he'd been silently judging the forger and the assassin for being what they were, it was *Slate* who had been willing to sacrifice herself to save the rest of them. Slate who'd been begging the assassin to keep her from giving them away to the enemy.

All the platitudes he'd mouthed over the years about self-sacrifice, and here he was being shown up by a forger who'd been arrested for treason.

As for Brenner…well. He still didn't know what to think of Brenner. The assassin was a weapon and Slate clearly had no qualms about using him as such. Even on herself.

Caliban rode his horse close beside Slate's and could hear the rasp as she inhaled. He listened to it like a penance.

I am a fool. Still.

Pride. It always came back to pride.

By now you think I'd have learned.

She glanced over at him, lips quirked. "What? Afraid I'll fall off the horse?"

"Should I be?"

"Oh, probably." She pressed the flat of her hand against her forehead. "My sinuses feel like they're full of lead. But we need to get farther away from the road before I fall down."

"I'm sorry," he said.

"Not your fault."

"No. Before…" He gestured behind them. "I didn't know what you were doing. I should have realized Brenner hadn't just decided to murder you in the middle of the afternoon. I made it harder. I'm sorry."

To his surprise, she laughed. "Don't worry about it. There's always a good chance that Brenner will decide to murder me in the middle of the afternoon."

"I resent that, darlin'," said the assassin, riding up on the other side. "The middle of the afternoon's when I like a nap. I'd at least wait 'til evening."

"Well, I'd hate to interrupt a *nap.*"

Caliban shook his head in disbelief. Slate grinned at him, then sneezed again, and then Learned Edmund called that the game trail they had been following had just vanished into a tangle of branches and mud and Caliban rode ahead to see what, if anything, he could do to help.

Riding through the woods was even worse than riding along the road. Slate got so used to having branches slap her in the face that she stopped even flinching. It was too early for mosquitoes, which was a small blessing, but just the right time for frequent rains. Water dripped off leaves and found its way unerringly down the back of her neck, no matter how many layers of clothes she wore, and her feet were so cold so much of the time that she started to wonder if she was wearing her socks wrong.

Don't be stupid. They're socks. There's only the one option.
Still...

They had to lead the horses much of the way. Caliban led them, but even the tireless knight wasn't used to this sort of travel. He held them on a mostly straight course, and that was all that anyone could hope for.

The horses were actually another set of problems. Slate was used to simply handing the reins to a stableboy or the farmer's son and walking off. Apparently, there was a lot more to keeping horses around than that.

You had to take their tack off and rub them down and check their hooves and their legs and feed them and water them and make sure they were tied to something where they'd be comfortable and not break their necks trying to run in the middle of the night. And then you had to rub the tack down, and fix bits and put oil on other bits, and by the time you were done, over an hour had elapsed when you weren't eating and weren't sleeping and weren't getting any closer to your goal at all.

Then in the morning you had to get up and do it all over again, pulling saddles on and bridles and shoving things in horses' mouths and tightening straps and then the horses would puff their bellies out so that you didn't tighten it very tight, except that if you fell for that, Brenner generally slid off the horse an hour later, and there'd be a lot of swearing and brandishing of knives.

Mules were worse. Mules were like horses who could *plan*.

Caliban dealt with the animals with his usual patience, but there were seven of them, and that was a lot of horseflesh to be tending every evening. Slate started helping, which required him showing her a lot of things, usually three or four times.

She never did figure out what a horse's hoof was supposed to look like, but that was okay, because it never actually looked like that anyway.

That aside, she actually found that she liked Caliban a lot better when they were taking care of the horses. He didn't mope, he didn't overthink, and there was almost no way for the conversation to segue dangerously. "Is this a rock in this hoof?" did not lead gracefully to "So, you over killing all those people yet?"

And he spoke to the horses the same way that he had spoken to Learned Edmund, in the gentle, trustworthy voice.

"Good girl," he said to Brenner's mare. "Come on...easy, easy...good girl. Such a pretty girl you are." And the horse would let him check each leg for swelling, lift each hoof, quieter under his hands than she had ever been under Brenner's.

Slate couldn't blame her. There was something about that voice. *I'd let him check my feet, too, if he talked like that to me.*

Hell, I'd let him check a lot more than my feet.

Which was idiocy, of course. Caliban was polite. He was always polite. And when they touched—as it was nearly impossible not to touch sometimes—it was impersonal. She could imagine him treating an elderly nun exactly the same way.

She wondered if the hypothetical elderly nun would be as vaguely annoyed by it as she was.

Not that it would have done her any good if he *had* been interested. There were no inns. There were no farmhouses. Consequently, there was no privacy.

They slept on the ground, in bedrolls. It was cold and the fire went out a lot because nobody was particularly good at banking it.

Brenner, entirely unconcerned about privacy, made a few quiet advances about ways to keep warm. Slate made a few quiet rebuffs, and finally suggested he go see if either of the other two were interested.

"Bah. I'm nothing if not open-minded—particularly in this weather—but the knight won't be, and the priest really isn't my type."

"Servants of the Many-Armed God are sworn to celibacy anyway," said Caliban, returning from gathering wood. Slate felt the tips of her ears get hot and was glad that her complexion hid blushes. She wondered how much he'd heard.

Brenner, as usual, had no shame at all. "Aww. Guess that limits my options. What do you say, paladin?"

Caliban raised an eyebrow. "Seriously?"

"What, afraid you can't keep up with me?"

He shook his head. "I'd like to say that was the worst proposition I've ever received, but unfortunately, I've had worse."

"Is that a yes?"

"No. Unless you can conjure up a hot bath. You don't *want* to know what I'd do for a hot bath right now."

"Well, I feel used..." muttered Brenner.

Slate patted his shoulder. "You'll live."

Celibate or not, Learned Edmund turned out to be the most useful of their companions. He had traveled alone, with his mules, for many days. He could tend to mules, read maps on horseback, find water, and do laundry on a rock.

And he could cook over an open fire, which was black magic as far as Slate was concerned.

He still had a hard time making eye contact with Slate, but as long as she ignored that, he was remarkably even-tempered. His earlier bitterness seemed to have passed off, and it was occasionally nice to talk to someone who did not have a sardonic comment for every occasion.

He still kept his bedroll as far away from hers as possible. He waited until she picked a spot for the night to even unload his mule. If she went down to the stream to sluice dirt off, he stayed in camp as if shackled to the fire.

Slate fought back an urge to ask how his bowels and genitals were doing. Breaking the fragile peace wasn't worth the brief satisfaction.

Brenner slipped away from the campsite one evening and returned a few hours later, whistling, with two rabbits slung over his shoulder.

"I didn't know you could hunt," said Caliban, impressed despite himself.

"Neither did I. Well, not animals, anyway." Brenner dropped them in front of Learned Edmund. "Can you do anything with these?"

"Certainly." The scholar eyed the two bodies thoughtfully. "I have a question for you, though."

"Yes?"

"You clearly shot this one..."

"Yes?"

"The other one appears to have been hit with a knife."

"I threw a dagger at it."

"You hunted a rabbit with throwing knives," said Caliban slowly.

"Was that strange?"

"It's certainly novel," the paladin admitted.

A day later, tired and disheveled from bathing in streams, they found the smuggler's road.

It was a narrow, winding track, but it was in good repair. Wagons were definitely using it, to judge by the ruts.

"That's a good thing and a bad thing," Brenner said, scratching at his beard stubble. "Where there are wagons, there are bandits, particularly up here, where there's no patrols. Still, it's the lean end of the season. The fat merchants haven't started coming through yet, and most of the bandits are probably still wintering over."

"That's what I'm counting on," said Slate. She started to kick her horse forward.

Caliban's hand on the reins stopped her.

The paladin searched her face, brown eyes much too sharp. "You were always planning on taking this road," he said.

Slate saw no point in denying it. "Yes."

"That's not what you told the Captain."

She rolled her eyes. "Your fine captain held me down and inked a murderous tattoo on me. Forgive me if telling him the exact truth about our itinerary wasn't foremost in my mi—ah!"

She slapped her arm. The tattoo in question, which had just bit her, eased its grip.

"I didn't betray anyone," she said, as much to the ink as to the man in front of her. "I haven't done anything to jeopardize the mission. In fact, this was the smartest thing I could have done. If there's spies in the Dowager's palace, now they won't know where to look for us."

"You lied to me. You lied to all of us. Why?"

"Because three can keep a secret if two of them are dead!" she snapped.

He looked disgusted. More than that, he looked disappointed. Slate hadn't experienced that in years. She hadn't missed the sensation.

"They'll notice when we don't show up at the front," said Caliban. "They'll be expecting us. They'll assume we're dead."

"Then think how happy everyone will be when we turn up alive!"

He didn't take the bait. He stood there, looking down at her, his gaze cool and judgmental and remote.

"If you'd been killed, the three of us would have just walked into the war zone," said Caliban. "Thinking that was the best way."

"Yeah, well." Slate shrugged. "I warned you that was suicide, didn't I?"

He turned away. His lips were set. She could not shake the feeling that she'd let him down, and that was stupid, because she didn't owe him anything, did she?

You got him out of his nice safe cell...

He ought to be damn grateful, then.

"Don't pat yourself on the back too hard, darlin'," said Brenner. "I'd been thinking there was supposed to be a smuggler's road. And that bandits are easier to deal with than monsters."

"See, there you go," said Slate to Caliban's back. "Besides, maybe this way we can find out what happened to the last group the Captain sent out. According to that last commander, they actually did go up into the hills." Which had had nothing to do with why she'd chosen this road, but it was convenient, anyway.

"The group that no one's heard from and is presumed dead?" said Caliban.

"That's them, yep."

The line of his shoulders did not indicate that this made him feel any better.

"Could they have been killed by bandits?" asked Learned Edmund.

Brenner set off down the road. "Nah. Mark my words—anyone out on the roads this early is probably either out of money, or had gone stir crazy and is looking for excitement, and either way, there aren't likely to be many of them."

Actually, there were about eight of them.

They had crossbows, and they turned up in the middle of the road while Caliban was off scouting down their back trail.

Of course there would be bandits. Slate felt very calm. She didn't know why she hadn't seen it coming.

"So what do we have here?" asked the bandit leader. He was tall and lanky, both hair and skin an indeterminate shade of grizzled blonde.

Slate sighed. This was annoying. It probably wasn't all that dangerous—bandits were masters of the cost-benefit analysis, and they would generally pass on a fight for a suitable bribe—but it was still one more irritation.

Worse, Caliban, and the very large sword, were still somewhere back down the road.

Well, no, maybe that's a good thing. If I can pay these guys off before he shows up…

"I believe you're on our road," said the man, slouching forward and catching her horse's bridle.

Brenner shifted a bit on his horse, an unobtrusive movement that no doubt set him up to kill several people in very short order, assuming the horse didn't do anything untoward, like breathe or take a step in any direction. Learned Edmund had a hand on his saddlebags, ready to sell his life dear in defense of his books.

"I'm sorry," Slate said, with carefully controlled pleasantness, "I didn't realize this was *your* road."

She could kick the bandit in the face and probably get a knife in him before he'd recovered, but then they would definitely have gotten into a fight, and that would be *really* irritating.

"It is. We would quite hate for anything to happen to anyone using it."

"Well, then." She drummed her fingers on her thigh. "I suspect we can come to some arrangement."

There were hoof beats on the road behind them. Apparently their knight had caught up with them.

"Quick!" she snapped at the bandit leader. "You've got five seconds to close this deal before he gets here!"

The leader blinked at her.

The hoof beats stopped. "Too late," sighed Slate.

"Unhand…that…horse."

Everyone, very slowly, turned to look at Caliban.

Brenner let out a single whoop of laughter, covered his mouth with his hand and dissolved into silent, shoulder-heaving hysterics.

So much for support from that quarter.

The bandit leader stared at Caliban, then turned back at Slate. They shared a moment of horribly embarrassed camaraderie—*did he just say that? Should we just pretend that didn't happen?*

"Ignore him," said Brenner, having gotten control of himself, "he has delusions of knighthood."

"Shut *up*, Brenner," Slate snapped. "And Caliban, let me handle this."

"Madam—!"

"I *said* I'll handle it."

"Sorry, *madam*," gasped Brenner, and went off again.

The bandit leader and Slate exchanged looks again. He had beer-colored eyes, and he looked about ten years older than most of his men.

"Do you ever feel like you're the only sober person in a room full of drunks?" asked Slate in a low voice, leaning forward.

"Constantly," he said, glancing back at the ragged line of men behind him, several of which had gotten bored and were picking at various parts of their anatomy. Crossbows pointed at the air, and occasionally at each other.

Slate glanced back at her rabble. They weren't any more inspiring, but at least no one was picking his nose.

"Right. Well, I think we could arrange for a suitable…hmm… road tax," she said.

He looked back at Caliban, who was glowering and running his hand over the hilt of his sword. "Fifteen."

"Five."

"Twelve."

"Seven."

"Ten—"

Caliban's horse took a few steps forward. He opened his mouth to say something in protest, and what came out was guttural and in no human language.

"Nine, and hurry it up, my friend here is not staaaable," Slate said, uttering the last word in a sing-song which caused the bandit's eyes to widen even farther.

"Nine sounds good."

Slate put her hand in her money pouch, counted out nine coins inside the bag—no sense letting the man see how much was really in there—and handed them over.

The bandit hefted the money, glanced at each member of the group in turn, then leaned forward. With his lips barely moving, he murmured "I wouldn't normally ask this, but are these men kidnapping you?"

Slate had a sudden desire to yell "Yes!" and throw herself into the bandit-leader's arms—he really did have lovely eyes—but she suspected that nothing would be left alive on the roadway by the time that had finished playing out.

Plus the tattoo would eat me.

"I'm beyond help at this point," she said instead. "But you're sweet to ask."

He nodded to her, looked as if he might say something else, then shook his head.

The bandits melted away into the trees.

"You're going to just let them get away?" Caliban demanded.

"Yep."

"They're bandits!"

"That they are."

"They threatened you!"

"For god's sake, Caliban, is there any particular reason you want to interrupt our trip with somebody getting stabbed? Just let it go."

He slid out of the saddle and grabbed her stirrup. His voice came out clipped and impatient, and Slate almost didn't register the words at first, which were "I'm sorry."

Slate blinked. "Uh."

"I should have been up here, not checking behind us. You could have been killed."

"No harm done?"

"It will not happen again, madam."

What do I say to that? "See that it doesn't?" "No, really, don't worry about it?" What will shake him out of his martyred knight mode?

She settled for a nod. He rode practically at her stirrup for the rest of the day, one hand always on his sword. She wasn't sure if she was comforted or worried or just annoyed.

He's miffed because I lied about which route we were taking, and now he's mad at himself because he was off sulking and I could have been killed by bandits. I swear, the man looks for ways to beat himself up. It's like some kind of weird hobby.

It was a surly group that made camp that night. Caliban was either still grim over not having killed the bandits, or still feeling guilty over not having been there to defend them from the bandits in the first place. Learned Edmund had finally snapped and yelled at Brenner, who'd yelled back, until Slate had yelled at both of them.

They all sat around the fire, nursing mugs of tea and their respective grievances.

"How far do you think it is to Anuket City?" asked Learned Edmund finally.

Slate shook her head. "There's no way to tell. We don't know where we joined up to the smuggler's road, and it's not really marked on the maps. At a guess—probably a week or more to Archenhold. That'll be the first sort of civilization we'll reach."

"Gonna be a long week," muttered Brenner, sliding a glance at Caliban through hooded eyes.

"Indeed," said Caliban, returning the assassin's glance with a steely one of his own.

Slate put her head in her hands and entertained a brief fantasy of leaving them all to rot, going back down the road and finding that bandit leader and seeing if he wanted to get nice and drunk together.

Her tattoo twinged. Apparently it had no concept of daydreaming. She slapped at it irritably.

When she looked up again, Caliban was watching her. She met his eyes squarely—*Yes, I might have been thinking something that jeopardized the mission. Want to make something of it?*

He looked away instead.

Slate sighed and figured she'd throw her guard dog a bone. "Archenhold's not really allied with Anuket. I mean, they *are*, but they like to pretend they're a sovereign nation. We can send word back to the Captain once we get there, if you're that worried that he'll think we're dead."

Caliban nodded, still not meeting her eyes.

When they went to sleep that night, her last sight was Caliban sitting up still, running a whetstone down the length of his sword, although whether he was watching her or watching *over* her was anybody's guess.

CHAPTER 11

They kept traveling.

There are practical considerations that arise when four people live in close proximity for very long. All the little questions need answers, like who did the dishes and who got the firewood and whether they could spend a morning beating clothes against a rock before they set out, because nobody owned anything clean to their names.

They dealt with it in their own ways. Brenner griped. Caliban brooded. Learned Edmund prayed.

Slate contemplated their approaching deaths with an increasingly unhealthy relief.

There was also another consideration.

There are only so many bushes in any given stretch of forest, and Slate's bladder wasn't helped by the pounding her nether regions took on horseback daily. She was starting to think that you could judge a man's character by how he reacted if he tripped over you attending to a call of nature.

Brenner would grin like a shark and saunter off, whistling. Caliban would say, "Excuse me," turn around, and walk off in the other direction. Learned Edmund would turn six shades of scarlet, gabble out something, trace a hurried sign of protection and fall over himself while retreating.

Likewise, there was the matter of changing. Sooner or later you had to put a different shirt on, and no one ever stayed out of the campsite for nearly long enough.

Brenner would watch and offer commentary. Caliban would turn his back politely and stand with his hands clasped behind him, and would even act as a lookout in case Learned Edmund wandered by, since the priest would again turn scarlet, make another sign of protection, and fall over—and that was only amusing the first couple of times.

Slate wondered occasionally if this would be any easier if there was another woman in their motley band, or if it would just make for twice as many unfortunate encounters. It would have been nice to have someone to lock eyes with and sigh occasionally. Slate considered herself enlightened, but there were still times when she wanted to throw her hands in the air and scream, *"Men!"* and then stomp off and kick something.

She did not do this, mostly because it would have confirmed all of Learned Edmund's fears. It was a near thing, though.

She was dead certain they got into belching contests when she was away from the campsite. She wasn't sure if she was grateful they were sparing her, or irritated that she wasn't invited.

Oh, well. Just a few more miles to Anuket City, and then it'll all be moot anyway...

They were half a week out of Anuket City when the storm hit.

The first raindrops weren't much, but they fell from a sky that boiled like lead between the leaves.

Caliban drew his horse up, and the rest of them followed suit.

"That doesn't look good," Brenner said.

They all studied the sky. Lightning flickered off in the distance.

"I'd say we should take shelter," said Learned Edmund, "but we're near the Vagrant Hills right here, and I hate to leave the road." Caliban grunted.

"What're the Vagrant Hills?" asked Slate.

The knight looked around. "Forests and low hills, more or less. We don't want to wander into them."

"Why not?"

"You know how magic makes you sneeze?"

"Sure."

"We'd probably have to tie you to the saddle."

"Lovely."

They watched raindrops make craters in the dust. Thunder growled around them, and a cool wind slithered between the trees.

"Maybe we can find something close to the road," said Slate, kicking her horse forward. "Keep an eye out."

They got about a quarter mile down the road without spotting anything likely, and the sky opened up with a cataclysmic ripping sound.

Everyone was instantly wet to the skin. Slate's hair plastered itself to the back of her neck.

"Damn."

"We should have oilcloth cloaks in the bags somewhere," Caliban said, shouting a little to be heard over the rain.

"We're going to have to get off the road," Brenner called. "We can't just sit through this."

The Learned Edmund opened his mouth to say something— possibly to protest leaving the road at all—and a crack of lightning hit the ground less than a hundred yards away. Thunder smashed around them, not just a sound but a physical weight that rang in Slate's brain and bowels as well as her ears.

Her horse bolted.

Slate was so blinded by the jagged afterimages of the lightning that at first she thought she'd simply fallen off the horse and that the sickening lurch was an after-effect of the thunder. But then a spray of pine needles smacked her in the face and she fell forward, and she realized that the horse was moving under her.

In a stumbling run.

Through the dripping forest.

Ohmygodohmygod

Its ears were flat against its head. The forest was a wall of black cut-outs, given brief, flickering depth by lightning.

Can horses even run in forests? Will it hit a tree? Is it about to fall down? Am I about to fall off?

She flung herself as flat along its back as she could, clinging to the reins and the saddle and the mane, her legs wrapped around the horse's belly, which she realized, rather too late, it might be taking as a signal to keep running.

Too late now. If I let go, I'll fall off. At high speed.

The world slewed at an angle. The horse put its hindquarters down and skidded down a slope full of wet bracken.

It occurred to Slate that, suicide mission aside, she was almost certainly going to die *right now* because no horse could run through dark wet woods without slipping or putting its foot in a hole or breaking a leg in some fashion.

And this caused her to make quite an unexpected discovery—namely that she didn't want to die.

Ohmygod I want to live I want to live I don't care I want to live!

And hard on the heels of that thought: *Well, this is a helluva time to figure that out!*

The horse stumbled and recovered. Slate's stomach did not. Wet grasses slapped at her legs and face like whips.

I could jump off. That's probably safer, right? Right?

Part of Slate's brain agreed. The part that was holding onto the horse was not convinced.

The slope leveled out. The horse staggered, caught itself, and ran. Rain poured into her eyes again.

It's an old river bed. Oh god, we might live after all.

If I can just get it to slow down—

She searched her clenched hands for the reins. There weren't any. Mane, saddle, a chunk of saddle blanket. No reins.

She'd dropped the reins at some point, or the horse had managed to flip them over its head, or something. Regardless, they weren't there. Shit.

If she let go, she could reach down and grab for them.

If she let go, she was going to fall off.

If she fell off, she was probably going to die.

Well, maybe just one hand... She pried her fingers loose.

The horse hit a patch of rock and skidded on two hooves. Slate shrieked and grabbed tight again.

I can't stop it. It's going to fall down and I'll break my neck and die or break my legs and die of exposure or—

There was a yell behind her.

She looked over her shoulder, and there, as she should have known he would be, riding like a lunatic or a demon, was (former) Knight-Champion Caliban.

That idiot. That wonderful idiot.

I take back all the times I thought about letting Brenner kill you.

His horse pounded down the streambed behind hers. Lightning sizzled, illuminating the whites of its eyes. Caliban didn't look much calmer himself. He was hunched over his horse, and if his sodden grey cloak hadn't been glued to his back and the horse's haunches by the rain, she wouldn't have known who it was.

Well, he's still on the horse, so it'd be a good bet it wasn't Brenner, and he's giving chase, so it obviously wasn't Learned Edmund. Okay, I could have figured it out even without the stupid cloak.

Her horse skidded again. Coherent thought dissolved briefly into a screaming welter of *IdontwanttodieIdontwanttodieshitshitshit—!*

Caliban was shouting something, but she couldn't make out the words. He was slapping his horse's rump with something—it looked like the flat of his sword—and it was running, ears back, and somehow, madly, he was gaining.

He shouted again.

"I can't hear you!" she yelled back.

Thunder smashed anything he might have said in response. Her horse squealed, and she had to stop looking over her shoulder and clutch desperately at it. She was hunched so low that every stride cracked the back of the horse's neck against the side of her head.

Could he really catch up to her?

Hey, it's a math problem. I'm good at math! If a horse traveling at twenty-six miles an hour going west is intercepted by a horse traveling at twenty-nine miles an hour going northwest, will their paths cross before or after the first horse breaks its rider's neck?

She giggled hysterically. Rain and the horse's mane lashed her face raw, and she giggled anyway.

Oh god, I don't want to die...

There was a shadow next to her. The paladin's horse was pulling alongside hers, neck to haunches, then neck to knee. She could see his hand, practically next to her face, as he groped forward.

If you think you're reaching over and pulling me off this horse in mid-run, you're even farther out of your mind than I think you are...

He might have been out of his mind, but apparently not that far. The hand passed her, swung down, and there was a sizzle of wet leather as he grabbed the flapping reins.

If Slate had somehow managed to get the reins, she would undoubtedly have hauled back on them with all her strength, and the horse would have bucked or reared or gone over or all three at once. But Caliban had a somewhat better notion of the stopping distance of a horse on a wet riverbed, and the two horses went pounding along together, side by side, until the desperate run dropped down to a gallop, and the gallop fell to a canter, and the canter became a kind of stiff-legged bouncing trot, and then the horses had stopped and he slid off and Slate fell off and he caught her.

It occurred to Slate, a few minutes later, that she was clinging to a knight in the middle of a rainstorm, her cheek full of wet chainmail, which wasn't very comfortable, and that she appeared to be sobbing uncontrollably. She wasn't actually sure. It was too wet to tell if there were tears. She might have been laughing instead.

Caliban was holding her upright. He still had his sword in one hand, and the pommel was digging painfully into her shoulder, but she didn't care, because she wasn't dead.

He was saying something, over and over, that she couldn't make out—it might even have been the demon muttering, for all she knew—but the rumble in his chest was soothing.

The thunder rattled. She was glad of it, because it meant he couldn't hear her, either. She had a horrible suspicion that what *she* was saying, over and over, was, "Oh my god, I don't want to die."

She wrestled herself under control at last, partly out of pride, and partly because the horses were moving restlessly and bumping into them both. She finally got her feet under her.

Carefully, possibly even reluctantly, Caliban released his hold and stepped back. She looked up. Rain sluiced down both their faces. Was he crying too? How could you tell?

He leaned down, and shouted, next to her ear, "We have to get out of here before it floods!"

Ah. Good thinking. Now that Slate looked down, the water did seem to be swirling perilously close to the tops of her feet. She nodded to Caliban, who took the tangle of reins in one hand and Slate's hand in the other and led them all squelching upstream, looking for a place to climb out.

The rain was still coming down in hard sheets. Visibility was nonexistent. But they found one at last, on the opposite bank, and none too soon. The water was threatening to come in over the tops of Slate's boots. The horses, already panicky and exhausted, were slipping and snorting and pulling at the reins.

She let go of his hand and dragged herself up the slope. The knight and the horses followed.

Her vision was better than his in the dark, and once they were under the trees, she took the lead. There wasn't a great deal of cover, but she found a fallen tree at last. It had crashed through the canopy and been overgrown by a spreading pine tree.

It formed a wall on two sides and at least a suggestion of ceiling, and the ground underneath was damp rather than sodden.

It'll do.

There was no real point in trying to start a fire. She crawled into the hollow and pulled her knees up to her chest.

Caliban tied the horses, draping their saddle blankets over them as best he could, then crawled in after Slate.

It was pitch black under the tree. Slate could just see make out the outline of the horses, black against grey, and that was all.

Squish. Squish.

What the hell...?

In the next flash of lightning, she caught a glimpse of Caliban trying to wring out his cloak.

"Well," he said, after a minute, "it's not dry, but it's what we've got."

With some grumbling and a few curses, and the removal of some armor and his sword, they managed to huddle together under the cloak. It stank of wet horse, but it was wool, so it held warmth in, and that made up for a lot of wet horse.

She sneezed anyway.

His sigh seemed to come from his toes.

"Sorry," she muttered, and sneezed again. The smell of rosemary was threaded in and around the wet horse.

He dug into a pocket and pulled out a handkerchief.

Slate started laughing. She couldn't help it.

It caught like a sob in her throat. She was going to cry again. Her hair hung in her face in damp strings, and she shoved at it futilely. *Why am I crying?*

I'm cold and exhausted and I don't want to die, and someone just handed me a handkerchief.

These seemed like excellent reasons.

Caliban wrapped his arms around her and rested his chin on top of her head, murmuring all the meaningless things that people murmur to console the weeping. As any paladin could have told her, the words didn't matter nearly so much as the voice.

The spate of tears passed off quickly. She was too tired to keep it up for long. She lay quietly, feeling his arms around her in the dark.

It was about the only way to keep them both under the cloak, and there was rather more metal that she liked, but she wouldn't swear she didn't enjoy it.

You're just giddy from being near death, that's all. You figured out you don't want to die. It doesn't mean anything. You'd feel the same way no matter who was in here with you.

Well...possibly not the Learned Edmund.

Still.

Her heart ached, and her head ached, and her sinuses...well, they always ached. She snuffled into the handkerchief. She tried to think of something clever to say, to deflect the fact that she was shortly going to be quite embarrassed for crying, and couldn't find anything. Her voice, when it came out, sounded thin in her own ears.

"Caliban?"

"Mmm?"

"I don't think I want to die."

He chuckled. Chain clinked under her ear. "That's good."

"But we're going to die."

"Let's try not to."

"Okay, then."

There was a lot more that she wanted to say, about Anuket City and what was waiting for her there. But it was all horribly complicated, and she would have had to explain what she had done and who wanted her dead, and about the Shadow Market and the Grey Church and the crow-cages. And she was very tired and the city was very far away.

The wet wool of his tabard was beginning to dry under her cheek. He'd unbuckled both shoulder guards and his gloves and either she was cold or his skin was as hot as a brand against hers.

She rather hoped he'd make a move of some sort. Hell, Brenner would have been smoking a post-coital cigarette by now, if she'd been curled up in his lap like this.

She could have used…well…*something.*

But Caliban was a former knight-champion, once sworn to temple service, and that meant either that he did not take advantage of mildly hysterical women who had just been dragged back from the brink of death or that he was incapable of recognizing a hint when it crawled into his lap.

One of the two, anyway.

Nothing ventured…

She stretched up a hand and touched his face in the dark. A day worth of beard stubble rasped under her fingertips.

She traced the long line of his jaw downward, then across. Her finger lay across his lower lip. She could feel his breath against her skin, sharply indrawn, and then released.

He folded his hand very gently around hers and drew it down, to lie loosely on his chest. And then, a moment later, he patted her hand, and withdrew his.

Or he's completely uninterested. Son of a bitch.

Slate's face burned in the dark.

She was too drained to be angry for long. She wanted to be furious and embarrassed but that would take energy and she had so little left to spare. It was dark under the tree, and very warm under the wet wool. She was either comfortable or too exhausted to feel physical discomfort.

The rain dragged on. They existed in a small, warm place outside of time. Slate dozed off with her hand clenched in an undyed tabard that was by now very much the worse for wear.

Knight-Champion Caliban—who had indeed been known to recognize hints, and who was clinging to what was left of his vows by will alone—leaned his head back against the damp wood of the tree stump and waited for the rain to pass.

Chapter 12

"Well," said Brenner, in a voice that could have etched glass, "isn't this *cozy*."

Slate pried her eyelids open. They felt dry and itchy. She was in somebody's arms, which wasn't necessarily a bad thing. Brenner's? It'd been his voice, and it wouldn't be the first time, but she didn't recall him being so sarcastic afterwards. Usually he just wanted to get breakfast.

It appeared to be early evening, and the rain had passed off. The world swam into focus, revealing pine needles, dirt, someone's arm, Brenner, the Learned Edmund, two horses and three mules, in that order.

Brenner looked furious, and wasn't hiding it well. Learned Edmund looked appalled. The horses looked like horses, and the mules looked bored.

By process of elimination, therefore, the arm I am using as a pillow belongs to…

Ah. Yes.

She sat up. Former Knight-Champion etc. Caliban lifted his arm politely to release her and got to his feet, scrubbing at his eyes.

Okay. We've both got all our clothes on. I didn't do anything stupid.

Not for lack of wanting.

Still, it's good. It's a good thing. The last thing I need is Brenner getting jealous, or any more complications on this bloody death march anyway.

It might be too late on the first count. Brenner was watching Caliban with death in his eyes, possibly wondering if he could get a knife into the knight before anyone moved.

Learned Edmund was also watching Caliban with something like pity. Had his bowels turned to water and his genitals withered already? Was it a gradual process?

Slate stood up, slapping bark dust off her clothes. She felt cold. The paladin's body had been very warm, with the cloak over them both like a blanket.

This was a line of thought that did not bear pursuing. "How did you find us?" she asked.

"The horses," said Learned Edmund, not meeting her eyes rather more obviously than usual. "When we got close, they whinnied to each other. We just followed them."

"Ah. Didn't hear it. Must have been more tired than I thought."

Learned Edmund stared at the ground. Brenner's stare grew even more lethal. Slate replayed the last statement in her head and winced internally.

Still, there were bigger concerns than the priest's assumptions or Brenner's petty jealousies. One big, serious, pressing concern.

"So!" said Slate. "What's for dinner?"

Learned Edmund was setting up camp. Brenner was starting a fire. Slate went to go help unload the horses, grabbed a pack, turned around, and found herself nose to nose with Knight-Champion Caliban.

They looked at each other. It became uncomfortable very quickly. He dropped his eyes first.

Slate felt her face get hot. She was blushing hard enough that not even her dark complexion could save her.

What am I embarrassed about? Crying? That's nothing, lots of people cry.

That I offered, and he didn't want anything I had to offer?

No. I didn't say anything. Nothing that'd stand up in court.

Caliban cleared his throat.

But you know. And he knows. And you both know that the other one knows.

"Madam—" he began.

Slate raised a hand, opened her mouth, found absolutely nothing to say, and closed it again.

He looked up at her finally, saw that she was burning scarlet, and his eyes widened.

"Ma—Slate—there's nothing to be embarrassed about."

It's an interesting conundrum, Slate thought, as blood pounded in her ears. *I am more embarrassed because I have nothing to be embarrassed about than I would be if I'd actually managed to do something embarrassing.*

"I haven't thanked you," she said, not looking at him. "You saved my life."

"You don't need to thank me."

"I'm not sure what else I can do." *Since any other offers I might have made seem to be of little interest to you.*

"I..."

"I'm sorry if I offended you," she said.

"Offended?" He actually looked up at that. "What? Oh! No. No, of course not. Not with—no. But you—when people are frightened—"

She didn't know what her face looked like but apparently it was not kind, because his eyes slid away from hers.

Unfortunately, he also kept talking.

"I took an oath," he said, staring back at the ground again. "The strong should not take advantage of the weak."

Slate parsed this mentally and came to a conclusion so outrageous that it took her several tries to get the words out. When they came, they were so calm they seemed to belong to someone else, a totally different Slate, who was not nearly dizzy with outrage.

"Did you just call me *weak?*"

"We're all weak sometimes," he said gently. "It's nothing to be—"

"*Ah.*"

She packed enough acid into that syllable to stop him cold.

Sonofabitch is patronizing me. Sonofabitch thinks I'm weak. Even Learned-bloody-Edmund is at least scared I'll fry his genitals off.

I suppose he thinks that I need to be protected from him.

I pulled you out of a stinking cell where you flinched every time someone moved. I led you blind because you were afraid of the sky. And you dare—you dare—to call me weak?

She did not say these things. They crashed in her head like stones, and if she tried to get them out, they'd all fall out together like an avalanche, and god help her, she'd start crying again, because she *always* cried when she was really furious, and god *damn* if she was going to give him the satisfaction.

"I just wanted to keep you from doing anything you'd regret," Caliban said, a man who had dug six feet down and decided to keep on going.

"You arrogant *jackass*," said Slate, her voice clipped and calm and almost pleasant.

He took a step back involuntarily. Slate felt a stab of triumph.

If Brenner had appeared behind him at that moment, and laid a knife across his throat, Slate wouldn't have sworn that she wouldn't have nodded. But the assassin was off collecting wood and missed his chance.

"Slate—"

"Don't talk to me," she growled, and turned on her heel and stalked back to camp.

Learned Edmund looked up, saw her approach, and retreated to a safe distance.

It was probably because she was on such a ragged edge, but his alarm was almost soothing. At least here was someone who was afraid *of* her, and not *for* her.

Slate barked a laugh, reached out, and caught at the air a foot from Edmund's face. He stared at her in alarm.

"Learned Edmund?"

"Yes?" he said warily.

"Thank you."

One eyebrow went up. He made half a gesture, possibly part of a benediction, thought better of it, and said "Uh…you're welcome?"

Slate pulled her hands through her hair. "Do you need anything?"

"I could use some water, if you want to go down to the river."

She looked around for the bucket. Caliban, who had been walking back into camp, reached down, picked it up, and walked off again, without speaking.

Slate gritted her teeth at his back.

I should have left him in the cell.

Well. Excellent job, Caliban congratulated himself. *The only way you could have made more of a hash of that was to accidentally run her through with your sword.*

I did what I had to do.

The empty bucket knocked against his leg. He stepped cautiously down the pine-needle encrusted slope to the river.

He'd had some kind of thought, when he started talking, of saying, "I wasn't sure if that was what you really wanted, but if you're sure…" Of seeing if she was actually interested, not merely high on adrenaline and the body's animal need not to die.

And then what?

He snorted. *And then I would have told Learned Edmund to watch the horses and taken her the minute we were out of sight. Up against a tree if I had to.*

Repeatedly.

She had been growing in his mind for weeks. Her anger and her stubbornness and the way she would grin suddenly when she worked out a problem in her mind. He wanted her to grin like that at him. He wanted to take her in his arms and feel the weight of her breasts in his hands and say things that made her laugh out loud and do things that made her cry out his name.

He knew better. He should have known better, anyway. He'd resigned himself to physical loneliness. The demon in his head would be an unwelcome third in any bed. But somehow his body didn't know that and it seemed to be dragging his heart along in its wake.

He had been wanting to say something for days now, but there was never a chance—not with Brenner like a jealous shadow at her heels.

And then he'd had a chance…and somehow the words had gotten tangled up and what had come out had been so painfully awkward that he was probably lucky she hadn't stabbed him on the spot.

I did the right thing. She would have regretted it. Who wants to bed a possessed murderer?

Apparently for a moment last night, Slate had. He could still half-feel the path her fingertips had taken across his skin.

Perhaps he should dump some freezing water over his head.

The strong do not take advantage of the weak.

So why do I feel like such an idiot?

Caliban dipped his bucket in the stream, straightened up, and felt steel lying in a cold kiss across the back of his neck.

In a way, it was a relief. He'd known it was going to happen, and at least they could get it over with sooner rather than later.

"Hello, Brenner," he said.

"I think I'd like to have a worrrrd with you," drawled the assassin.

"I'm sure you would." He set the bucket down. "You're not planning on killing me or you'd have done it already, so perhaps you could move the knife?"

"Mmmm." The knife pressed a little harder, the point creasing the skin just under his left ear, then moved away.

Caliban turned around, letting his hand drop to the hilt of his sword.

"Getting a bit comfortable with our Slate, are we?"

Dreaming God's bones. We're on a suicide mission, we've got carnivorous tattoos, we're supposed to stop monsters that are like nothing I've ever seen...and now we're going to have a fight because we're both interested in the same woman.

On the one hand, it probably said something inspiring about the human spirit that it could rise above such things in pursuit of love.

On the other hand, it was pure bleeding *idiocy*.

"I'm sorry, would you have preferred I let her freeze to death in the rain? Or perhaps just let the horse carry her off to a broken neck?"

Brenner frowned. It was a different expression from his habitual scowl, and Caliban liked it a lot less. Dark hair fell into his face like a curtain.

Is this jealousy, or something else? How close are they, anyway?

"If you're getting any ideas," said Brenner softly, "I would keep them to myself, if I were you."

Caliban put up an eyebrow. "Why do you care, anyway? You're sleeping as cold at night as the rest of us." He shifted his feet, and heard pine needles crunch underfoot.

Why am I baiting him? This is stupid. I should just say, "No, no, I'm not interested, all yours." Do not bait the assassin. Did I take a blow to the head when I wasn't looking?

Brenner tilted his head. His eyes flickered, but the point of the knife never wavered. "Oh, I won't deny I wouldn't like another chance at our Slate. She's a dear thing when she's not waiting to die."

Caliban wasn't surprised. He'd been more than half sure they'd been lovers once—there were too many intimacies between them that friends never achieved. This was only confirmation after all.

What *did* surprise him was the sudden knot in his stomach, and the hot, dizzy feeling inside his head.

What the hell is wrong with me?

What a stupid question. You'd need quite a list.

Nha, ghaa, ngh'aa…

The demon's voice alone should have stopped him, but he could still taste the knot of—yes, *fine*, it was jealousy, or maybe only envy, that the assassin had done what he could not.

How had she looked at him when they were together? You could read every emotion on Slate's face, usually from a mile off. What expressions had crossed it when the assassin had been in her bed?

Oh Dreaming God, we're being fools and she'd kill us both if she knew.

"Fine," he rasped. "Plead your case to her, not me. She won't be best pleased if we stab each other."

"Oh no. That's not my point," said Brenner, smiling now, which was even more ghastly than the frown.

"It isn't?"

"It's an odd thing," he continued in a light, conversational tone, "but every killer I've ever known who killed for pleasure rather than money—and I've known a few—had the same thing going on in their heads. They got sex and death all tangled up, and if they couldn't get the one, they'd have the other."

Caliban had expected anything from a brotherly threat of bodily harm to a former lover's outrage, and had thought he was prepared to weather it.

He hadn't expected this.

"What?"

"Now if there was ever a repressed lot in life, it's temple paladins, and frankly, I don't care what you may have done. But if you start getting all tangled up about our Slate, and I come back one fine evening and discover that you chopped her into little pieces, I am going to be *pissed.*"

The knight raked a hand through his hair. "Are you—my *god,* you're not serious!"

Can't he just wave his knife around and say, "I saw her first!" like normal men?

"I'm very serious," said Brenner, in a voice that was low and almost friendly, the paladin's voice through a black mirror. "Killing I know very well. And believe me, my fine knight-champion, I can make you die slow."

"I would never—" He groped for a phrase, found "randomly dismember Slate" on his tongue, and couldn't get it out.

Well, I wouldn't.

"Never? Seems to me you did it once already." The assassin was circling him now, still with the knife out. Caliban realized that he was no longer sure that Brenner wasn't just going to kill him. "Oh, excuse me. *Eight* times."

"I was possessed!" the knight shouted.

"I don't believe you," said Brenner.

Caliban drew steel. Brenner came up on his toes with a wild smile on his face.

They circled each other, once, twice.

"It's a neat trick," said Brenner. "The demonic voice thing almost had me fooled. But I don't buy it. Probably you got a taste for killing people you claimed were possessed. You killed those people, and you enjoyed it and you found an excuse that kept your neck out of the noose—"

"Burning," rasped Caliban. "The punishment for apostate paladins is burning at the stake."

"Then I don't blame you for trying to avoid it," said Brenner, grinning, "but you're not trying it on our Slate."

He made a sudden dash forward. Caliban fended him off with a sweep of the sword.

A net dropped over both of them.

Caliban's first thought was that this was some trick of Brenner's. Then he saw the assassin was also struggling under a net.

His second, wilder thought was: *Couldn't Slate find a bucket of water to throw on us?*

He tried to get his sword the rest of the way out of the sheath. A foot stepped on his hand—no, it was a hoof?—and someone kicked him in the ribs. A few feet away, Brenner was being relieved of his knife in a similar fashion.

Someone green stepped into his field of vision. Caliban looked up into a face that wasn't human, and the sharp end of a sword.

There was a loud and unmistakable *shing!* of steel being drawn and someone shouted.

Aw, shit. Brenner really did try to kill him.

Slate snatched up her knife and ran for the river, Learned Edmund hot on her heels.

Hell if I know what I'll do once I get there. Help whoever's losing, maybe. Shit, shit, shit...

She dodged around trees, skidding through the mat of pine needles. *Goddamn, how far away did they go?*

A minute later she slowed. "This is crazy. Where are they? No one would go this far for water." The sounds of a struggle had ended almost as soon as they'd begun, and now only silence greeted them.

"Brenner! Caliban! *Where are you?*"

No reply.

"Brennerrrr! Helloooo!"

The stream gurgled by. Leaves hissed softly in the wind. There were no shouts, no moans, no sounds of two people cutting each other to pieces.

They can't be fighting somewhere. Fights aren't quiet things.

She turned and looked at Learned Edmund, who spread his hands helplessly. "I have no idea."

"They have to be here somewhere!"

"Could one have killed the other?"

"We'd still find one of them, and a body."

"Could one have stabbed the other and run? And the other gave chase?"

"I suppose, but—"

Slate stopped.

The discarded water bucket lay at the edge of the water. The ground was trampled and scuffled, pine needles kicked up in great gouts, which could have meant something or nothing at all.

"I'm no kind of tracker, but they were here and…something happened."

"Brenner seemed angry with Sir Caliban," observed Learned Edmund.

"Yeah, but if he killed him he wouldn't try to hide it, and if Caliban killed *him,* he wouldn't try to hide it either."

"What's that?" asked Edmund, pointing.

She turned.

Something lay on the ground, a bit of gaudy green twine laced with small black and white feathers. The white quills gleamed, even in the failing light.

"Woodpecker feathers," said Edmund, picking it up.

"What does that mean?"

"I have no idea, but I'm guessing that they didn't leave under their own power."

"Hmm."

She stared at the twine. It looked like some kind of bracelet, but it had been ripped off.

"Well," she said. "At least there's no blood. They took them alive, I think."

"Should we go after them?" asked Learned Edmund.

"I'd love to. Pick a direction."

"You can't tell which way they've gone?"

"Can you?"

"No."

"Well, then."

They looked for signs, in a broadening circle around the river clearing. There weren't any or there might have been dozens. The wood was full of things that looked like trails and weren't. Any one of them might have been real, if they'd only known how to look.

They slogged back to camp. It was too dark to see, even if they knew what they were looking for. Slate dropped down next to the fire and put her face in her hands.

What do I do now? I can't rescue them if I don't know where they are!

She waited for Learned Edmund to say something snide, but instead he handed her a roasted potato. "No good will come of us starving ourselves, Mistress Slate."

"No, I suppose not. Thanks." It was indeed an excellent potato. She choked it down through a throat gone thick.

What do I do? I can't leave them!

What if they're already dead?

Caliban has to be alive. He has to be alive so I can think of something really cutting to say to him, the metal-plated ass.

She gnawed on a fingernail. She wouldn't cry, because that would be useless, and it would also confirm all of Learned Edmund's worst fears about her.

Slate glanced at him, a slim, miserable-looking figure hunched inside his robes. Something about his posture, and the way he kept blinking, made her think that he might be worried about crying too.

Somehow that was cheering. Not because she wished him ill, but because there are few things in life as steadying as someone you have to be brave for.

"Well, a fine pair we are," she said. "And we thought the hard part would be *in* Anuket City."

He smiled weakly. "I suppose—"

The horses lifted their heads. Even the mules pricked up their ears.

"They hear something," said Learned Edmund.

A breeze rippled through the trees, and after a moment, over the crackling of the fire, Slate heard it too.

It was music.

There were drums in there, and pipes, a low beat and a high skirling whine threaded through it. It wasn't a pleasant music— every now and then the beat would skip, which jolted the listener as if their heart had skipped—but the fact that it was music at all, in the middle of the woods, fired Slate with relief.

"Come on." She got up and kicked dirt over the fire.

"Where are we going?"

"After the music."

"You think the musicians took the other two?"

"I think it's the best lead we're going to get."

They left the horses tied up and picked their way down to the river. Slate wasn't sure if the music was coming from there, or if the sound just carried better over water, but they had to start somewhere.

They got partway down the slope and the trees opened up. Learned Edmund reached out and caught her arm.

There go your bowels and your genitals, m'boy.

"Look!" he hissed. "Something's moving!"

Something was indeed moving, a regular undulation that seemed to slither down the slope a dozen yards to their left, and move out across the rocks that spanned the river. Slate squinted. The starlight wasn't very bright, but it looked like a thing of parts, like a column of ants, rather than a single snakelike body.

They were much bigger than ants, but still not very big. They didn't look like anything that could overpower a man, although there were a great many of them. More streamed past, every moment, moving out of the woods and crossing the stream.

The music skirled. The drums skipped a beat, and the whole column lurched briefly, then took up the step once more.

They inched closer.

"God's mercy," breathed Learned Edmund, "I think they're rats."

"I think you're right."

They were indeed rats, or at least mostly. There were several varieties, from rotund cotton rats to big-eyed deer mice, and even the occasional chipmunk, but primarily they were plain, ordinary rats, the sort that Slate saw every day going about their business in the alleys and gutters of the capital.

Unlike those sleek urban rats, however, these were not quietly pursuing their own rodent interests.

They appeared to be dancing.

With each beat of the drum, the rats would take a step forward on their hind legs. Their whiskers and tails moved, and they shuffled back and forth to the high skirling of the pipes. A step at a time, hundreds, if not thousands of them, they danced and squirmed and stepped across the rocks and up the opposite hillside.

That's really quite horrible.

A single dancing rat might have been cute, a line of several dancing might have been amusing, but this constant, slithering stream was deeply unsettling. If they stopped and turned, Slate and Learned Edmund would be ankle deep in squirming bodies.

Now that's a pleasant thought.

"Well…" she said, trying to keep her voice even, "I suppose it could be worse."

"I think it is," said Learned Edmund weakly. "That one there doesn't have a front."

Slate looked.

The back end of a rat, the sort of thing that a cat might leave as a present to its unfortunate owner, was stepping merrily along in the line. The fact that its waist ended in a kind of bloody rag of fur didn't seem to bother it.

Slate put a hand over her mouth. The potato wasn't sitting very well at all.

Ohhhh…

Now that her eyes were adjusting, she could see that many of the rodents were much the worse for wear. Some of them were obviously dead, missing heads, entrails, or other vital bits. Some might simply have been badly wounded. Despite this, they capered as fluidly as the others dancers in the line. If the body had feet, it seemed to be able to dance to the music.

The only mercy to the whole thing was that she had absolutely no desire to sneeze.

"I'm going to be sick," said Learned Edmund, and was.

Slate reached over and held his hair with one hand. She didn't take her eyes off the line of tiny dancers.

If the sound of a scholar dry heaving bothered the rats, they gave no sign. The column showed no sign of tapering off. Rat after rat came dancing down the hillside, to cut a grotesque saraband across the river.

A few minutes slid by. By the time Edmund had stopped heaving, and was wiping his mouth, Slate had made a decision.

"Learned Edmund," she whispered, "I want you to go back to the horses."

"Mistress Slate?"

"Go to the horses. If we're not back by noon tomorrow, take them on the road, and go back the way we came. Once you get to a large enough town, send a message to the Captain of the Guard. Tell him we're all dead and to send someone else to help you."

"You can't be serious!"

"I'm very serious."

"I'm not going to just leave you all!"

She could have growled with frustration. The music beat in her head like a pulse. "Listen to me, Edmund. Of the two of us, I can't handle the horses, and I *can* sneak into places."

"But—" He blinked at her. The moon was rising, and she could see his pallor, and the determination of his expression under it. "Sir Caliban is my friend. I can't let you go alone. You're—"

"Expendable," she said.

"A woman."

"That, too. Regardless. All three of us are expendable. You are not."

"But—"

"That's an *order*, Learned Edmund," she said, and filled her voice with every ounce of steel she possessed.

He stared at her. She stared back, unblinking. The rats danced and skittered behind him.

"If they're expendable, why are you going after them?" he asked her.

Slate jerked. On her shoulder, a sudden spike of pain, as if small ink jaws had clamped down on her skin.

No! I'm not betraying the mission! I have to go after them! The odds of success are much better with them than without! And I'm not risking Edmund, see? See?

Perhaps in response to her frantic thoughts, the tattoo loosened its grip. The painful pressure eased.

"*Go,* Learned Edmund," she growled.

He rose to his feet, and then, slowly, bowed his head. Slate nearly sagged with relief herself.

"Where are you going, then?" he asked.

She rose to her feet, already moving down the slope to the river. The knot in her stomach had loosened. She knew what she had to do.

"To follow the rats, of course."

CHAPTER 13

Right about the time the Learned Edmund was losing his potato, Caliban and Brenner finally exhausted their mutual recriminations and looked around for something else to do.

They were hog-tied on a dirt floor, inside an earthen lodge that looked like it was built by a magpie with ambition. The wattle-and-daub walls were studded with junk: bits of straw, feathers, small stones that might have been a mosaic if there had been more of them, snake skins, bright glass and colored string. Nets with glass fishing weights hung from the ceiling, illuminated by the flicker of a fire near the entrance.

There were also bones. Some were individual bones and some were whole articulated skeletons, from a number of small, unfortunate animals.

Brenner and Caliban were in the middle of a sunken circular area. Wooden posts rose to waist height around them, holding back the rest of the floor. Their captors had taken their weapons and, for some odd reason, their shoes.

"You know," said Brenner, for approximately the fiftieth time, "none of this would have happened if you hadn't been—"

"Shut *up*, Brenner," said Caliban, who was learning why that was Slate's favorite phrase.

"I'm just saying."

"You were trying to kill me!"

"...I was only gonna cut you a little."

After they'd been netted, their captors had shoved gags of splintered bark in the men's mouths, tied their hands, picked them up, and begun to run through the forest. They were inhumanly fast, which made sense because they hadn't been human.

Flattened against the bottom of his net, all Caliban had been able to see was a sickening lurch of landscape going by. If he craned his neck, he saw…legs.

Green legs, with fine swirls of brown hair on the calves, ending in large, cleft hooves.

That did not fill him with confidence.

When they had finally been dumped out onto the ground, he looked up into a circle of a dozen faces, none of which were human and all of which were green.

They looked like deer, mostly. They had long-muzzled faces and broad, flaring nostrils. The spacing of their eyes was wide and unsettling, but the eyes held a deep and uncanny intelligence. Mobile ears flicked back and forth at every sound.

The males were broad-chested and had antlers. Two of them carried Caliban between them as if he weighed nothing. The females were slenderer, with shallow breasts and patterns of dark green scars circling their eyes. Both sexes wore necklaces, armbands, and loincloths. All carried spears.

They did not look friendly.

A spear came in and prodded Brenner, who had managed to work his gag out. He cursed the spear-holder in no uncertain terms.

The deer-creatures spoke to each other in high-pitched voices, like bird calls. Even the deep-chested stag-men had shrill, lilting voices. It didn't make them sound any friendlier.

Another spear poke, this time directed at Caliban.

He gritted his teeth.

The spear poked again, more insistently.

Pride had always been his besetting sin. Damn if he was going to scream in front of Brenner, after that little scene at the river.

The spear got in a solid jab. It didn't penetrate the chainmail, but there was going to be a bruise under there in the morning.

Assuming we live so long.

One of the stag men reached down, grabbed his hair, and dragged his neck back. One blunt-fingered hand made an unmistakable gesture across the knight's throat. The spear lifted.

Caliban didn't break, but his demon did.

"Nghaa! Ha, ha, ngha'aa, halikaliha!"

The deer jerked back as one, with squealing gasps.

"That was either brilliant or incredibly stupid," said Brenner.

"I don't think it was brilliant," Caliban muttered.

The deer gabbled to each other, with many hand gestures. One approached and checked the ropes.

Then the deer left them face down in the center of the floor. Caliban heard the woosh of hides being moved aside, the thump of hooves...then nothing.

After a while they had an argument. Actually, they had the same argument, in about three variations, about who was to blame for their current predicament. It was somewhat cathartic, but at the end of it, both men were still tied up and Caliban had sand in his mouth.

About an hour after that, the music started.

"What's that?"

"Music."

"Where's it coming from?"

"Outside."

"I don't like it."

"Finally, we agree on something."

It wasn't painful to listen to, it wasn't bad, it was just...*uncomfortable*. It got in your head and started pushing things around. Every time the music skipped a beat, Caliban felt his stomach lurch.

His demon didn't like it at all. Whenever the pipes rose to a crescendo, the muttering voice became a shriek, as if it was trying to drown out the noise.

What sort of noise can bother a corpse?

Brenner fell silent. Caliban worked his legs against the ropes, not because he had any hope of getting out—he didn't—but because his feet were falling asleep. They'd tied him well, and he didn't have Slate's reckless disregard for joints.

"Can you get out of the ropes?" he asked the assassin.

Brenner pushed against the ropes and got a bit farther than Caliban had, but not enough to make a difference. "No. I've been trying."

"Hmm."

"I really, really want a cigarette."

"I really, really don't care."

They lapsed into silence again. Caliban's cheek was going numb from being plastered against the dirt, and he wiggled around until he could turn his head. Unfortunately, this meant he was looking at Brenner.

Dreaming God, if you still have any scrap of kindness for your servant, please don't let him be my last sight on this earth.

"What do you think they are?" asked Brenner.

"What?"

"The things that captured us."

"I'm pretty sure they're rune."

"Rune?"

"Forest people. What you get when dryads mate with stag men for a few hundred generations, or something like that. I'm not really sure." He'd seen them in illuminated manuscripts, but never in real life. Up until a few hours ago, he hadn't thought they existed anywhere but a monk's feverish imagination.

"Look about right for that."

"Yeah."

It was strange, but he hadn't remembered reading that rune were anything but shy and harmless creatures. Apparently the monks had left the bit about kidnapping out.

"They seem very angry about something."

"That they do."

"Looks like this is their village."

"Does it?" Caliban wondered if he could gnaw through Brenner's ropes, or vice versa. It seemed unlikely.

"There was a whole circle of these little dirt huts. They must dig a hole and then build the walls up around it."

"Oh. You've got better eyes than I do. Or they were holding you right-side up."

"Mm."

"Don't suppose you saw a way out?"

"No."

Having thus exhausted the conversational possibilities, they lay there. Caliban wiggled his fingers. They burned as the blood flowed back into them.

He wondered what Slate would say if she were here, and was extremely glad she wasn't.

Assuming she doesn't take it in her head to come after us...no. She wants to live now, and chasing after mad deer people isn't a good start on that. And after that charming little display on your part, I doubt she'd walk across the street to save you, let alone stage a daring rescue on a village full of demented deer people.

Thank the Dreaming God. We're going to die, but at least she and Edmund will get away.

Hopefully.

It was a tiny, mean emotion, entirely unworthy of a paladin, but he was glad that Brenner was here with him.

"Caliban?" said Brenner, in a rather different voice than anything Caliban had heard him use before.

"Yes?"

"I think I'm losing my mind."

"What, only now?"

"Look up around us and tell me if you see what I see."

Caliban opened his eyes.

188

Rats—and pieces of rats—were lining the edge of the sunken circle. He craned his neck as far as he could, given his position, and they went all the way around, rank on rank. They were shuffling, one step at a time, in time to the throbbing drums. When they crossed in front of the fire, tiny headless shadows danced across Caliban's face.

The drum skipped a beat. The whole line of rats stumbled pitifully, and then the beat picked up again, and they fell back into the dance.

"Dancing rats. Some of them with no heads," said Caliban.

"Oh, thank god. You see it too."

"It's very disturbing."

"I'm glad I'm not the only one who thinks so."

"I wonder if they're going to eat us."

"Always an optimist, our paladin."

"Shut *up*, Brenner."

The dance was distressingly hypnotic. Caliban watched it until his eyes burned and he had to look away.

What could call them here? There can't be this many rats in the village—there have to be hundreds of them—and you can't tell me that a rat with no head walked here under its own power!

Step…step…step…*lurch*…step…

It might have been the demon riding his senses, or all the years in the service of another sort of power entirely, but Caliban could feel some kind of force to their dance, something rising off the tiny, wretched bodies.

If it was magic, it was no kind he understood, and yet there was definitely something there.

I'm not imagining things. The demon feels it too.

Every time the drum paused, it clenched like a fist.

Nghaaaaaakalikalaakkalaaknggggaaaaah!

Shut up, demon. I don't think we want to be noticed right now.

Ngha ngha…

Step…*lurch*…step…step…

The power was driving the dance, but the dance was *feeding* the power. Caliban didn't know how much energy it took to make a dead rat dance—it didn't come up much at the temple—but all those bodies dancing together were doing *something*.

Like water through a millwheel. Somehow they're getting more out than they're putting in.

That shouldn't be possible.

Caliban, however, took the view that when something impossible was going on, it was best to deal with it as you found it, and not stand around claiming it wasn't happening.

Brenner jackknifed against his ropes. "Can't you *do* something?"

"Like what?"

"I don't know, something paladin-y!"

Caliban smiled sourly. "Sure, I can take your confession and grant you absolution so you die with a clean conscience."

"Very funny."

"I wasn't joking."

Step…step…step…*lurch*…step…

"I'm not confessing anything to *you*."

"Suit yourself." He wasn't entirely sure he could have done it anyway—the Dreaming God had broad definitions of what constituted confession, but Caliban really didn't want to die listening to a recitation of the assassin's sins.

The door to the earthlodge opened.

Rune filed in behind the rats. Foreshortened as his view was, Caliban could only see their faces and the heavy antlers of the males, rising like winter trees above their brows. Firelight painted lurid orange across their green cheekbones.

After a moment, he realized that they were moving in time to the music as well. They were not as awkward as the rats—they froze, ears upswept, at the missed beats, instead of stumbling—but it was the same dance.

Whatever's got the rats has them, too.

"Brenner?"

"Yeah?"

"If you've got a knife stashed anywhere, this might be a good time."

"I don't. If I did, I'd have used it by now."

"Sorry."

"Might even have cut you loose, too."

"You're too kind."

One of the rune, a stag-man taller than Caliban, stepped down into the circle. The rats parted before him then danced back together to fill the space.

The rune lifted a knife. His antlers were wrapped with beads. Black and white feathers and bits of bone swung as he knelt down behind the knight.

Dreaming God, I commend my soul into your hands, assuming you still want it—

The ropes between his feet were cut. Caliban sagged, partially from relief and partially from the scream of blood back into tormented muscles.

A surprised grunt next to him indicated that Brenner was receiving the same treatment. Then a heavy hand was lifting him up, and Caliban found himself on his knees, the assassin beside him. Their hands were still tied behind them, but just to sit up was an excruciating relief.

The stag-man stood behind them, the knife still in his hand. Caliban looked over his shoulder and saw that alone among the rune, the knife-bearer was not moving in time to the music.

A dark figure appeared behind the circle of rats. It walked forward with excruciating slowness, approaching the edge of the circle.

Shaman. Has to be.

The music stopped. The rats dropped simultaneously, as if dead, which many of them already were. A wave of tiny bodies fell at the figure's feet, a sweeping rodent obeisance. Their bones crunched under the shaman's hooves.

"NGGHAAAA—!" Caliban's demon clawed at him, screaming so loudly that the knight bit his tongue to keep from yelling aloud. Blood welled up under his teeth and filled his mouth with salt.

Along the walls, the rune shuddered, their ears drooping.

The shaman stepped down into the circle.

At first, Caliban thought it was another stag-man. The rack of antlers over its head was huge, twice the size of that of any of the other males, hung with bones. Round stones with holes in them clicked against something that looked disturbingly like human fingerbones. It wore a cloak of woodpecker feathers that dazzled the eye with spots and stripes until the shape under them seemed to swim in the firelight.

Then it spread its arms, and the stag-man behind them rushed to take its cloak away, and he saw that it was a female.

An antlered doe. Shaman—and judging by the number of points, a very old one.

The doe's face did not wrinkle like a human's would, but the long planes of her muzzle were sunken, the bones in fine relief, and the hairs had gone white, turning her skin a frosted green. Her spine was bent slightly forward, possibly under the weight of those magnificent antlers, and her breasts were flat sacks against her chest.

The doe's eyes were milky with cataracts, but they narrowed with unnerving clarity on his face.

Caliban swallowed a mouthful of blood. The demon had gone so silent that it was like being alone in his head for the first time in months.

"You," said the antlered doe, in a low, throbbing voice, mourning dove rather than sparrow. "Why here, you?"

Caliban had to swallow again before he could speak. "It was an accident. We were on the road, and the storm drove us off."

"Lie, you."

"No lie."

"Bring demons here, you."

Uh-oh.

"We didn't mean—"

She took a step forward, her eyes narrowing, and struck him across the face. The strength in those delicate limbs was astonishing. His head snapped back. The demon yammered, briefly, and then fell back into that terrified silence.

"Lie, you! Demon *inside* you, you!"

Despite the fear and the pain and everything else, Caliban felt a sense of vindication so powerful that it was practically a venial sin. He turned his head and stared at Brenner.

The assassin said "Heh," and made a kind of full facial shrug. He had the decency to look embarrassed.

"The one inside me is dead," Caliban said, turning back to the rune. "I swear, it is no harm to anyone."

The rune-shaman's nostrils flared. She put her face down practically next to his and inhaled.

"Could be, you. Or could be lies, you."

"No lie. I swear it."

She tilted her head. "Ye-e-es. Maybe, you. What other demons though, you?"

Is she asking if I have any other demons? God, isn't one enough?

"What other demons?" asked Brenner.

The antlered doe turned and looked at him, then stepped forward, her head darting forward. She walked like a bird or a lizard, oddly jerky. "Others, you. Clanking, clicking, tearing. Four-leg, six-leg. Know, you?"

Brenner inhaled. "I think she means the Clockwork Boys."

"The Clockwork Boys? Have they come here?"

She glowered. "Not know *clokwerk*, me. Know demons. Demons come, rune territory, *my* territory. Kill rune. Want kill *me*. Know, you?"

"We're not with them," said Caliban. "Not our demons. We want to *stop* them."

Her ears went back. "Lie, you."

"No. We're going to where these demons come from. To stop them."

The antlered doe fell back and paced around them in a circle. Caliban got a crick in his neck trying to watch her, and looked at Brenner instead. The assassin shook his head minutely.

"I wonder why she thinks they're demons," Caliban murmured.

"Maybe they are."

Her face thrust next between them. "Those demons kill me, take territory. Kill me, take territory, you?"

"We haven't killed any rune. We don't want your territory. We're just passing through."

"Lie, you! Else bring demon why, why, you?"

"I swear, I don't want your territory. My demon is dead. It doesn't want anything." *Except maybe to be left alone.*

She wrinkled her muzzle. "Not believe, me."

"I don't know how I can prove it to you."

She grinned. Her teeth were flat and herbivorous, but she had wickedly sharp canines. "Know, me." She turned away, leaping out of the sunken circle, kicking up the bodies of dead rats like dust.

And just like that, watching her move, he knew.

Oh, Dreaming God...

"There's a demon in her," he said aloud.

"What?" Brenner stared at him.

Caliban tried to swallow, found his throat tight, and spat blood on the dirt floor. "There's a demon in her. A live one. I should have realized from the rats—some of them can control vermin, but I never saw anything like this. She's possessed."

Shit, I must be out of practice. A year ago I would have known the minute I looked in her eyes.

There was a slim possibility that the rune shaman had accepted possession willingly. It did happen. Not often, but it did happen. Such demons were nearly impossible to spot, as Caliban knew to his sorrow.

"I wonder if they know," said Brenner, glancing at the other rune. They were as silent as the rats.

"I doubt it." Caliban's heart ached for the rune, that their shaman, who should have been wise, was host to a monster instead.

"Well, so, you're a demonslayer, then," said Brenner eagerly. "What do we do now?"

Caliban sighed. "We die."

"What? You're the bloody Knight-Champion!"

"I'm the *former* bloody Knight-Champion, and I don't have a sword to kill her, or salt and holy water to exorcise her, and my purity of heart with which to exhort her has been pretty shaky lately, as *somebody* keeps reminding me!"

"Bloody hell," said Brenner, with feeling.

The rune returned. She was carrying an abalone shell which trailed a thin stream of smoke.

A collective moan went up from the rune watching. They were sagging where they stood, their mouths open and panting. Whatever force had slain the rats did not seem to be treating them much better.

The demon rune crouched before Caliban, her antlers hanging over him. Bands of shadow crossed his face like bars. He could see inside the abalone shell now, a pile of leaves burning atop a bed of clear white salt.

Nghaaaaaa…!

For the first time, the knight felt a rush of almost camaraderie for his demon. *I'm scared too, believe me…*

He licked his lips. Salt and holy water were only there to focus the mind. If your heart was pure, you didn't need them.

The sword…well, the sword would have been very useful.

He had not felt the Dreaming God's presence in a very long time. Without it, what use was he?

Still…

He took a deep breath and said, in the paladin's voice, *"Halt."*

She paused. Just for an instant, just long enough to hope.

Then: "Think you command me, you?"

"Well, it was worth a try," he said, not looking at Brenner.

"See now, me," she said, and grinned with those wicked sharp teeth. Far down in her pupils, something alien looked out at him and laughed.

The antlered doe bent her muzzle to the abalone shell and inhaled deeply. Smoke rushed into those broad nostrils, and the coals flared.

She lifted her head and exhaled the smoke in twin streams into his face.

Caliban tried to hold his breath, instinctively. The rune behind him caught his hair and jerked his head sharply back. He gasped at the unexpected pain, and smoke rushed in.

It smelled sweet and acrid, like burning hay. He coughed and with each cough the world lurched sideways and farther away, as if he were moving backward, except that he was still kneeling in the dirt, unmoving.

Darkness closed around him.

CHAPTER 14

Slate had followed the line of dancing rats for what she thought was over a mile. She wasn't used to thinking in such distances, particularly not when they twisted and turned and doubled back, but it had definitely been a long, scrambling way. Her face had been slapped by so many pine needles that she felt as if she'd been flogged by miniature whips.

It would have been a dozen or so blocks, anyway. About the distance from the gutterside docks to Archivist Street, I'd say.

The moon was out, but she hardly needed it. The drums drew her on, and the slithering line of rodents was as clear as a signpost.

I hope I'm actually going the right way, and that this isn't some kind of random phenomenon—the Running of the Rat Bits—that happens occasionally in this part of the world.

Seriously, though, what are the odds?

She was standing in the middle of the rune village before she actually saw it. The sunken mud huts were so far from her idea of houses that if she hadn't seen the rats vanish into a doorway, she would have taken them for hills. Once she realized that she was standing in front of a door—and that there were a good dozen huts around her—she stepped back into the shadows, heart pounding.

No one seemed to be moving. If anyone had seen her, they were keeping quiet about it.

She examined the building beside her carefully. It was some kind of mud-and-straw construction, like a bird's nest. The walls looked thick and knobbly. When she dug her fingers into one, experimentally, it didn't give at all.

I could climb on one of these if I need to.

Slate made a careful circuit of the village. There were eighteen houses all told, although some of them were so small they looked like storage sheds rather than living quarters. There didn't seem to be any people in the village, except for the largest earth lodge.

This final lodge was a good forty feet across. The music was definitely coming from inside, and she could see a dull red glow through the doorway. If there were people in the village, they were likely inside.

The rats had finally stopped entering the doorway. Perhaps it had filled up. Instead the newcomers formed circles around the perimeter, six or seven deep.

It didn't follow, however, that if Brenner and Caliban were prisoners, they were inside as well. Possibly they'd been dumped in one of the other huts.

Slate slunk from doorway to doorway, peering inside. Each hut had been dug down, some of them quite deep and surprisingly spacious. A few had hide curtains in the doorways, and she had to twitch them aside a fraction to peer inside.

The smoke holes at the top of each building provided a circle of moonlight, and a good thing, too, or she would have had to go through and check by feel, and that didn't bear thinking about. Slate got through eleven houses, seeing nothing but firepits, bedding, baskets, and all the various flotsam of people's lives. No one appeared to have thoughtfully left an assassin and a paladin out.

She peered into the twelfth, saw what looked like a pile of rags in the moonlight, and was dropping the curtain back when the rags said, "Hssst!"

There was a knife in her hands. She didn't actually remember drawing it.

"Brenner?"

"Hey, lady! Help me out here!"

Slate winced. *That's definitely not Brenner. Whatever it is, it's seen me...*

She couldn't risk it yelling and raising the alarm. She let the curtain fall behind her and slid quickly into the circle of moonlight, where the pile of rags was sitting up.

It wasn't human. It looked like a cross between a badger and a haystack. It had a broad striped head, small almost-human ears, and a dozen layers of different bits of clothing. They were wrapped and tied and bound together in an intricately knotted tangle. Slate had never seen anything quite like it.

"Do you live here?" she whispered.

"God's claws, lady, do I look like I live here?"

"I have no idea! What are you?"

"I'm a gnole."

"What's a gnole?"

"One of me! Please, lady, untie me quick before the rune come back."

"What're rune?"

The gnole rolled its eyes wildly and wiggled. Its hands emerged briefly from the tangle of rags. They looked to be roped together, although the gnole's eccentric clothing made it hard to tell what was rope and what was more rags. "Rune are the things that live here, and they've gone crazy, lady! Now untie me and let's get out of here!"

"I'm looking for some friends of mine—"

"You come back to Anuket City with me, lady, I'll get you all the friends you want! Hurry up!"

Slate's lips twitched. She crouched down and cut the creature's bonds.

It rolled to its feet, wringing its hands frantically. "Thanks!" It was only about three feet tall, which put them at eye level when she was on her haunches.

It leaned in and a tongue swiped over her cheek, a warm, doggy kiss. Slate choked back a laugh and raised her hands to fend the gnole off. His breath stank of garbage and old meat. Also, it tickled.

"Come on!"

"I can't leave yet, I have to find my friends."

"Lady, you don't want to stick around here—"

Something happened. The air seemed to change, pressing down around them. It took Slate a minute to realize what it was.

The music had stopped.

The gnole flattened himself to the floor and moaned. Fur spiked along the thick neck.

"Oh, god, she's doing it again…"

"*Who's* doing it again?"

"The rune! Rune in charge is wicked bad, got them all worked up."

"I've seen it." Slate rose, looking around the earthlodge. If they kept the prisoner here, perhaps there was something else useful. "At least, some of the magic, I think."

"Wicked boss rune doing it. It's bad, lady."

Aha! A tangle of irregular shapes resolved itself into a familiar pile of weaponry. Caliban's scabbarded sword was nearly buried under Brenner's personal armory, and both pairs of boots.

I suppose they must not expect them to walk anywhere, then.

"What were you doing out here?" Slate asked, strapping knives to her belt.

"Oh, well, you know. Whole column of clocktaurs, so a couple gnoles go along."

"What the hell's a clocktaur?" Slate tried to belt the broadsword to her waist and smacked herself painfully on the ankle.

The gnole rolled its eyes at her. "God's stripes, lady, where you been? You know, eight feet tall, coupla extra legs, made out of little fiddly machine bits?"

"A—you came with the *Clockwork Boys?*"

My god. My god. It works for the Clockwork Boys.

I've found one of the enemy.

It didn't look like much of an enemy. It looked like a lost dog that had wandered off and didn't know how to get home.

The tattoo on her shoulder seemed to throb. "How are they made? How do you control them? What are they made of?"

"You get me out of here, lady, a gnole will *bring* you a clock-taur! We don't have time for this!"

"Right…right…" Slate grabbed for the next lump on the floor, picked it up…and paused.

It was a helmet.

Caliban didn't wear a helmet.

She turned it in her hands, baffled. There was something familiar about it, but what was it doing here?

"Lady…!"

"Where's this from?"

"God's scat, lady, it was here when I got here. You want to know about the rugs, too?"

There was a shout from elsewhere in the village. It sounded like Caliban and it sounded like pain.

Slate peered out the flap of the door and thrust the helmet in front of her, into the moonlight.

It was a perfectly ordinary metal helm, round, with a short nose guard and a coat of arms stamped on the side. Slate had seen dozens of them. Hundreds. She'd looked down at the top of them from drainpipes and rooftops.

She'd had occasion to examine one most closely, recently, when the wearer had her pinned down in the Captain of the Guard's office, while she sneezed and sneezed and sneezed.

She rubbed her nose and stared at the Dowager's guardsman's helmet.

She started laughing. She couldn't help it.

Well. Now I know what happened to the last group they sent out, anyway.

She slid back inside the hut and dug through the gear on the floor. Swords, knives, a mapcase.

The mapcase was locked, but with the kind of simplistic lock that Slate could have cracked in her sleep. She popped it, one-handed, and went back to the strip of moonlight.

It opened like a clamshell to reveal a rolled map and a worn leather book. Slate flipped the book open to reveal cramped, nearly unreadable handwriting and drawings of everything under the sun.

Brother Amadai's journal. Well, well, well.

Slate shoved the mapcase in her pack and left the rest.

I could take the gnole and run. Let these rune break their teeth on Caliban and Brenner. By the time they crack those nuts, the gnole and Learned Edmund and I can be well out of here, and it knows something about the Clockwork Boys. I have Brother Amadai's journal and the scholar to translate it. The odds of success just went up amazingly.

I could do it.

I should do it.

The tattoo eased. There was no question what course of action it approved.

She couldn't do it.

Brenner was a rat bastard and she trusted him as far as she could throw him, and he'd still never failed her, never sold her out, never turned her in. And Caliban was an arrogant jerk and he'd ridden down a flooding streambed with lightning crashing down around him and caught her horse and saved her life.

And he always had a handkerchief.

"I'm going after them," she said, and winced as ink teeth dug into her flesh. "Can you wait for me outside the village?" *I have to take the sword. I can't leave it here.* She slung it awkwardly over her shoulder, hissing as the straps brushed the tender flesh of the tattoo.

The gnole frowned. It had immense lower canines, like a badger, but it looked more worried than fierce. "Don't do it, lady—if she's got them, they're old meat anyway. That boss rune is *bad*."

"Yeah, well, they've said I was dead meat a time or two, too." She pulled the curtain back, peering into the village. It was still deserted in the moonlight, and the rats were laying down in piles.

"Is it clear?" The gnole's snout peered over her shoulder, pressing close between her cheek and the hilt of the sword. Its fur was bristly and rough against her skin.

"Looks clear. Go on."

"How long am I s'posed to wait?"

"Use your best judgment. If it looks like I'm going to get caught, get out of here, go south of here, and cross the river. You'll find a man and a bunch of horses. His name is Learned Edmund. Tell him that I sent you, and he'll take you back to Anuket City."

The gnole paused in the entrance of the hut. "You sure about this, lady?"

"Unless you want to come with me."

It grimaced. "You help a gnole, maybe a gnole helps you sometime, but I ain't going up against that boss rune for nothing."

"Then stay out of my way." Slate rubbed her hands on her trousers, hunched her shoulder to keep the sword up, and turned toward the largest hut.

Pain spiked up her arm. She missed a step and staggered.

A small, solid body braced her up on that side. The gnole barely came up to her waist, but it steadied her with graceless ease. "God's scat, lady, you okay?"

"I'm fine," she lied. The tattoo was really gnawing now. Her arm tickled, which was almost certainly a sign that she was bleeding.

It'll be okay. If I rescue them, it'll let up, and if I die it won't matter.

I hope it'll let up.

I'm not betraying the Dowager, you stupid thing! I'm helping my friends, but that doesn't mean I'm betraying the mission!

The pain subsided a little, but there was still a definite pinch. It wasn't quite buying her rationalizations.

That makes two of us.

"Go on," she told the gnole. "I'll be back or—not."

"Good luck, crazy lady," said the gnole, and melted into the dark.

Slate turned back to the largest earth-lodge. The door...no, the door was right out.

She crouched down and rubbed her hands in the dust. Then she hitched the sword in place one last time, and began to climb.

Caliban hung alone in the dark. The earth-lodge was gone, Brenner was gone, the rune was gone. He clung to the ache of his knees as long as he could, but it spun away from him, and then he might not have had knees or a body at all.

"Ngha..." his demon murmured in the dark. He still had that, at least. *"Ngha, ha kalikalikaliha..."*

He had no time to dwell on what that might mean. The darkness broke apart and the rune was in it—or not quite the same rune, because she was younger and her face was more human. She was beautiful, in a terrible way, but her eyes were still too wide apart and antlers rose from her brow in a great arching sweep of bone.

It was impossible to tell how far away she was. There was nothing in this dark place to provide any reference.

She walked toward him. Her feet looked human, but they left hoof prints across the faceless dark, which drifted smoke behind her.

Caliban had a body again. He was still kneeling, and he still seemed bound. His knees didn't hurt, however, and he could feel his feet, which was probably a sign that something else was going on.

"You carry one of my kind here, shining one," she said. The cadence was strange, as if she still spoke with the broken syntax of the rune, but the meaning came through clearly.

Hallucination. It's a hallucination, that's why I can understand her, and she's controlling it. My god, she's strong. Where did she get the power to do this?

"Why did you bring your demon here? I can smell lies, shining one!"

His heart thudded against his ribs like a drum.

The drums. That's where she got the power—she called the rats and drained them dry. She's draining the rune to do this too, I bet. Oh, Dreaming God, this one is strong.

He licked his lips. Whether they were real lips, or a phantom, he wasn't sure. Perhaps it didn't matter.

"I didn't mean to. The demon is part of me. A storm drove me here. I did not know you were here."

Her nostrils flared. Her face was next to his, close enough to bite or kiss.

Let's hope it doesn't come to that.

"If you can smell lies," he said, "then you know I'm telling the truth."

"Sssss…" Her breath hissed out, and then her lips parted and a stream of guttural demonspeech came out.

Caliban had no idea what she was saying—the translation of this hallucination apparently did not extend so far—but his demon clawed frantically at his throat, and he heard himself crying *"Ngha, ha! Kalaakalaak ha!"*

The demon wanted to cower back and cover its head. Caliban gritted his teeth and did neither.

The antlered doe laughed, highly delighted. Fingers caught his chin and lifted it. "It *is* dead, then. You carry a corpse inside you, shining one."

"Yes."

"Shining one" must be how she translates "paladin" or "knight" or both. It's probably a good thing Brenner can't hear that.

Her voice dropped, became throatier. The fingers stroked against his skin. "Would you give me your demon, shining one, if I asked?"

"What?"

The rune stood over him, her hands clasped on either side of his face. Her thumbs moved over his cheekbones. "Give me your demon. I can take it from you, shining one. It need not trouble you any longer..."

Was she telling the truth? Could she set him free? Not even the exorcism had been able to wrench the demon loose—whatever sins it had set its claws in were lodged too deep. They'd left him with a corpse wrapped around his soul, rotting in the back of his head, and not even death had stopped its mouth.

Oh, god, to give it up, to be alone in his own head again!

"Give it to me!"

He wanted the demon gone so badly he could taste it, as strong as the taste of blood in his mouth.

Caliban lifted his head, met her wide burning eyes and said, "No."

We are paladins. We do not deal with demons. Ever.

His heart ached in his chest. His demon gibbered in disgusting gratitude.

She smiled. The fingers slid up into his hair.

"Are you sure, shining one? It would please me...greatly..."

Her form was almost entirely human now, except for the great bone scaffolding rising from her brow. She was straddling his knees, and her skin was feverishly warm against his.

He almost laughed. Demons were not subtle creatures. "*Quite* sure."

The rune woman's mouth covered his, her tongue flicking at his lips. Her breath smelled like burning hay. Caliban bore this as stoically as a martyr being tortured.

It wasn't the first time. They threatened, they bargained, they seduced. He had always half-suspected that the reason the temple did not require celibacy of the Knight-Champions was so that they did not leap at what the demons so often offered.

"Give me your demon."

"No."

Her eyes narrowed. "No? Perhaps you would bargain with another..." Her thumbs swept across his eyelids, and when he opened them again, startled, it was Slate.

His stomach sank, but he gave no sign. You could never show weakness to demons, or they knew they had you.

His eyes must have flickered, though, because the antlered doe smiled with Slate's mouth. It was not Slate's smile, which relieved him greatly. Slate did not smile like that, and she had never been that beautiful.

"This shape is much in your mind, shining one. Your demon knows it. Would you give *her* your demon?"

"We could skip right to the threats, if you like," said Caliban dryly.

"Not just yet, I think..." Her hands were on him again, sliding down his chest and along his arms. If he had a tattoo in this place, he could not feel its teeth.

Ngah, said his demon worriedly.

You said it.

"You say no, but your body says yes..." purred the rune.

"Yes, well. My body's an idiot." He stared straight ahead and tried to remember a catechism. Any catechism. *Dreaming God, who holds us all within his dreams...*

207

Ngha, ha, kalikaliha…

There was an oddly familiar quality to the demon's voice. If he hadn't known better, he'd think that it was praying too.

"Give me the demon," Slate's voice breathed in his ear.

"Why do you want it?"

Her mouth was moving down his neck, but her voice was clear, which was proof enough that this was not real in any sense he understood. "Does it matter, shining one?"

Did it matter? He could be shed of the demon.

His muscles twitched from strain. The demon soothed them down with scarred, ink-stained fingers.

He had not touched Slate because he had taken vows to protect the weak from the strong, even when the strength was his and the weakness was a fleeting anguished moment. He had thrown away his chances with the real Slate, but this creature was not weak—not remotely.

The temple had cast him out. No real vows constrained him any longer.

He could give up his demon, and in return, he would have something that looked a great deal like Slate, and no one would ever know—

Caliban forced a smile. "Nice try," he said hoarsely, recognizing the touch of the rune-demon scratching behind his eyes. "No."

God, she's strong, and subtle, too. She wants the demon. Why? You can't fit two demons in one soul, they're insanely territorial, if she took mine then she…

Could she jump to me?

The rune woman snarled, jerking backward. The knight shuddered. Is that it? *Is her demon looking for another host? Does she want to pry my demon out so that she could take its place?*

Is my dead demon protecting me from being possessed again?

"We could do well together," she hissed, not touching him now. "Your oaths are all broken anyway, and I am far more civilized than that sniveling corpse you carry around now—"

"Why? You have a host—a whole tribe following you—"

The rune's face was melting now, back into the deer, the beauty running back into the merely alien.

"She will not leave!" hissed the rune. "The old doe is bound here, her bones rotting around me, and the rune will not leave this place! There is nothing that will compel her out of these hills! I am trapped here, do you understand, shining one? Trapped!"

The old doe is holding her here?

Not willingly possessed then.

And he remembered, suddenly, that morning in the temple, when he had gone stalking through the halls with his hands red to the elbow. His demon had tired of such quick deaths, and wished for sport, like a cat with a mouse.

Her name was Selena. He barely knew her—she was one more fixture of the temple, not someone he spoke with more than a few times a year. She had been tall and spare and grey-haired, and her hands had been full of the white pillar candles they burned in the sanctuary.

She had heard the screaming and come running, still with her arms full of candles, and the demon had seen her through his eyes and purred and lifted the sword to cut her, only a little, to make the dying last.

And Caliban, who had been nearly mad and screaming behind his eyes, had thrown every ounce of himself behind the sword, and the cut had dropped her, dead before she hit the floor.

Denied, the demon had raged at him, frothing, his own voice screaming obscenities and curses down upon him. He could not have stopped the sword, he had no power to do that, but there was enough of him to bend it a little—only a little—to his will.

Was the old doe in there, still? Was she bending the demon a little, only a little, but enough to hold her trapped in place, no threat to the other tribes of rune that must surely populate these hills?

Caliban felt a fleeting admiration for the strength of the old shaman, completely dominated by the demon, yet holding the creature here nonetheless.

I wish I could have known her.

He looked up into the rune's face, hearing the demon rant, and he could have sworn, for a fleeting instant, that something looked out of her face and winked at him.

I must have imagined that...

The demon's voice cut off. It flung its hair out of its eyes and stood, chest heaving, until it seemed to calm itself.

That was, in its way, frightening. A demon with even that much self-control was rare.

Still. She can't seduce me. She can't compel me. Perhaps I can still find a way out—

"Come now, shining one," the demon-rune said, trying to find its feet again. "Surely you feel some pity for my plight? A maiden in distress, I am. You need only take me to the nearest city, and I will flee, and trouble you no more. I can be so quiet that you will not even know you carry me. Surely you cannot deny me aid—"

We are paladins. We do not deal with demons. Ever.

He didn't realize that he had spoken aloud until the demon shrieked and flung herself at him. Inhuman fingers scrabbled at his throat, and closed around his neck.

I guess she can still kill me.

It was frothing at him, snarling obscenities, while the grip on his neck got tighter and tighter, and even the hallucination began to seem distant and unreal, a shadow of a shadow.

He would have welcomed death, even now. Slain by a demon, defiant to the end—it was a good death. It was a knightly death. It was how he had always expected to die.

One thought alone held him, and made him struggle feebly. *If she can't get me, will she possess Brenner? Oh god, what if she does, and she goes back to Slate and Edmund, and they don't know?*

No! Dreaming God, no!

It was a futile effort. He had no real body in this place. Was he even fighting for breath? He couldn't tell.

"I'll eat your *death*, shining one!"

Kalihalikalaakhali…ha… breathed his demon, and wrapped itself around him like a lover.

The world went out like a blown candle.

CHAPTER 15

Caliban's first thought was that he wasn't dead, and that this was somewhat surprising.

His eyes were open. He had fallen on his side, and his hands were still bound. His throat ached, but the demon-rune was flat on the ground in front of him.

Did I do that? I don't think I did that...

And Slate, who had just dropped through the smokehole and landed on the old shaman, staggered to her feet.

She had a sword in her hands. His sword. It was amazing she hadn't cut herself in half falling on it. The scabbard was slung across her back and looked about to strangle her. Her hair fell in a wild tangle across her face. Blood welled from a dozen sluggish punctures across her breast and shoulder.

She set her feet, raised the naked sword in both hands, and sneezed.

Sweet god, she fell on the thing's antlers. She must have dropped onto it and broke the trance—

The stag-man, who was still standing behind Brenner and Caliban, roared and leapt forward at the intruder. She staggered back and raised the sword in both hands. The point got maybe a foot off the ground.

Caliban heard himself shouting denials in a voice shattered by the rune's hands. "No! Slate, no, look out—*no!*"

She can't possibly fight with that sword, she can barely lift the thing, he'll kill her, oh god—

Slate, apparently agreeing with him, threw the sword at the stag's legs and dove out of the way.

When someone throws a broadsword under your feet, you have to stop. The other options aren't worth considering. The sword didn't do any damage, but the rune had to pull up in

212

mid-stride to avoid it and that gave Slate enough time to get out of the way.

"Get him, Slate!" shouted Brenner from somewhere near the floor.

"Shut up, Brenner! Slate, *run!*"

Slate ignored them both, flipped one of Brenner's knives into her hand, and paused. He wasn't sure if it was a taunt or a moment of weakness. He could see her shaking, but that could have been blood loss or adrenaline or both.

There was blood trickling down her left arm in thin skeins.

"Slate—"

"Shut *up*, Caliban!" she snarled.

The stag-man charged.

Slate dived out of the way again, and the stag discovered too late that she had been standing directly in front of the shaman. He tried to change direction to avoid trampling the old doe, and ran directly into Caliban instead.

Ooof…

The stag-man went down in a welter of flailing limbs. The knight felt hooves drum against his ribs.

She did that deliberately. I wonder if she's hoping we'll kill each other.

The stag tried to rise. A hoof scraped down Caliban's back, leaving a welt.

I've got to keep him down. I've got to help. He tried to roll on top of one of the stag's legs.

It scolded like a jay, an incongruous sound, and struck out with the knife. A hot line went across his thigh. Caliban hissed.

Slate stepped in, her face as cool and detached as a woman doing long division. She caught the stag's antlers in one hand, hauled its head back, and jammed Brenner's knife into its throat, up to the hilt.

Blood fountained out. Caliban's armor was awash in it. If they lived through this, his chainmail would take hours to clean.

The creature thrashed atop him and died.

Slate stepped back, nodded, and cracked her knuckles.

It occurred to Caliban that he had been nattering about his oath to protect the weak to a woman who had apparently just tracked them through the woods, found their weapons, climbed up the outside of the hut carrying said weapons, dropped fifteen feet through a hole in the ceiling onto a shaman, saving his life and possibly his soul in the process, and then proceeded to fight and dispatch a stag-man twice her size.

My god. I am *an arrogant jackass.*

Slate rolled the rune sideways off him, pulled the knife free, and sawed through his ropes. By the time he managed to sit up and get the blood back into his hands, she'd also freed Brenner.

"And now—" Slate said, turning, and then, "God's balls!"

All around the perimeter of the room, the rune were rising to their feet.

"I didn't see all *them* from up there," said Slate, turning in a slow circle. Then she sneezed.

Caliban got to his feet, feeling his wrists and ankles screaming. His feet were coming back to life and felt like they were on fire. He looked around, found his sword and picked it up.

Slate sneezed again and wiped at her nose, never taking her eyes off the circle of rune. Caliban limped to her side, and looked up at the deer-people in despair.

There had to be two dozen of them. Even if his legs weren't about to buckle, even if his throat didn't feel as if it were full of shards of glass, even if Slate weren't bleeding and if half of the rune were too groggy to fight, there was just no way.

The deer were advancing toward the pit.

"It was a good rescue," he rasped, lifting his sword.

"Pity it didn't work," she muttered, and sneezed again.

The rune were moving slowly. He groped in a pocket and found a handkerchief. Slate took it with a choking laugh.

Ranks of green bodies circled the pit. The sounds that they made were high-pitched and dangerous, like the screams of hunting hawks.

"I'm sorry I said you were weak."

"You damn well *better* be."

She shoved the handkerchief into a pocket. There were bloody fingerprints across it.

"Everybody back off," said Brenner behind them, in a voice so cold and brittle that it sounded as if it might shatter, "and I mean it."

The rune drew back, hissing.

Caliban turned.

Brenner was holding the antlered doe up with one arm around her waist. The other held a knife at her throat. The old shaman's eyes were rolling, and blood made a red mask over her face. Several tines had snapped off her antlers, perhaps when Slate had slammed her to the floor.

"Brenner, be careful! There's a demon in there!"

"Well, there's a whole lot of those bastards out *here*, so we're taking our chances." He brandished the knife at the rune, then set the point back against the shaman's throat. "Now. Everybody backs off, nice and easy, and my friends and I are going for the door."

Whether the rune understood what the assassin was saying, or if the gestures were enough, they backed away from the edge of the pit. Caliban boosted himself out of the sunken circle and pulled Slate up after him.

"Take her," growled Brenner, never taking his eyes off the rune.

"What?"

"Take the hostage!"

His conscience twinged like a bad tooth. Good paladins did not take hostages, particularly not old women.

Brenner must have seen it in his face. "Take the goddamn hostage or you can stay here with the rune!"

Slate gave them both a disgusted look, reached down, and grabbed Brenner's knife in her good hand. "Set her on the edge," she ordered, steadying the silent shaman against her body. Antlers poked at her like tree branches, and she turned her face away.

Shamed for more reasons than one, Caliban pulled the doe upright. Brenner leapt up after her, light on his feet despite the long confinement, and took his blade back. The hilt slipped briefly in his fingers.

"You're bleedin' pretty good, Slate, darlin'."

"Yeah, I know. The tattoo wasn't keen on this idea."

Both men winced.

The rune were watching them with big, worried eyes.

"Back towards the door," said Brenner, taking possession of the old shaman again.

They backed.

The noise of a man stepping on a carpet of dead rats in bare feet is "squii*ckrunch*." Caliban felt that he could have gone his whole life without learning this particular fact.

"Your boots are outside," said Slate.

Caliban glanced at the demon, but it wasn't saying anything.

I bet it's hoping we'll take it out of here as a hostage.

We might not have much choice.

Of the three of them, Brenner was the only one in any shape to fight if the rune got restive. If they dropped the shaman, the rune might follow, and then what would they do?

At the door to the earth-lodge, Brenner paused. He pointed the knife at the assembled rune. *"Stay."*

The leather curtain fell down. The demon still didn't say anything.

"You think they understood that?"

"Works on dogs."

They made it to the edge of the village. Slate ducked into a shadow and came out with their boots.

"I've got a friend around here somewhere," she said.

"A friend? What?" Brenner looked up. "Where'd you find a—"

"God's stripes, lady, you did it!"

Brenner whipped the hostage closer, the knife digging painfully into her throat. The rune uttered a high moan of pain, but did not flinch.

"Stay back!" the assassin ordered.

"Cut it out, Brenner, it's not one of those deer things! It says it's a gnole."

"A gnole, that's me." It blinked up at them in the moonlight. "You want to cut that wicked boss rune's throat, you do it. I'm not gonna stop you." It spat on the ground. "Probably safer for all of us."

Caliban, trying not to think about the bits of dead rat still on his feet, shoved his boots on. No socks. The gods only knew what the rune had done with them.

Brenner, in a display of agility unique to assassins, stepped into his boots without taking the knife away from the rune woman's throat.

"Let's move."

They moved.

The rune didn't follow. None of them emerged from the earthlodge for as long as it was visible through the trees.

"Why are they letting us go?" Slate asked. The tattoo had stopped gnawing, blessedly, but every time she took a step, a jolt shot up the side of her body that had impacted the deer-creature's antlers. The holes weren't deep, but they were oozing steadily, and the pain was making her list sideways.

"I think she told them to," said Caliban. "There's a demon in her, and it wants to get out of here."

"And we're *helping* her?"

"If you have a better idea, darlin', I'm open to suggestions."

Slate opened her mouth, took another step, felt pain leap from puncture to puncture as if they were stepping stones, and went a bit green.

Caliban tried to get his arm under her shoulders to act as a crutch, but the disparity in their height was too great. The jolts were twice as bad, and she waved him off, growling.

The gnole came to her aid instead, putting an arm around her waist and shoring her up on that side. The creature reeked of garbage and old goat, but it helped. Oddly enough, it didn't make her sneeze.

"Thanks," she said, as it helped to haul her up a slope.

"Don't mention it, crazy lady."

Slate's gnole-crutch didn't slow them up to any significant degree, since Brenner was already hampered by his grip on the antlered doe, and Caliban's breathing was coming in slow, painful rasps. Slate figured she'd arrived just in time.

She'd watched through the smoke-hole for several minutes, while the old deer woman had been glaring into the knight's face, and he sat staring into the distance as if drugged. She hadn't been sure whether to drop down or not, and she'd had no idea that there were dozens of other rune in the lodge, standing outside of her field of vision.

Then the old rune had started strangling Caliban, and she'd done the only thing she could think of.

I could have wished for a better landing, but at least we're all still alive.

They were most of the way back to the river when they halted, and stood listening.

"Hear anyone after us?" Brenner asked.

They strained their ears.

"Nope," said the gnole after a minute. "Not hearing nothing."

"Me, neither," said Slate.

"Nor am—*Brenner!*"

Slate turned, following the paladin's shout, just in time to see the assassin lower the old rune to the ground. Her throat was slashed with black in the moonlight. As they watched, the blunt-fingered hands closed convulsively on Brenner's sleeves, then relaxed and dropped away.

"You killed her!" Caliban said.

"You said yourself she was a demon," growled Brenner. "What were *you* planning on doing with her?"

"Dammit—there's a rite—" The paladin dropped to his knees next to the deer woman. He put his free hand on the creature's forehead, the other locked around the hilt of his sword.

A moment slid by. Caliban stared into the dead rune's eyes, speaking in a language that Slate had never heard before.

Even not knowing the words, Slate felt the hairs on the back of her neck standing up. It was the voice he was using, the calm, trustworthy one, but it had a timbre to it that she didn't understand.

Is that how he does it? Does he actually talk the demons into hell?

Apparently in this case he could not. He fell silent.

"Did you do it?" asked Slate quietly, afraid to interrupt him.

"No," said Caliban bitterly. "Her soul is gone, and the demon fled unbound." He closed the rune's eyes with his fingertips. "No time to catch it. Brenner was quite…efficient."

"*You* were going to do it," said Brenner. "You ought to be grateful, paladin. This way you keep your hands clean."

Caliban stared at him. And reached down. And drew about an inch of steel.

Oh my god, they're really doing it.

They're really going to have a goddamn dick-measuring contest right here in the woods with a bunch of murderous deer-people after us.

Slate pushed the gnole back, stepped between the two men, and said "Stand down, both of you, and *that's an order.*"

Neither of them obeyed. She hadn't really expected them to.

Oh, well, at least they're both looking at me instead of at each other.

"You got crazy friends, crazy lady."

"I'm gonna have *dead* friends in a minute, if they don't come to their senses!" She put her hands on her hips and glared at all and sundry. "Need I remind you that there's a whole tribe full of deer-things that are gonna be bloody furious when they find out we've killed their shaman, so can I suggest we get the *hell* out of here before you two go back to pissing in a circle around each other or whatever the hell this is supposed to be?"

It was quite a speech and she didn't stop for breath once. Hoping for both men to break into spontaneous applause or abject apologies was probably too much, but they did have the decency to look embarrassed.

Someone came thumping and scrabbling down the opposite bank of the river. Slate turned and saw Learned Edmund skidding the last few feet down the slope to the water's edge.

"Mistress Slate! Is that you? I heard yelling—"

"It's us. Saddle the horses. We need to get out of here now." She turned her back on Caliban and Brenner. Let them kill each other if they wanted to, she'd done her job. The gnole's arm went around her waist. Slate leaned on the little creature and limped down the slope to the river.

She was trying to figure out how she was going to get across the river—there wasn't room for two on the stepping stones—and someone reached down and scooped her up.

She expected it to be Caliban—it was such a typical knightly thing, and she was prepared to get very cutting if he said anything about weakness—and was rather surprised to get a whiff of tobacco instead.

"Chivalry rubbing off on you, Brenner?" she asked.

The assassin smirked down at her and strode out lightly out across the rocks. The hands curled around her knees and shoulders were wet with blood, but she was too tired and too bloody herself to care.

"You'd better hope not, darlin'."

"That was some pretty quick thinking with the hostage," she said.

"I thought so."

He set her on her feet on the opposite side, but left an arm around her shoulders. Caliban followed them across the river, his eyes unreadable. Slate stifled a sigh.

This is probably just another example of pissing in a circle. Oh, well...

The gnole bounced up to her, and she abandoned Brenner's embrace for her small, foul-smelling crutch. They limped up the hillside together.

"Do you have a name, crazy gnole?"

"Yeah, crazy lady. Name's Grimehug."

"I'm Slate."

"Crazy Slate. Good name. Could almost be a gnole name."

"Yeah?"

"Yeah."

Learned Edmund led her horse forward. Slate scrubbed at her eyes. "They've all got saddles on. You struck camp. They're ready to go."

The scholar nodded, and then, much to her surprise, leaned down and offered her his hands as a mounting block.

"Why'd you saddle them all? I told you not to leave until noon…"

He was much slighter than Caliban, but he held steady enough as she climbed into the saddle. "I knew you'd be back with them. I thought we should be ready to move when you were."

"How'd you know that? I was sure I was a goner."

The scholar sketched a benediction in her general direction. "I had faith."

Huh.

"Bowels turned to water yet?" asked Brenner snidely, passing the scholar on the way to his own horse.

"It appears to be a very slow process."

There are limits to what horses can do in the dark. They could not go at a canter, nor even a trot. They went at a steady, shambling walk instead. Learned Edmund led, with the bright-eyed gnole before him. It had excellent night-vision, and it kept up a cheery stream of talk to the scholar. Oddly enough, they seemed to be getting along.

Slate clung to her saddle. Her clothes were stuck to her wounds, making crude bandages, so she wasn't going to bleed to death any time soon. She was dreading getting the shirt off when they finally stopped.

We just have to get away. If we can reach the road, we can put enough distance between us and the rune. We've just got to keep moving.

It seemed much darker on the back of the horse than it had when she was moving under her own power. She couldn't see where the animal was setting its feet. This would have worried her, but she was rapidly too exhausted to care.

It had been at least an hour, probably more, and she was sunk in a dumb haze of pain and exhaustion and feeling generally ill-used by the universe when Learned Edmund pulled the horses up.

"We haven't hit the road," he said worriedly. "We weren't that far off it, and we've headed straight for where it should be. We should have been there half an hour ago."

This sounded bad. Slate lifted her chin off her chest, wincing as dried blood pulled at her skin. "Are we lost?"

"I'm not sure."

"Could we have passed the road in the dark?" asked Caliban.

"I don't think so. The ground hasn't changed at all."

Slate realized that the scholar was looking at her to make a decision. *Oh, sure, now he trusts me…* She waved a hand. "Let's keep going for another half hour or so. If we don't hit the road, we'll assume we're lost and look for a defensible place to hole up."

Learned Edmund nodded.

Slate was dreading what she'd do when the half-hour was up, but within ten minutes the sound of the horses' hooves changed, from the chuffing of pine needles to the thudding of a roadway. Slate sat up a little straighter.

It was a narrow path, barely a lane, and badly overgrown. It did not look like the hard-packed smugglers' road. Between patches of grass and horsetail rushes, the mud and packed pebbles glittered like the reticulated hide of a lizard.

"This isn't our road," said Caliban.

"No," said Brenner, "but it's *a* road."

Everyone looked at Slate.

Shit, do I have to be in charge again? She rubbed her forehead.

"Any road is better than no road at this point. Let's follow it."

Learned Edmund nodded, and kicked his horse into a brief, brutal trot. Slate sank her teeth into her lower lip to keep from shrieking. Her shirt pulled away from one of the punctures, and she felt a new wetness of blood slide over the already layered stickiness.

My torso has got to look like raw ham.

The light began to grow. *Dawn already? Really?*

It was. Her horse's ears stopped being a black cut-out and became infused with brown and pink. The black mane that washed over her hands separated into individual hairs. Green began to leach into the grey of the grass on the roadway, and the gnole's cloak became a ragged patchwork of violet and carmine and dun.

In a way she was astonished, and at the same time the night seemed to have lasted at least a thousand years already.

We've got to stop soon. If I don't stop soon, I'm going to fall out of the saddle.

The road opened up before them.

Learned Edmund led them forward into an empty clearing as broad as a sheep meadow. Trees lined it on three sides, and on the fourth, it rose up into a hillside, and…something else.

Slate couldn't figure out what it was. It could have been a building or a statue or a strangely symmetrical rock formation.

It looked for all the world like a man, crouching belly down, with his hands curved in a circle before him. His head was down, half-buried in the ground, his mouth open in a silent yell.

"What the hell is *that?*" said Brenner.

They rode nearer. Slate pulled up at a safe distance, but Learned Edmund spurred his horse forward.

It wasn't until she saw the horse and rider approaching the strange statue that Slate realized exactly how huge it was. The thing was the size of a house. Its open mouth could have held a team of horses.

Learned Edmund practically fell off his mount in front of the thing, tossed its reins to the ground and ran forward to touch it.

"Well, it looks like someone knows what it is," said Slate.

She reined in a few feet from Learned Edmund. He was stroking the material of the statue, which up close didn't look like stone as much as it looked like ivory, except that was impossible because you couldn't get a piece of ivory the size of a house, and if there were any seams, they were hidden well.

"Is it a building? Some kind of temple?" Slate asked.

Learned Edmund didn't so much as glance back at her. "No. I think it's a…wonder-engine." His voice was full of awe.

"What's a wonder-engine?"

"Nobody's really sure. Some of them do things." He stretched up a hand as far as he could, and ran it tenderly down the ivory surface.

I've been made love to with less enthusiasm than a celibate guy is fondling a big ivory…thing. Possibly it's time to rethink my life.

"What sort of things?" Brenner wanted to know.

"Miracles. Marvels. Completely useless things. It doesn't seem to follow any particular pattern."

"Learned Edmund," she said tiredly, "is it going to try and kill us?"

He had to stop and think about it. Slate pinched the bridge of her nose, feeling a hysterical bubble rising in her throat. It was going to come out as a sob if she wasn't careful.

"I don't think so, no. It doesn't seem to be moving." He frowned. "I suppose it's remotely possible it might kill us. But no more than a house or a wagon or a windmill might."

"Good enough." The bubble went back down. "Let's set up camp. I'm about done in, and this is as defensible a spot as we're going to get."

Nobody argued.

It's a miracle.

They made camp in the bay formed by the circled arms of the wonder-engine. The gaping mouth behind them was unsettling—if it had been an open cave, Slate would have insisted on setting up somewhere else—but it ended in a smooth, tongue-like sweep a few feet back. The only hole was a narrow, drain-like opening at the top, a tiny throat for such a large mouth. With the horses picketed in a wall across the open side of the bay, they were as well protected as they were likely to get.

It took only a few minutes to get a fire going, which was a good thing, because Slate didn't think she had more than a few minutes left in her.

"Sit, sit," said Learned Edmund. "Let me see to your wounds."

"Slate first," said Caliban, although he was practically swaying on his feet. "She took the worst of it."

Bloody chivalry again, but he's probably right. Slate sat down onto a rock. The shirt pulled where it stuck to the punctures. Learned Edmund knelt in front of her, frowned, and turned to dig through a saddlebag.

All at once. All at once is better. It's like a bandage. Do it fast.

Slate took a deep breath, grabbed the hem of her shirt, and ripped it off over her head in a single savage yank.

Her shriek was not noticeably slowed by her clenched teeth, but she managed to bury most of it in the folds of the shirt around her head.

"Mistress Slate!"

Slate opened her eyes blearily. *Am I dying? Did I just give myself a mortal wound?*

Learned Edmund had fallen over backwards, and had a sleeve over his eyes.

Did I hit him?

"Mistress Slate—you cannot—you—modesty forbids—"

Brenner's howl of laughter tipped her off. *Ah. Yes. Those.* She glanced down at herself. There were ugly bruises across her torso, and several shallow oozing holes. Blood had painted her skin with a thin, irregular layer of clotted red. As an object of erotic interest, her breasts currently rated somewhere below a dead flounder.

226

"Look," she said tiredly, "I don't have anything Brenner hasn't seen before, Caliban's a paladin, you're sworn to celibacy, and Grimehug's the wrong species. Just sew me up."

"But—"

"Hey Edmund, I hear that if you hold your breath, it keeps your genitals from withering."

"Shut *up*, Brenner."

The scholar rubbed his forehead. "Yes. You're right. It is shameful for me to be concerned with such things when you are in pain."

She patted his shoulder absently, too tired to be gratified when he didn't flinch.

Learned Edmund looked a little green by the end of it—whether from being forced to touch feminine flesh, or the task at hand—but he managed. Most of the antler wounds hadn't actually penetrated the skin, leaving ugly round bruises instead. Only a few actually required bandaging.

Despite his difficulty in looking directly at the injuries, Learned Edmund did a skillful job patching her up. Slate had been treated by licensed healers with a touch that wasn't half so delicate.

The tattoo was actually the worst. A thick line of blood had crusted under its teeth and the skin gaped open. Cleaning it was excruciating and Slate had to chew on a knuckle and look away.

"I barely know what to do with this," said Learned Edmund honestly. "I should sew it so that it doesn't scar, but—I don't think it'll let me."

"Leave it," said Slate. "If I get out of this with just a scar there, I've been lucky."

She looked away, and saw Grimehug sprawled out on his side by the fire, like a dog. He smiled at her with all his sharp teeth. Firelight reflected orange in his eyes.

"Should use gnole medicine, crazy lady."

"Gnole medicine?"

"Lick it till it feels better. Then eat grass. Works every time."

"As your physician," said Learned Edmund testily, "I do not recommend that."

Slate grinned.

The scholar ran his hands over her ribcage to make sure nothing was broken, a process he undoubtedly found more uncomfortable than she did, despite the bruises.

"What do you recommend, then?" she asked, as he finished and began scrubbing his hands furiously.

"Keep your wounds clean. And sleep. As much as we can arrange."

Slate was only too happy to obey.

CHAPTER 16

They stayed in the wonder-engine's valley the next day. Slate was in no shape to move. Caliban had lost his voice almost completely, and was speaking in hoarse whispers. The horses were exhausted.

And Learned Edmund? He was in rapture over the wonder-engine anyway. He'd filled a notebook with meticulous sketches and measurements, which had mostly involved a patient Caliban, a snide Brenner, and a very long ball of string.

"I don't think anyone's ever described this one," he told Slate excitedly, waving a book at her. "It's a completely new wonder-engine!"

"Is that good?" Slate asked, wrapping her fingers around a cup of tea.

"It's wonderful! There are only about thirty wonder-engines known to exist in the entire world! To find a new one—our names will live forever in history!"

He can actually utter that phrase with a straight face. I have definitely fallen in with the wrong sorts of company.

"Do they all look like people?" she asked.

"Doesn't look much like my kind of people," said the gnole, who was laying on his back by the fire. Slate had been very warm last night, with the gnole sleeping in a ball at her feet like a hairy rug. She'd offered him his own blanket, and he'd looked hurt. Apparently gnoles slept in piles. Since both Slate's feet and her love life were cold, this was fine by her.

"Sorry, Grimehug. Do they all look like human people?"

"No, actually. Some of them do look like humans. Some look like animals, apparently, and some resemble buildings, or are more abstract conglomerations of parts." He made vague gestures with both hands, defining a shape Slate couldn't even begin to recognize.

"Any gnoles?"

"Not that I know of."

"Their loss." Grimehug closed his eyes again.

"Who made them?"

"No one knows."

"How old are they?"

"Good question."

Slate pinched the bridge of her nose and tried once more.

"Do they know what any of them do?"

"A few. One on the coast turns salt water to fresh water. One in Moldoban incinerates everything they put into it—they worshipped it as a god with human sacrifices for many years. Now it's a waste disposal system."

Slate chuckled into her tea, though she was pretty sure he wasn't joking.

"And there's one that, if you put in gold, turns it into fresh pears. I'm not sure how they figured that out."

"What a waste," said Brenner, who was lying stretched flat on one of the wonder-engine's arms, like a big dark cat. He propped his head on his crossed arms. "Any of them turn fresh pears into gold?"

"Not that I know of. Although this one might, for all we know. We could try it, if we had any fresh pears." He consulted his notes. "It seems inert to everything I've tried. It doesn't respond to being fed rocks, grass, handkerchiefs, tea leaves, horse hair, human hair, gnole fur, copper coins, iron filings, leather, blood, saliva, semen—"

Slate put her hand over her eyes. *Well, we can't question his… ah…passion for science…*

"—water, wood, fire, charcoal, potatoes, parchment, ink, fingernail clippings, bread—"

"Okay," Brenner broke in, "I get the point. You don't know what to feed it."

"Do they all work like that?" Slate asked. "You put something in, and something else comes out?"

"Most of them. The incinerator is the only one that they're not sure about, and it's arguable that you're putting something in and getting fire out." He shook his head. "The authority on wonder-engines, ironically, is Brother Amadai. If we can find him in Anuket City, he will be excited to hear of this one."

"Do you think we'll find him?" asked Brenner.

"There is no value to despair," said Learned Edmund primly. "We must hope."

Brenner gave him a look.

The dedicate sighed. "He was known as an eccentric genius. He went to Anuket City after some ancient writings turned up in the markets there. His first few correspondences were full of notes, theories, addendums to papers, that sort of thing—and then they tapered off. For two years, there has been nothing."

"Took you awhile to send somebody after him," said Brenner.

Learned Edmund shrugged. "In truth, we thought he was probably busy and had forgotten to write."

Brenner laughed.

Slate took another drink of tea. It was peppermint, laced with the last of their poppy milk. Her eye was caught by motion, and she gazed down the slope, to where Caliban was slicing at shadows again.

"Your big friend do that a lot?" asked the gnole.

"Do what?"

"Chop up air with that crazy big sword."

"Temple knights of the Dreaming God are required to practice their swordwork for at least two hours a day when not on specific assignment," said Learned Edmund idly, turning a page.

"No wonder they're all so stiff," said Brenner. He rolled over. "Anyway he's not required to do that temple knight stuff anymore."

"I wonder if he knows that," said Learned Edmund.

"Mmm." Brenner sat up and slid off the ivory wall, slouching off across the grass. Down the hillside, Caliban finished dismembering a shadow and had dropped to his knees in prayer.

"I hesitated to ask with our friend here," said Learned Edmund carefully, "but you seem troubled, Mistress Slate."

Slate glanced up, surprised.

"It is none of my business, of course." He flicked an imaginary spot of dust off his sleeve. "But I have taken confessions for many of my brothers over the years, and if there is anything you wish to confide…well, I am good at keeping other people's secrets."

Slate had a strong urge to yell "Over the years? You're *nineteen!*" but didn't because that would have been unkind. Instead she said "I'm surprised you noticed anything, with the wonder-engine here."

"Ah. But you have a very methodical mind, Mistress Slate, and when I asked you about taking measurements, you offered no advice, nor did you demand to double check my figures. And Brenner has said several cutting things to you in the last few hours, and you have not replied in kind." He put his fingers together. "From this, I deduce that something is preying on your mind. But if it is not something you wish to share, I understand."

Slate gazed down into her tea. *A misogynist practically half my age offering to take my confession. Oh, well, it's no weirder than anything else…*

"I have been, yes." She set her teacup down. "I suppose…if you're not afraid that hearing me talk will turn your bowels to water."

Learned Edmund spread his hands ruefully. "So far it appears to be a *very* slow process."

"Mmm." She laced her hands behind her head and leaned back on the grass. The sky was blue, framed by the yawning ivory mouth of the wonder-engine. Grimehug wiggled around to lay his head across her feet.

"Well…thing is…hmm, where to start." She frowned up at the clouds. "See, back when I was first sentenced—they got me for treason, by the way—I expected to die. My life was over. It was pretty much just a matter of filling in time before they hung me.

"Then I got this reprieve—except that it wasn't really a reprieve, I just had to fill in even more time before I died, you know? I still felt like I was walking around dead."

"That must be hard," said Learned Edmund gently. *He can't do the voice as well as Caliban,* Slate thought wryly, *but it still isn't bad.*

"Actually, no." She ran a hand through her hair, raking out bits of grass. "It felt almost liberating. If you know you're going to die, you don't have to be afraid of anything. The worst has already happened. What more can they do to you? So I didn't have to worry about going to Anuket City, I didn't have to worry about wandering around with a psychopath and a guilt-wracked paladin and an insufferable priest—"

He made a polite scoffing noise. She flicked a blade of grass at him.

"And then, my horse ran away with me." Her smile faded. "And I nearly died. And I realized I…really didn't want to. I'm not done with my life yet." She frowned up at the sky.

"Living is always hard," said Learned Edmund.

"Yeah, but most of the living don't have to go back to Anuket City."

"Unfinished business there?" the scholar asked.

"Oh, yeah." Slate pinched the bridge of her nose. "And frankly, Edmund, that scares me half to death."

"You have done very well, though." He reached out and patted her on the shoulder, and barely hesitated at all. "Your first act after rediscovering your fear was to charge after friends in danger. That's not the act of a coward."

"Oh, well, that." She flushed. "Didn't do much, really."

"Not to hear Caliban tell it." Learned Edmund considered. "Have you told him of your fears?"

"Caliban?" She sat up, rolling Grimehug off her feet. The gnole squawked. "No, thank you! He already thinks I'm weak, the arrogant sod, hell if I'm rolling over and showing *him* my throat."

Learned Edmund's eyebrows went up. "I...hmm." He steepled his fingers. "I doubt he really thinks you're weak. But— well, I can see him saying something unfortunate, yes." The priest sighed. "He is proud. But he carries an enormous load of guilt for his crimes, and pride is part of what motivates him. And he is so afraid of failing again."

"Hmmph." Slate folded her arms. "Well. He did apologize. I'll give him that."

Learned Edmund eyed the stubborn set of her jaw and sighed again. "I don't know. I'm only a scholar, and sometimes not much of one. I sit under the greatest discovery of my life—" he gestured to the wonder-engine, "—and all I can think is that it would be good to sleep in a real bed again. Perhaps we're all weak."

Slate unbent enough to smile a little. "You're not the only one, Learned Edmund. I'd give my hope of heaven for a real bed at this point."

"Well," he said, sniffing, "hopefully nothing *that* extreme will be required."

Slate laughed. And then sat up, suddenly, her laughter cutting off. "Oh! Gods! I forgot—can you imagine? I *forgot!*"

"Forgot what?" asked Learned Edmund, startled.

"The second team they sent. The journal. The rune caught them." Learned Edmund stared at her in non-comprehension. "Oh—look—here!"

She dug into her packs and came up holding the map case.

"This is a military case," said Learned Edmund doubtfully.

She snapped it open and pulled out Brother Amadai's journal. *"Mistress Slate!* Is that...?"

He snatched the book from her so quickly that he didn't even seem to care that their fingers touched. His bowels were clearly not nearly so important as the journal.

A few minutes later, they were all gathered around. Slate leaned over Learned Edmund's shoulder, which he hardly noticed, and Caliban had sheathed his sword and come to investigate.

Brenner, virtually illiterate and not particularly bothered by that fact, was consulting the map that the second group had left behind.

"This is it," said Learned Edmund. "This is the journal. This is his."

"What are the odds?" asked Slate.

Caliban frowned down at her. "Not dreadful," he rasped. "Not as bad as they could be. I suspect the rune demon was drawing in any travelers she suspected of having something to do with the Clockwork Boys."

"Crazy rune," muttered Grimehug.

"That would account for both us and this group, and even Grimehug as well." He nodded to the gnole. "She was speaking about demons in her territory. If you accept that she thought the Clockwork Boys are demons and that columns of them had gone through the Vagrant Hills before us..." He spread his hands.

"It makes sense," said Slate slowly. "A kind of sense. But how would she know we had anything to do with the Clockwork Boys?"

"She could read minds," said Caliban.

Slate stared up at him. *"Really."*

"Yes. She...ah...plucked a memory from me, when we were speaking." It was hard to tell with his voice so wrecked, but she thought he sounded embarrassed. "And tried to convince me to work with her. I doubt she could have such a great influence on minds at a distance, but if we entered her territory with thoughts of the Clockwork Boys uppermost in our minds…" He trailed off, coughing. Slate tossed him a waterskin.

"But what did she *want?*" said Slate, frustrated.

Unexpectedly, it was Brenner who spoke up. "Isn't it obvious, darlin'? The same thing the Captain wanted, and all the rest of us. She wanted to get the Clockwork Boys out of her territory, and she didn't know a damn thing about them. She's probably been pullin' people in ever since they started stomping through the Vagrant Hills, tryin' to find somebody who knew what they were and where they came from."

It made sense. It made a lot of sense. Slate exhaled slowly.

Learned Edmund finally looked up.

"There is no doubt," he said. "This is the journal. And it is in Brother Amadai's hand, and with his codes."

Slate raised an eyebrow. "Can you read it?"

"Not *here*," said Learned Edmund, gesturing to the wonder engine and the valley and the woods. "I need to work out a key and for that I need paper and ink—more than I have with me—and time and a surface that isn't a mule or a flat rock!"

"Fair," said Slate. She thought about trying to forge a document while sitting in the middle of the wonder-engine's valley and shook her head. "Yes, that's completely fair. Well. I suppose we'll need to leave the Vagrant Hills for that."

"Believe me, darlin'," said Brenner, with great feeling, "it can't be soon enough."

Slate had two private encounters before they left the valley, both of which were either damned odd or inevitable, she wasn't sure which.

The first was Caliban, who caught up with her when she was off changing the bandages, which, out of a sense of mercy, she was doing out of sight of Edmund.

She was sitting at the rear of the wonder-engine on what looked like a giant ivory hip bone. She'd spread rags and a water-skin over the hip bone and was trying to re-bandage her raw shoulder wound one-handed. It wasn't going well.

Who knew it was so hard to patch your own arm? Possibly if I hold this end in my teeth...

Sword-callused hands reached in and held the square of cloth flat. She got it wrapped and he tied off the end, then sat down on the hip bone next to her.

"Thanks," she said, wondering what he wanted. *You better not be thinking of lecturing me about last night's rescue, buddy...* "How's your leg?"

"Fine," he said, in that creaking whisper. "It only grazed me. My throat's in worse shape, but Learned Edmund thinks I'll get my voice back in a day or two."

"That's good."

"Mmm."

They sat together in silence for a moment. Swallows skimmed low over the green hillside, picking up insects from the grass.

"I haven't thanked you," he whispered finally. "You saved my life."

Slate choked back a laugh. It had surprisingly sharp edges. "You don't need to thank me."

"I'm not sure what else I can do," he said.

Slate opened her mouth to say something—she wasn't sure what—and caught a sly gleam in his eye. *Was that a joke? Good lord, if he develops a working sense of humor, I'll start to worry he got possessed again when we weren't looking.*

She had a sarcastic response all thought out, and then she caught a wave of rosemary from him and sneezed violently instead. By the time she stopped sneezing and managed to pry her eyes open again, he already had a handkerchief out and was dangling it in front of her.

"Thangks."

"Don't mention it."

"How many of these things do you carry?"

He lifted his chin. "Leave me some small mysteries."

She snorted.

"Actually, I buy a dozen any time we stop at a town large enough to have a dry goods store."

"I always lose them."

"I know. That's why I keep buying them."

He helped her gather up the bandages. She started to rise, but he held out his hand.

"Slate…"

"If you apologize again, you'll probably make a hash of it and then I'll let Brenner kill you," she warned him.

He shook his head. "It's twice now," he said. "You gave me my death back in that cell. Last night you gave me my life back."

Slate hunched up one shoulder. *He shouldn't be able to do the voice with his throat like that. Dammit,* how *is he still doing it?*

He stepped back and unsheathed his sword.

Slate looked down the length of the blade and raised her eyebrows.

He drove the point into the earth at her feet and dropped to one knee.

"Oh god, no," said Slate involuntarily.

It was Caliban at her feet, but the Knight-Champion looking up at her. "The church cast me out. The city locked me away. And I prayed, when I was in the cell," he said. "I prayed for weeks. And no one came and I knew the Dreaming God had turned his back on me."

Slate swallowed hard.

"But you saved me," he said. "And I no longer have a church to serve. So I will swear to you, instead."

"You can't. I mean, you *really* can't! Dear god! A paladin swearing to a forger?"

"You are my commander," he said, unruffled, and bowed his head.

Slate sank back down onto the wonder-engine's hip bone, trapped.

He spoke a few words only, in a form of the language so old that she'd only read it in books. It seemed she had been wrong about half the pronunciations, too.

Am I supposed to say something?

Apparently not, because he sheathed his sword and knelt at her feet and said "I am yours to command."

Shit. Shit. Shit.

"What does that even mean?"

He looked up at her again and even if he was using the voice, he had a small, sardonic smile.

He knows perfectly well that I don't know what the hell to do now. Dear god, I think he thinks this is funny.

"I would give my life for yours. Your enemies are my enemies."

"They already *were* your enemies!"

"Well," he admitted, "that's true. But I'll be here if you make any new ones."

Slate gripped her skull in both hands. "Wait, you're not going to go around trying to defend my honor, are you?"

"...I *am* a paladin."

"Yes, but I haven't *got* any honor!"

"I'll try to keep the duels over your virtue to a bare minimum, then."

This was even worse than she'd imagined. "Um. Uh. Okay. Go take care of the horses, I guess?"

The former Knight-Champion, now, evidently, *her* Knight-Champion, rose to his feet.

"Caliban?"

He looked over his shoulder. "My liege?"

She winced. "Don't you dare call me that in front of Brenner!"

"As you command."

Slate groaned. "Maybe you *could* have just apologized."

The paladin's smile grew just a little.

"I'd only have made a hash of it," he said, and went to take care of the horses.

The second encounter was rather different. Slate had wandered out to the tree-line to take care of certain private business, and was wandering back when someone grabbed her from behind a tree.

Slate slapped a hand to her dagger. *Shit, shit, it's the rune, I didn't hear them coming, shit—*

Strong fingers clamped hers to the hilt, keeping her from pulling the blade out, and then Brenner had pulled her tight against him and covered her mouth with his.

The strength of her physical response startled her. Instinct took over for a heartbeat—it had been a *very* long time, and Brenner, whatever his many faults, was warm and solid and *there*.

He had been an...interesting lover. Her mother had always said you could tell a lot about a man by the way they conducted intimate business. The ones who thought they were amazing in bed, the ones who were afraid that they weren't, the ones who expected you to do everything...

Brenner had been none of those. Brenner had made a very careful study of what her body responded to and then he had done it, quite ruthlessly, until Slate could hold nothing back at all. Then he would take his own pleasure, just as ruthlessly.

It had been exhausting and oddly transactional, very much like Brenner. It left her sated and a little bitter afterwards, as if they had used each other.

Her body remembered it differently. Her body felt his palm on the back of her neck and his teeth against her lips and was instantly, shockingly ready.

Right here. Right now. I am alive and I want to feel... something...

Brenner let go of the dagger hilt and slid his arm around her waist, pulling her off balance, just a little, just enough so that she had to either grab at him or step back.

And then, for no particular reason, she remembered Caliban holding her up in the streambed, until she could get her feet under her.

Slate stepped back.

"What was *that* all about?"

Brenner grinned down at her. "Just sayin' thank you, darlin'."

"You could just *say it*, like normal people."

"Ah, where's the fun in that?" He wiped his mouth. "And you were right there for it, too. For a moment, anyway."

"Yeah, well..." She glanced away. "Old habits die hard."

"Can't blame a man for trying. Still dreaming about tall, blond, and guilty? It's a bad idea. Never date a man prettier than you, it never ends well."

Slate snorted loudly. "Are you daft? I never come between a man and his self-loathing."

"You're a poor liar, darlin'. I'd say stick to figures, but that *was* a pretty sweet rescue the other night, even if you should look before you leap."

She dug an elbow into his ribs. "I looked for a good twenty minutes! It's not my fault that they were all tucked around the edge of the building like that."

"Yeah, yeah. I'm not complaining." He slung an arm around her shoulders as they walked back down the hillside. "Just want you to know, you ever find yourself getting cold at night…"

"With Grimehug sleeping over my legs like that? I'll let you know."

"You do that."

They were halfway back to camp, where Learned Edmund was trying to do the dishes without Grimehug helping, and Caliban was doing something obscure to the horses' tack. Brenner began rolling a cigarette. "One other thing…"

"Hmmm?"

"Our paladin."

"What abou—gaah!" Slate sneezed several times in rapid succession. "About him?"

"You okay, darlin'?"

Slate rubbed at her nose. "Dunno. Allergies, probably. But what about the paladin?"

Brenner shrugged. "Probably nothing. But that demon-rune was awfully interested in him. She was muttering into his ear in god-knows-what kinda language for a good few minutes before she started strangling him."

"Yeah, I saw some of that. Well, and so?"

He put the cigarette in his mouth. "Like I said, probably nothing." A match hissed, and he lit the end quickly, then shook it out. "But he didn't talk in his sleep last night."

Slate had her sleeve over her nose, but looked up startled.

"You think something happened to his demon?"

Brenner shrugged and flicked the match away. "What do I know about demons? Just thought I'd mention it, darlin'."

More unsettled than she wanted to admit, Slate kept an eye on Caliban's distant figure all the way back to camp.

"Well," said Learned Edmund, their second night in the wonder-engine's valley, "I have the proverbial good news and bad news."

They were sitting around the fire. Grimehug was stretched out full-length on his back, looking like a hearthrug designed by incompetent weavers. Brenner was sharpening his knives. Caliban was oiling his scabbard. Slate was starting to feel a little uncomfortable with all the small deadly noises going on to either side of her, and was wishing she had a harmonica just to drown them out.

She seized on Edmund's pronouncement instead. "So what's the good news?"

"I've figured out more or less where we are in relation to the rest of the world," said Learned Edmund.

"And the bad news?"

"There's a lot of the Vagrant Hills in the way."

"How did we get that far off track?"

The scholar sat back, rubbed at the back of his neck. "Well... we should never assign to malice what we can assign to our incompetence..."

"Hear, hear," muttered Brenner.

"But near as I can tell, the Vagrant Hills reached out and grabbed us."

"Can they *do* that?"

"Apparently so."

"There's another possibility," said Caliban. His voice was still hoarse, but had most of its timbre back. He had been staring into the fire, but he looked up now. The flames left his face backlit with orange, and woke unpleasant highlights in his eyes.

"Yes?" said Slate.

"The rune demon. I don't know how much power it had, but it's possible that it might have warped the landscape. It felt my demon as soon as we entered the Hills. Perhaps it wanted to bring it closer."

"Might be right, big man," said Grimehug. "Don't know where your smuggler's road is, but clocktaurs went in maybe twenty miles from Anuket City. Only cut a little through the hills when a gnole fell off and rune caught me."

"And we were nearly sixty miles away from Anuket City," said Slate. "So—what, the rune-demon managed to make the horses run forty miles in five minutes? Or she pulled the landscape out from under us like a rug? That can't be possible."

Caliban shook his head. "I don't know. Some demons are supposed to be able to twist the world around them. It's how they levitate and do some of the other tricks. And she was incredibly strong, and for her kind, very subtle."

"Couldn't do much about a slit throat, though," muttered Brenner.

"I don't know if that's what happened. I'm just saying that it's possible she was behind it."

"The Vagrant Hills are notoriously malleable," Learned Edmund said. "A demon might not need as much power here, in order to change things. It may even account for why we did not encounter any great oddities once we entered. She may have wanted to bring us as quickly as possible, and smoothed the way."

They all stared into the fire in silence for a while.

"Still," said Slate finally, "the demon's gone, right?"

She was looking at Caliban when she spoke. He nodded, slowly, the fire painting shadows under his skin.

Brenner caught her gaze and jerked his chin a quarter-inch toward the paladin.

Yes. I know.

Slate gnawed on the edge of a fingernail. "I suppose it doesn't matter. Might even work as a shortcut, if we're only twenty miles from Anuket City now. Learned Edmund, can you get us to the road?"

He met her eyes. Despite everything, Slate was pleased.

If I can get a scholar of the Many-Armed God to at least make eye contact with me, surely the rest of the world can't help but fall into place.

"Probably," he said. "I don't promise it won't get, um, strange."

"Stranger than it already has?"

"Oh, yes. In fact, I think the wonder-engine is…hmm…. grounding some of the oddities, like a lightning rod. Once we leave here, some very odd things might start to happen. Or nothing at all might happen. There's no way to tell."

"Okay. Good to know, I guess." Slate sneezed, started to dig in her pockets for a handkerchief, and took the one the knight handed her instead. "Okay. We'll move out tomorrow, and we'll follow your best guess."

"Are you sure you're ready to travel?" asked Caliban, glancing at the rag tied around her shoulder.

"I'll be fine."

"We could wait another day—"

"I'll be fine, Mother. I'll wear a sweater and I won't go home with any strange boys."

Brenner snickered. The paladin's lips twitched, and he turned back to the fire. "Very well."

Slate woke up in the middle of the night, at some small sound. She lay awake listening to the people sleeping around her.

The fire popped and crackled. Learned Edmund snored. Grimehug made faint doggy noises where he lay draped across her legs, scuffling at the blankets occasionally with his feet.

From Caliban's bedroll came no sound at all.

Bad enough when he's gibbering, but when he's not…now I really am *worried.*

Slate stared up at the stars. They crept slowly by overhead, and had no voices either. It was a long time before she got to sleep.

CHAPTER 17

They were less than two hours from the wonder-engine's valley when things did indeed start to get strange.

Caliban took point, with Learned Edmund just behind him to call directions. Slate and Brenner followed with the pack mules. It was a cool, pleasant day, blessedly free of insects, and they followed the road for an hour, before reaching a point where Edmund said that they should split off and head southeast.

"There should be a river a few miles along. We want to make for it. We'll follow it most of the way if…err….nothing happens."

The sounds of the river came up to meet them soon enough. It was a broader, shallower waterway than the one they'd crossed to reach the rune. The horses splashed across it, and they dismounted to drink and water the animals.

Grimehug dunked his whole head in the river and pulled it out again. He paused, his small ears pricking up.

"You hear that, Crazy Slate?"

"Hear what?"

"Kinda grinding noise. Like a big millstone."

Slate cocked her head. After a minute she heard it too, very faintly, a rumbling, scratchy noise. "It's coming from downriver."

The other three heard it soon after. Caliban pushed between the pack mules, coming down to join the woman and the gnole at the water's edge.

"Think it's coming closer," said Grimehug, leaning out over the stream and nearly falling in.

Caliban caught him by a handful of rags. "Should we get out of here?"

"I'd like to know what it is," said Learned Edmund.

"So would I, since we're planning on traveling downstream anyway. We'll run into it anyway, and I'd rather pick the ground."

Slate chewed a nail. "Let's move the horses away from the river. Then we'll wait—from a safe distance—and see what it is."

The horses seemed oddly unconcerned about the strange noise, even as it grew louder. They moved up the bank anyway, until they found a vantage point, and sat down to wait.

It took nearly half an hour, and when it finally arrived, it was so bizarre that Slate wasn't entirely sure she hadn't fallen asleep while they waited and dreamed it instead.

There was a stone fish in the river.

At first, Slate thought it was merely stone-like—its skin hard and grey, patchy with lichen and wet with moss. But the sheer weight of the creature was rapidly obvious, as it ground its way up the rocky riverbed. Stone screamed on stone as it pushed through a shallow patch of rapids. Sparks jumped and flashed from the contact.

In shape, it resembled an enormous salmon, nearly six feet tall at the humped back, at least twenty feet long. The stone tail thrashed in slow motion, driving it forward, and a mossy, under-slung jaw clapped with a sound like an avalanche. Its eyes were broad, fist-sized lumps, and the scales appeared to have been carved.

"That's a crazy big fish," said Grimehug.

"It's not moving very fast," said Slate, after watching it rumble by for nearly a minute.

"Yeah, but it's doing pretty good for a rock," said Brenner.

Nearly ten minutes later, it had passed the rapids and was partially submerged again. Once in the water, it made somewhat better speed, and eventually vanished around a bend in the river.

It left behind a trail of round stones, spherical as geodes. Learned Edmund reached into the water and picked up one up, examining it from all angles. It fit neatly into his palm.

"Is that an *egg?*" asked Slate.

"I…many-armed lord, you know, I think it might be." Learned Edmund's eyebrows drew together. "If you figure that creature was like a salmon spawning…" He gazed at the rock.

"Is it going to *hatch?*"

"Only one way to find out, I suppose." He tucked the stone carefully into a saddlebag. "Assuming it doesn't hatch on a geological time scale, in which case none of us may be around to see it."

Privately, Slate thought that the way things were going, they'd be damn lucky to be around to see it hatch on even a normal flesh-and-blood time scale, but she kept that to herself.

After that, the Vagrant Hills started to get truly odd.

They followed the river as well as they could. The trail left by the stone salmon was obvious downriver, scrapes punctuated by the round egg-stones. Learned Edmund scribbled rapidly in his journal

Every time they had to turn aside from the river, to avoid a bluff or detour around an impassable thicket, it got weirder.

Most of the things they saw were, like the stone fish, unsettling but harmless. There was the clearing full of spiders, weaving a long and intricate mural detailing the rise of an arachnid civilization. There was a gully full of stones, each one with a keyhole in it. (Brenner tried to pick one with a pin. After forty-five minutes, he succeeded, and it crumbled into dust in his hands.) There was a tree with broad fleshy leaves that made kissing noises as they passed, and one that pulled vines tight in around itself and moaned.

It was nearly noon, and they were following an old game trail, when a rabbit hopped slowly into their path.

It was large and brown and leggy, and it sat up to look at them. Its nose twitched.

"Bunny!" said Grimehug happily.

The rabbit flicked its ears, looked up at Brenner, and said, in a deep, thoughtful voice, "You'll die laughing, you know."

They stared at the rabbit. It flicked its ears again.

The assassin's hand went for the hilt of a dagger, and the rabbit bounded off the track, kicking up mulch and bits of bark. By the time his blade cleared the sheath, it was long gone.

Brenner was left sitting on his horse, holding a knife, with a bemused expression.

"Look on the bright side," said Slate. "At least it didn't say *when*."

They passed through one band of trees and into another. Pine needles gave way to rotted leaves. The woods seemed darker and denser, and the brambles got thicker and required longer and longer detours. The ground sucked at the horse's hooves.

"This is not a good place," said Brenner.

"It feels…unholy," said Caliban gravely.

"You'd know."

"Indeed."

Slate heard a rustling in what looked like a blackberry thicket. She looked over into it, and something looked out at her and giggled.

She started to warn her companions and was seized with a sneezing fit so explosive that she thought the top of her head was going to come off. She put out a hand to thin air, as if to ward off the suddenly excruciating scent of rosemary, and Caliban put a handkerchief into it.

Where the heck is he keeping all these, anyway? I know I never give them back. And they're always clean, too.

"Thanks, but—snrrk—something's in the bushes. Magic. *Ackchoo!*"

"Hmm."

Another giggle came, off to their left. Slate sneezed again.

"'Ware the bushes," said Caliban, as calmly as if shrubs laughed at him every day. He pulled his sword free.

Something flashed between the trees ahead, running low to the ground. It got ten feet and dropped with a squeal. A blade quivered upright in it.

Brenner drew another knife and nudged his horse forward.

The giggles were replaced with angry, squirrel-like chatters.

"Perhaps we should not antagonize them," said Learned Edmund.

"Does killing them count as antagonizing them?" asked Brenner, holding up his quarry on the end of his knife. "And what the hell is this thing? It looks like I just knifed a turnip."

They crowded the horses together in the center of the clearing. Learned Edmund peered down at the bulbous brown thing on Brenner's blade. "I think it's a mandrake root."

"Do they often run around?"

"Never, as far as I know."

"I think we want to go, guys," said Grimehug worriedly. "Bad vegetables in the trees, now."

Slate clutched the handkerchief to her raw nose and followed the gnole's gaze.

Something that looked like a cross between a rat and a potato was clinging to a tree trunk at head height, chattering at them. It had a number of beady black eyes and two separate heads.

Another one skittered up a tree trunk as she watched, then another. Slate looked around, seeing the straight trunks grow lumpy boles as mandrake after mandrake scurried upward.

Brenner got back on his horse, sprawled awkwardly across its back for a moment, then managed to get upright. Learned Edmund tugged on the mules' lead rope.

A pebble bounced off the back of Caliban's head. He winced and ducked.

"They're throwing rocks. *Hurry.*"

The next one took Brenner in the shoulder, and then a veritable rain of stones came showering down from the trees. The horses stamped, neighing furiously as pebbles stung their hindquarters.

"I can't hold them!" yelled Learned Edmund, as the animals crowded him, a tangle of hooves and outrage.

"Then stop trying!" yelled Caliban back, and spurred his horse forward, trying to cover Slate.

They fled. It was not glorious. It could only be described as a complete rout. The mandrakes chased them, herding them with showers of stones. They did not dare strike back for the river. Every time they tried, rocks pelted down, and the horses bolted back for the safety of the woods.

When they ran out of rocks, they threw nuts. When they ran out of nuts, they threw owl pellets, and after that it was almost a relief when they went back to rocks again.

The mandrake roots appeared to have a particular loathing for Caliban and Brenner, pelting the men with so many stinging stones that they looked as if they'd been attacked by angry wasps. Slate and Learned Edmund came in for less abuse, and Grimehug got away almost unscathed.

"They're herding us!" shouted Caliban.

"I noticed!" yelled Slate. "What do you want me to do about it?"

Her horse took an acorn to the haunches and lunged a few feet forward. Its feet slipped, and Slate clutched at the saddlehorn with a shriek. The animal lunged, caught itself, and then it was half-galloping, half-sliding down an embankment.

Slate had time to think, *Oh, no, not again!* and then the horse was prancing and jittering to a halt in the center of the open road.

Learned Edmund and the line of mules, with a squawking Grimehug, came crashing down behind her. The mules in particular were not pleased: they were cow-kicking at the air and braying, while the gnole clung to his makeshift saddle.

The stones stopped.

Slate looked down the road, which was broad and dusty and possibly the most beautiful thing she'd ever seen. She was just in time to see Caliban and his horse come charging down a few hundred yards away. His horse reared up. The knight clung with his knees, still holding his broadsword in his free hand, despite the weapon's demonstrated ineffectiveness against thrown nuts.

A minute later, Brenner's horse came down behind them, with an empty saddle. A minute after that, the sound of cursing announced the arrival of Brenner.

And so it was, flailing at the air, the horses neighing and stampeding under them, in complete disarray, bloody and cursing, they arrived at the end of the road, less than five miles from Anuket City.

"We made it," said Slate. "We made it. We...can't have made it. This is impossible."

They had followed the road, arguing about where it might be, until it had joined up to another, larger one. People and animals streamed by them: ox teams grunting and horses high-stepping around them, carts laden with squawking chickens in cages, people on foot with baskets piled high on their heads.

Then they had all argued some more, until Caliban had simply walked out into the road and asked a woman with trays of bread on her head where they were.

"The west gate of Anuket City," he said, returning to them. "And she looked at me like I was an idiot and I said we'd been in the Vagrant Hills, and she said, 'Ohhh...' and offered me a sweet bun."

He took a bite of the sweet bun in question. The other three humans stared at it with envy. Grimehug said, "A gnole said that's where it was."

"So that's it," said Slate. "We made it. We lived." And then, staring at the distant gates, with the heartfelt intensity of prayer, she said "Well...*shit.*"

She got off her horse, rummaged in the saddlebags, and pulled out a hat. It fit low over her eyes and she honestly hadn't expected to live long enough to need it.

"So now what?" said Caliban. "We just...go in?"

"Why not?" said Brenner.

"Because we're...uh..." He gestured at all of them. "We're... well, you know."

"No one will even notice us," said Slate.

She tried to get back on her horse. It didn't go well. After three tries with her foot not even reaching the stirrups, Caliban dismounted and came over to her.

He knelt down. "My liege," he said, under his breath.

"Don't start," Slate warned and he chuckled.

She stepped into his linked hands. There was a moment, just before he lifted her into the saddle, when she gripped his shoulder and felt the muscle underneath, and Caliban turned his head and met her eyes.

He smiled in a way that made her heart turn over just a little.

Stupid to think that when we're going to die... she thought reflexively, and then another thought intruded. *We've made it this far. Who knows how far we'll get?*

She turned her head and saw Brenner watching her, his face unreadable.

A wail went up suddenly from Learned Edmund. Everyone started.

"What's wrong?" said Slate.

"If we're here…" said the dedicate, staring at the map unrolled across his saddlebow. "If we're here, then we're not here…" His finger skipped back and forth, trying to reconcile their location. "Which means we could have been anywhere in the Vagrant Hills! Anywhere at all!"

"Okay?" said Slate.

"You don't understand!" wailed the dedicate of the Many-Armed God. "If I don't know where we were, I'll never be able to tell anyone where to find the wonder-engine!"

Brenner rolled his eyes. Slate shook her head. Learned Edmund looked ready to turn around and ride into the woods, mandrake roots and all, but Caliban leaned over and grabbed his reins.

"Later," he said. "We have other things to worry about. And your Brother Amadai to find."

"Yes…" said Learned Edmund slowly. "Yes, I suppose we do. And the rest of his journal to translate. I'll need to find the key to the second cipher." He sighed. "I suppose it will have to wait, then. But I hate to leave work undone."

"Trust me," said Slate, spurring her horse forward, "there will be plenty of work for us in Anuket City."

The others followed. Slate rode looking up at the gates, and slowly, step by step, the city reached out and swallowed them.

"The Single Most Embarrassing Acknowledgement Section I Have Ever Written"

I started this book during Nanowrimo of 2006, which makes it eleven years in the writing. My books frequently take several years to write, but even for me, that's extraordinary.

2006 was a bad year. I was extremely depressed and in denial about my first marriage failing. In that dreadful emotional pressure cooker, I kept starting books and abandoning them after about twenty thousand words.

I don't recommend this method of inspiration.

When I am depressed, I play video games. In particular, I started playing Neverwinter Nights 2.

NWN2 was a weird flawed game in many regards, but it had some really entertaining writing. There were characters that you really enjoyed spending time with.

And then there was the goddamn paladin.

The love interest if you played as a female character was a self-loathing paladin who was guilt-wracked over…something or other, I don't know. He moped a lot. He had no evident sense of humor. This was supposed to be attractive.

This is an ongoing problem with just about every paladin ever. Everybody seems to want to write them like crapsack Jedi—endlessly teetering on the brink of damnation, one bad thought ready to turn them over to the dark side, all of them as moody and self-absorbed as teenage boys.

In a burning rage about how paladins were being written wrong, I hammered out forty or fifty thousand words that would later form the bones of Clockwork Boys.

A few years went by and then a few more and life got better and once in a blue moon I'd put a few more words on what became known in my head as "the thing with the paladin and the ninja accountant."

Then I started playing the Dragon Age games, and damned if we weren't back in the land of self-loathing paladins again, knights with dark and terrible secrets that were blaming themselves for everything, blah blah blah. (Blackwall, I am looking in your direction!)

In the back of a car driving through south Texas, chasing rare birds, I turned on my laptop and wrote the vast majority of what would become The Wonder Engine. By this point, the story was alive in my head and it was going somewhere, but we were careening past 130K with no end in sight and I realized if I tried to make this one book, it could be used to club burglars to death. (I had already had this experience with the Digger omnibus and did not wish to do it again.)

So I split it in half and send the first half to my editor, saying "I think this is a light swashbuckling love story?" and she sent back a lot of words about how apparently those don't include carnivorous tattoos and dead nuns and rotting demons in one's head and no amount of banter was going to get past that.

Great thanks go, therefore, to K.B. Spangler, for editing it anyway, even if her margin notes occasionally just said things like "You should be screaming and running now!" and "eating a stick of coping butter."

Even more thanks to my long-suffering husband, Kevin, who had a manuscript thrust at him with "Tell me if the dudes work!" and without whom, Brenner would have even fewer redeeming qualities.

Thanks to my copyeditors, who have suffered untold indignities over the years, with no end in sight.

Thanks to all my readers, since those long ago Nanowrimo days, who have checked in occasionally to see if I ever finished that thing with the paladin and the rosemary.

I suppose thanks must also go to the writers of fantasy paladins, lo these many years, without whom there would be no tradition to enrage me and force me to tackle the issue myself. Inspiration knocks now and again, but spite bangs on the door all year long.

Thank god.

ABOUT THE AUTHOR

T. Kingfisher is a pen-name for the Hugo-Award winning author and illustrator Ursula Vernon.

Ms. Kingfisher lives in North Carolina with her husband, garden, and disobedient pets. Using Scrivener only for e-books, she chisels the bulk of her drafts into the walls of North Carolina's ancient & plentiful ziggurats. She is fond of wombats and sushi, but not in the same way.

You can find links to all these books, new releases, artwork, rambling blog posts, links to podcasts and more information about the author at

www.tkingfisher.com

When Gerta's friend Kay is stolen away by the mysterious Snow Queen, it's up to Gerta to find him. Her journey will take her through a dangerous land of snow and witchcraft, accompanied only by a bandit and a talking raven. Can she win her friend's release, or will following her heart take her to unexpected places? A strange, sly retelling of Hans Christian Andersen's "Snow Queen," by T. Kingfisher, author of "Bryony and Roses" and "The Seventh Bride."

THE RAVEN AND THE REINDEER BY T. KINGFISHER

$12.95 ISBN 978-1-61450-389-7

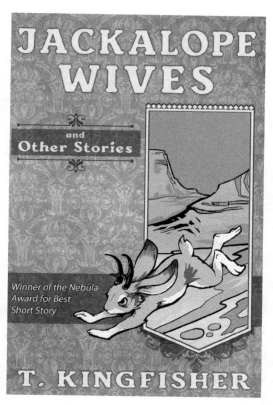

Winner of the Nebula and WSFA Short Fiction Awards. Includes "The Tomato Thief" winner of 2017 Hugo Award - Best Novelette From award-winning author T. Kingfisher comes a collection of short stories, including "Jackalope Wives," "The Tomato Thief," "Pocosin," and many others. By turns funny, lyrical, angry and beautiful, this anthology includes two all-new stories, "Origin Story" and "Let Pass The Horses Black," appearing for the first time in print.

JACKALOPE WIVES AND OTHER STORIES BY T. KINGFISHER

$12.95 ISBN 978-1-61450-394-1

CPSIA information can be obtained
at www.ICGtesting.com
Printed in the USA
BVHW050744240423
662923BV00014B/630